THE
Ring of Fire

Books by Shirley Rousseau Murphy

The Grass Tower
Silver Woven In My Hair
The Ring of Fire

by

Shirley Rousseau Murphy

*Atheneum * New York*

1977

LIBRARY OF CONGRESS CATALOGING IN PUBLICATION DATA

Murphy, Shirley Rousseau. The ring of fire.

SUMMARY: Although the children of Ynell have always been subject
to death because of their occult powers,
they suddenly are threatened by a greater evil.
[1. Science fiction] I. Title.
PZ7.M956Ri [Fic] 77-1576
ISBN 0-689-30594-X

Copyright © 1977 by Shirley Rousseau Murphy
All rights reserved
Published simultaneously in Canada by
McClelland & Stewart, Ltd.
Manufactured in the United States of America by
Fairfield Graphics, Fairfield, Pennsylvania
Designed by Mary M. Ahern
First Edition

Contents

Part One
The Curse of Ynell
1

Part Two
The Runestone
55

Part Three
Fire Scourge
117

Part Four
The Luff'Eresi
175

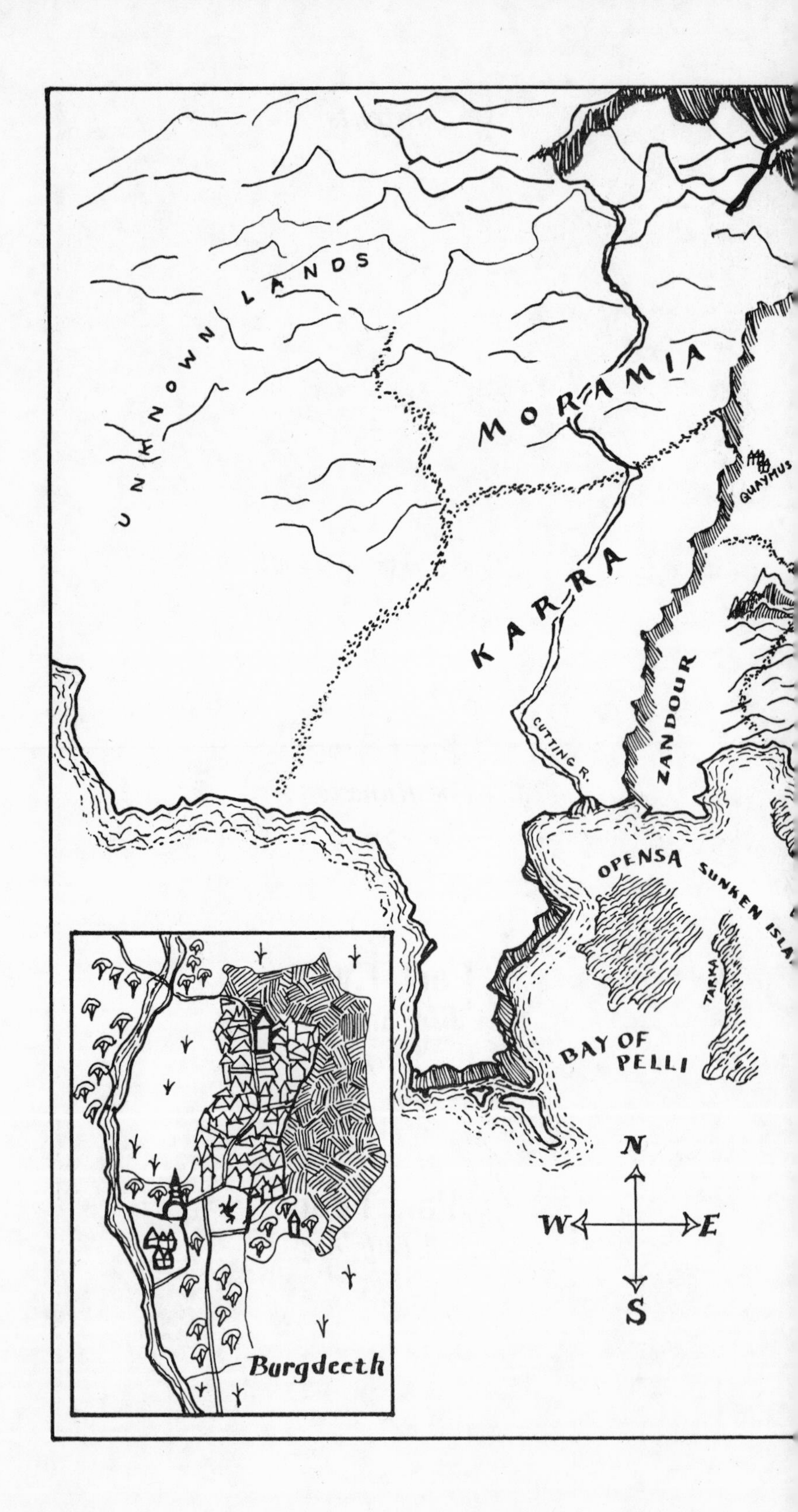
UNKNOWN LANDS
MORAMIA
KARRA
QUAYMUS
CUTTING R.
ZANDOUR
OPENSA
SUNKEN
TARKA
BAY OF PELLI
N
W
E
S
Burgdeeth

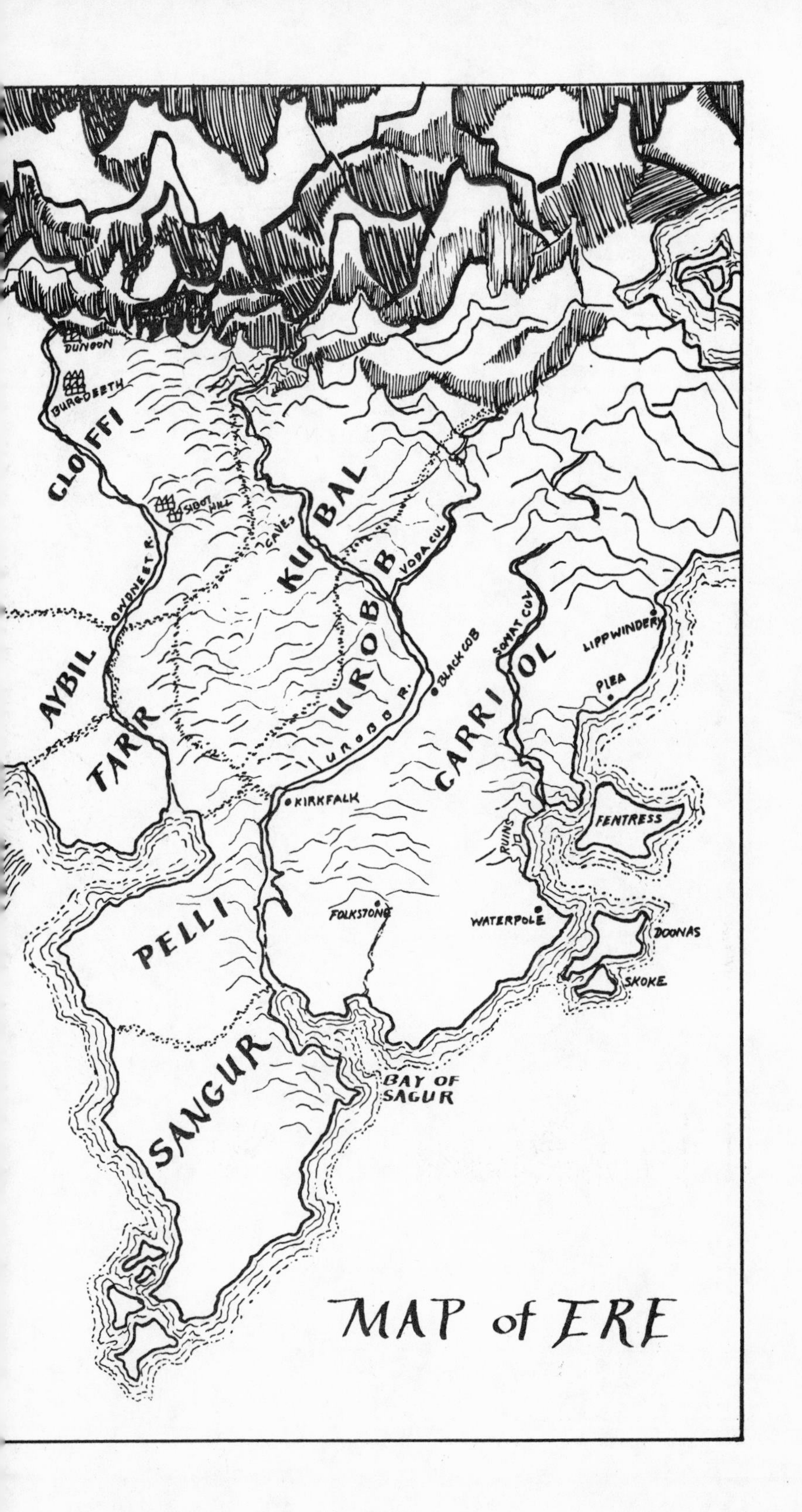
DUNOON
BURGDEETH
CLOFFI
SIBOT HILL
CAVES
KUBAL
OWDNEET R.
AYBIL
TARR
UROBB
VODA CUL
UROBB R.
BLACKCOB
SOMAT CUL
CARRIOL
LIPPWINDERY
PLEA
KIRKFALK
RUINS
FENTRESS
FOLKSTONE
WATERPOLE
DOONAS
SKOKE
PELLI
SANGUR
BAY OF SAGUR
MAP of ERE

The Curse of Ynell

The mountains were jagged and black, a circle of volcanic peaks a hundred miles across. No man of Ere ventured far into them, or knew what lay beyond. Ere's eleven countries crowded at their feet, pressed in by the empty sea and by the barren high deserts to the west; beyond the mountains were the unknown lands. Or perhaps nothing lay beyond. The countries of Ere were Cloffi and Kubal; Urobb and Carriol and Farr; Pelli and Sangur and Aybil and Zandour; and on the edge of the high deserts where life was barely possible, Karra and Moramia.

The history of Ere was violent with raiding and with war, just as the mountains themselves were violent sometimes in their eruptions of lava and fire that would spill across the warring nations, when the gods were angered.

In the old times it was the Herebian tribes who killed and tortured and took slaves, who hung the heads of their enemies from the center poles of their bivouc camps. But since the Herebian had formed themselves into a nation, driving out farmers and herders from a hilly section and naming this land Kubal, their warring had become less frequent. The eleven nations lay quiet: Ere was poised in a time of peace; though dark Kubal humped in eternal threat there between the borders of Cloffi and Urobb.

It is Cloffi where this story begins.

High up the mountain, above Cloffi's three cities, lay the little herd village of Dunoon, its pastures scattered like green velvet among the black lava ridges. A small nest of freedom, Dunoon, maintaining stubborn truce against the tyranny of the Landmasters of Cloffi who ruled the nation below.

Chapter One

Thorn readied an arrow against the string of his sectbow and searched the moonlit mountain above him. The guard buck stirred again, restlessly. Wolves, likely, moving in the darkness of the lava crags. And yet the herd's unease was different than when they faced approaching wolves. The buck's spiralling horns caught the moonlight as he shifted nervously. Thorn tried to see movement in the dark images cast by the moons but nothing stirred.

Finally the buck settled and turned to grazing. Thorn lowered his bow, keeping the arrow taut with one hand. Below him the village slept. He moved stiffly: his body still pained him from the beating he had taken. He scowled as he looked down past his own village to the far lights of Burgdeeth: the larger town lay so steep below he could have spit on it. "Goatherd!" The three boys had shouted, taunting him. "Goat dung burns on your hearth!" No older than he, strapping lads they were for all their city ways. "And your mother's a fracking brood milker!" He had piled into them, had fought well enough until the six red-robed Deacons dragged him away to beat him with a ceremonial staff, at the Landmaster's direction. The towns-folk of Burgdeeth had crowded into the square to smirk and whisper, remembering their own beatings, Thorn supposed, so taking great pleasure in his.

Ere's two moons hung low in the sky, washing their light across the eleven nations. The dark smudge in the south would be heavy cloud lying over the far sea. He watched the river Owdneet slip rushing down the mountain past his own village, then past Burgdeeth, and on toward the two more southerly Cloffi cities. The buck stirred again; a doe bleated; Thorn could hear the hush of tall grass disturbed. He turned quickly, but saw no shadow move. The animals acted as if something alien were there above them, yet they did not show fear; nor did they bellow the quick challenge the Dunoon goats were famous for. One buck muttered softly, then was still. Thorn stared up at the shifting, moonwashed clouds riding above the mountain and felt a familiar eagerness grip him, a longing for the sky that, though forbidden, he would never quell. Once again something stirred, he took a breath—then his blood went cold as a tall man stepped silently from the shadows and stood staring down at him. He had come without sound; Thorn's sectbow sought the man's middle; the moonlight shone full on him, a slim, well-made figure. But old; his hair white and shorn close to his head. His eyes, in the moonlight, looked yellow.

The man came silently toward him, disappearing in shadow then appearing again. He said no word, but Thorn divined a sense of urgency about him, and when he challenged the stranger it was almost reluctantly. "How did you come here? What do you among our herds? You do not come from Burgdeeth, I would have seen you climb the mountain."

"I came from there," he said, pointing to the jagged crags, "along the mountain from the east. It is a lonely way. I like the loneliness. I have come seeking you, Thorn of Dunoon."

"How do you know my name?"

"Your name came to my thoughts just as the scent of

rain speaks on the wind. I sensed it, long ago. I could not have done so had you not possessed the gift for which I search."

"What gift?" Thorn said, stiffening.

The stranger paused and studied him. "I search," he said slowly, as if weighing his words, "I search for those with the gift of seeing. I search for the Children of Ynell."

Thorn stared, his blood turned to ice: to pronounce a man a Child of Ynell was to condemn him to die.

"In Cloffi they call it the Curse of Ynell," the old man said. "I do not call it that. But you have the true gift, Thorn of Dunoon, as surely as I stand before you."

How could this man know such a thing? Yet Thorn could not refute it. The gift of seeing had come on him three times in his life, without warning, though it was inaccessible when he would try for it.

"I think you do not know, yourself, the strength you have within you."

Thorn looked deep into those disturbing yellow eyes and said nothing.

"Oh yes, I know how it is in Cloffi. I, too, have read the Edicts of Contrition. I know that the Gift of Ynell is considered a sin without redemption. I, too, have seen the Children of Ynell dressed in rags and filth and strapped across the backs of donkeys and carried up the mountain to the death stone. But I do not come to you to carry word of your talent to Cloffi. Nor to ask anything of you—not yet."

"What commerce would you have with me, then?"

"I come seeking the runestone of Eresu. And the spark for that stone is in you, young Cherban, for surely it is that spark that has led me here. I seek the lost runestone, a shard of jade of great power. There is a taut linking between it and you, a strength I can almost touch. Do you not know the stone, have you never seen it?"

"Never. I don't understand what you speak of."

"It is a stone that will bring the true gift of seeing strong in one who holds it, if such gift is in the blood. You are Cherban, red-headed Cherban. So was Ynell. And so are many of the true Children. A stone greener than Karrach jade, greener than your own eyes, and hidden here in the north of Cloffi, it is sworn. Hidden in a dark place." He glanced above him at the mountain. "In the caves of the ruined city of Owdneet, perhaps. Or perhaps not.

"The stone can grant a great power. And the time to wield that power may be soon, for there are rumors across the land that Kubal may soon be on the march." The old man's gaze was flinty, with a strength Thorn liked.

"We have heard one such rumor," Thorn said slowly. Then, "You know I would be killed in Cloffi for what you have just said of me."

The old man lay a hand on Thorn's shoulder. "I said I would not tell your secret. Why do you think I came secretly, and not marching up through Burgdeeth in the middle of the day, past six Deacons and the Landmaster and that staring populace? But remember, Ynell had the power and found it nothing to be afraid of. Ynell knew joy all his life."

"The Cloffi tale of Ynell does not tell that, old man."

"No, but my tale does. And so does yours, the old Cherban telling. The Cloffi tale has been altered by the Landmasters to suit their own desires."

"Tell it your way then. Let me hear it," Thorn challenged, for few knew that story. He had never heard that it was told outside of Dunoon—except perhaps in far Carriol.

"It is an ancient tale, as old as the tribes of Ere." The old man seated himself against a stone outcropping, and a doe came to muzzle at his pack. He fondled her ears and spoke to her until she lay down at his feet; the moonlight caught across her pale spiralling horns and bleached his hair whiter still.

"It came that Ynell, while tending his goats, saw the grazing covered with darkness as if the sun had gone from the sky. In the sun's place was a movement as of hundreds of dark clouds, and Ynell was sore afraid. He kneeled, and the blackness above him writhed and shifted. His goats bleated in terror and ran away down the mountain.

"Then one ray of sunlight touched Ynell. A crack had been cleft in the darkness, and he could see what the darkness was. And so wild was Ynell's amazement that he forgot his fear as a hundred winged gods descended to the field beside him.

"Now the field was bright with sun, and the sunlight shone upon the gods. They were the colors of saffron and otter-herb and evrole, and the leader stepped forward. 'Be not afraid, Ynell of Sap Vod,' He spoke not with words that Ynell could hear, but with words that rang silent between their two minds. And the god said. 'You are the first, Ynell of Sap Vod. The first who can speak with us in our own way. You are born blessed. You may come with us and dwell in our cities.'

"And so Ynell went with the Luff'Eresi, and he dwelt with them, and he served them, and he was blessed for all of his days. He flew on the backs of their winged consorts through the endless skies, and he saw all the lands, and the men, below him. He heard men's thoughts, and he knew their sorrows, and he knew their fleeting joys."

The old man ended the story and sat silent, his head bent. Then he looked up at Thorn. "Ynell was the first. But there have been others with the sight. The Landmasters of Cloffi fear them. The Kubalese fear them, too, perhaps even more at present, if Kubal is preparing for war. Tell me what you know of the lone Kubalese who has come to live in Burgdeeth. Why is he there?"

"They tell in Burgdeeth that he has come to improve his skill at iron working. He is apprenticed to the Forge-master. It's true the Kubalese are clumsy smiths, but it seems strange. The Landmaster of Burgdeeth seldom allows an outsider to bide overnight, yet this man, Kearb-Mattus, he is called, has lived in comfort at the inn all summer. My father does not trust him, nor do any of us."

"Your father is Goatmaster of Dunoon?"

"Yes, my father is Oak Dar," Thorn said, pondering the old man's knowledge. Then he added, "It is said that the widowed inn woman of Burgdeeth finds the Kubalese companiable, but that is only gossip. And that would be no cause for the Landmaster to make him welcome." He studied the stranger and felt the man's calm sureness. "Why would the Kubalese fear the Children of Ynell if they plan war?"

"Those with the sight could fathom their plans and could spread warning, might even thwart the Kubalese intentions. With the runestone," he added softly, "that might well be made to happen. With the runestone, more might be saved than you can guess.

"It is said the stone will be found by the light of one candle, carried in a searching, and lost in terror. That it will be found again in wonder, given twice, and accompany a quest and a conquering. That is the prophesy. A shard of jade that was part of a stone as round as the egg of the chidrack, a stone that was split asunder by a great power. And each shard bears the runes of Eresu and the power of Eresu. With the runestone, Thorn of Dunoon, one would have the true sight which is in him—which has touched you three times in your life." A hint of longing lit the old man's stern face. "One who holds the runestone will touch the sky one day." Thorn started; the old man had known what no man could have known; of the three visions certainly—but had he only guessed at Thorn's longing for the sky?

The stranger's look turned dark. "The stone's power would demand much of one. In weak hands, it could surely be turned to evil."

The old man took his leave at the first hint of dawn, as the star Waytheer set on the horizon, following in the wake of the two moons. No one else in Dunoon saw him, nor did he go down through Burgdeeth. He went back up the mountain, losing himself almost at once among the outcroppings as if he knew them better than the wolves who roamed there.

Before the stranger turned away, Thorn said, "Will you tell me how you are called?"

"I am Anchorstar."

"And do you go now to the caves above Dunoon, to search further?"

"I will search to the west of Dunoon, on into the unknown lands," Anchorstar said, making Thorn start. "You, Thorn of Dunoon, will search these crags well enough. When we meet again, perhaps the stone will link our two hands," he said, placing his hand over Thorn's for a moment, then turning to fade into the shadows.

Thorn gathered the goats in a preoccupied manner and came down the mountain. He was quiet all through breakfast. His father looked at him quizzically, for Thorn was not usually so silent. His mother gave him an anxious glance. His little brother Loke was too busy planning how to spend the silver he would earn on market day to notice Thorn's preoccupation.

All day his thoughts were troubled by the old man, and by the thought of the runestone; and when evening came he stood staring absently down over the land, only to turn every few minutes to look up the mountain as if Anchorstar would reappear—though he knew that would not happen. He watched the river Owdneet lose its sheen as the sun sank. Its foaming plunge down the mountain always sounded louder in the silence of dusk. The thatched roofs of his village shone pale in the last light, and smoke from the supper fires rose on the windless air. In the east, Ere's two moons tipped up low against the hills that bordered Kubal. Thorn could hear the younger children splashing in the river behind him. The mountain dropped away, the eleven nations at his feet; and the sky swept up in vistas that towered and breathed above him, that stirred in him the longing the old man had seen, that terrible longing for the sky that was forbidden as sin in Cloffi. Darkness came briefly, then the land was lit by the rising moons.

Down the mountain, in Burgdeeth, the thatched roofs were struck across with black chimney shadows, and the cobbles gleamed like spilled coins in the moonlight. The stone houses, crowded close, had been shuttered against the night air. Beyond the houses, the Husbandman's cow and chicken pens were a tangle of fence stripes; the patchwork of housegardens appeared as intricate as a quilt, plots of dill root and love apple and tervil, of scallion and mawzee and charp all shadowed patterns in the slanted moonlight.

Beyond the housegardens stretched the neat whitebarley fields of the Landmaster; and such a field, too, separated the town from the forbidden joys of the river—though the Landmaster's private Set, in the clearing in the woods south of town, had a fine view of the water. Next to the Set, the dome of the Temple shown white, rising alone into the sky. And behind the Temple stood the burial wall, with one small grave open, gaping.

Chapter Two

ZEPHY SAT ALONE in the deep loft window, four stories above the town, its pale, thatched rooftops washed with moonlight, and black shadows picking out doorways where the buildings crowded close along the cobbled streets. The cool wind felt good after the heat in the fields. She stared south past the houses to the gaping grave in the burial wall. Nia Skane's grave. In the morning before first light, Nia would be sealed into that wall to stand forever motionless in death.

How could such a quick, bright child, even if she was only six, have fallen from a tree so simple to climb? One minute alive, her blue eyes seeing everything; the next minute dead. Zephy shivered and remembered how she had tried to turn her attention away from the viewing services that had been held that afternoon. The open plank coffin with the little body strapped to stand forever upright. The light of the sacred flame playing across the dead child's face in a mockery that made her seem to be listening to the Deacons' Plea of Supplication that Nia's spirit dwell with the gods in Eresu. Zephy felt a dismal uncertainty. Would Nia really dwell in Eresu? *To question the edicts of the gods is a sin. To pry into the ways of the gods is to sin.*

Nia's death had focused all her questions into a painful rebellion; she stared up at the mountains above her: Eresu lay deep behind the peaks, the very core of the Ring of Fire. The very core of Ere's faith, the core of life itself.

Clouds blew across the moons so the sky was a place of shifting images. She stared above her, searching, but she could never be sure: were there winged forms sweeping behind that shift of clouds? Or was it only blowing clouds? She sighed. To truly see the gods would be wonderful—though other Cloffa didn't yearn so. They simply accepted the edicts, did as they were bidden, and had no time for the sight of wings: a good Cloffa didn't yearn after things forbidden. But twice she had seen the god's consorts, the flying Horses of Eresu; far off, indistinct, and almost as wonderful as seeing the gods themselves.

Behind her, the loft was brushed with moonlight, the sparse furnishings, the two cots, the chest, the few meager clothes hung on pegs. Shanner's empty cot. Her brother was still out, dallying with a girl again in the moonlight. Well what could you expect? Let Shanner get a girl pregnant, that would fix him. Cloffi's Covenants decreed marriage for such, and the Cloffi Covenants did not yield. She tried to imagine her brother married and settled to the stolid Cloffi ways. Wild as Burgdeeth's young men were, once married they changed completely to dull, obedient, settled men as Cloffi custom decreed.

And for a girl, the quicker pregnant and married the less the trouble she was to the town. A woman was *a vessel and a creature of duty*, the Covenants said, *commanded to submit, commanded to fulfill her role as servant of the Luff'Eresi, and of man, with humility and obedience.* Zephy scowled. I'll be servant to no man. And if that makes me sinning, I don't care!

"You're not docile enough," Mama said often. "You've had not one offer of marriage, Zephy, and you'll be grown soon! What will you do if no man wants you! And no one will with that bold tongue in your head. And that bold stare! Look at you! And not only in this house. You stare at the Deacons too boldly, you look at everyone too boldly. And you say things—you . . ."

Tra. Eskar did not have to say, if you don't marry, there's only one place for you. Zephy knew that far too well. But to go into the Landmaster's Set as a serving maid—never. And Mama *knew* she could never. The girls who went there to live were docile as pie. She could never be like that, nor would want to.

Grown girls, not allowed to stay in a Cloffi city unmarried, must go into the Set or were banned from Cloffi to make a living as best as they could in some other country, though few girls left Burgdeeth. But, there's something else to life, Zephy thought rebelliously. Something besides plant and hoe and weed, cook and scrub. Become a woman, put on a long skirt under your tunic, and be some man's servant forever!

Not until this summer had she felt the agony of Cloffi's binding ways so bitterly, nor rebelled so at Cloffi's rules, and at the way Mama prodded her about them.

Was it because she was growing up that she was suddenly so crosswise with Mama? They had never been before. Or was it Mama? Maybe the gossip about Mama and the Kubalese made Mama at odds with everything, too, though she would never admit it. Zephy reached out with her foot, snagged Shanner's blanket from his cot, and drew it over the sill to wrap around herself. Her brown hair, tumbled half out of the knot she pinned it into to work in the fields, shone tangled in the moonlight. Under her hearthspun nightdress she was as slim and lithe as a bay deer. There was a smear of dirt across one ankle, and a long scratch from mawzee briars down her arm. She pushed back her heavy hair, then stopped abruptly, her hand half-lowered—there were torches being lit at the Landmaster's Set. She could hear men's voices on the wind, and the faint jingle of spurs and bits. They weren't out to hunt the stag on the night of a funeral!

But they were. She could see six riders coming up from the Set with their sectbows. Well, what was a dead child's funeral to the Landmaster? A girl child—less than nothing.

In spite of her disapproval, the clatter of hooves made her yearn to be down there, mounted on that plunging steed in place of the fat Landmaster. The Landmaster's pudgy daughter, Bagriba, sat her gelding like a sack of meal. Only Landmasters' women were considered clean and allowed to ride a mount. A common girl could drive her donkey or lead him in the fields, but never straddle him, and must never touch a horse. For the horse was a creature that shared in a meager way the sacred image, and so shared its holiness, too. For a woman to touch a horse was to blaspheme that which was akin to the gods.

"You could ride to the hunt if you married the Landmaster's son," Meatha had said once. "No other girl cares about horses the way you do, you would be . . ." Zephy had stared at her until Meatha broke off in mid-sentence. Her friend looked innocent and serious, her pale-skinned, dark-haired beauty framed by the greening mawzee stalks. "Elij will be Landmaster one day. A Landmaster's wife—"

"Like marrying a trussed-up hog from Aybil!" Zephy had snapped, thinking Meatha meant it. "Besides, why would he want *me!*" Though sometimes she had caught Elij Cooth staring at her so strangely she became uncomfortable. Then she saw the laughter in Meatha's eyes, and they collapsed together in a fit of mirth.

"Besides," Meatha had said at last, "you'll marry no man of Burgdeeth, neither of us will."

The hunt was below her, the horses' hooves striking sparks on the cobbles. The quick jingle of spurs made a fire in her blood. Elij, tall and blond, was having trouble with his horse, which had begun to shy and stare behind into the shadows. Zephy looked back down the street as two figures stepped out from an alley, glanced toward the hunt, then turned away as if the riders did not exist. The boy dangling the jug and walking unsteadily was Shanner. You might know! With the Candler's oldest daughter again. Elij steadied his horse and laughed. "Swill the moons, Shanner, my boy. What do you feel for in those dark alleys! Does she feel up good, is she warm and soft on this cold night?" There was a roar of laughter from the hunters. Crisslia's face would be red. Zephy felt embarrassed for her, though she didn't like her much. Shanner must be drunk as a lizard to be so silent. Sober, he would have charged out to pull Elij off his horse, the fight ending in laughter.

Kearb-Mattus, the dark Kubalese, sat his horse silently, watching the episode with contempt. How elegantly he was dressed for a hunt. You'd have thought he was riding in a festival, the dark heavy cape the man wore flowing out over his saddle. The wind caught at Zephy's night dress so she drew back. When she looked again, the Kubalese was smoothing his cape carefully. What was tied under it behind the saddle to make such a lump? Maybe it was a sling for the stag they hunted. The hunt moved on, and Shanner and Crisslia were alone on the street. Shanner stepped across the gutter, pulled the Candler's door open roughly, slapped Crisslia on her backside, and was gone before she got the door closed. Zephy watched her brother come up the inn's steps, heard the wrench of the door that would never close quietly, and could picture Shanner glancing at their mother's door that faced the inner entry as he began to climb the stairs. Then she sat looking at the empty street, feeling a mixture of uncomfortable emotions she could not name or sort out.

The dallying of the boys—and most of the girls—was common enough. Why did it upset her so? Maybe it was the attitude of the boys, Shanner's attitude. She felt a sudden surge of satisfaction at the black eye Shanner had earned testing young Thorn of Dunoon. Sometimes her brother was too arrogant even by Cloffi standards. Dunoon boys were not so self-important as the boys of Burgdeeth. Nor did they play so loose with their girls. They were laughed at in Burgdeeth, made fun of for their reticent ways. Well, Dunoon boys fought well enough all the same. There was a long black welt across Shanner's cheek, and his lip was cut and swollen. Zephy thought of the beating Thorn had received in the square, fighting the Deacons, and her blood rose hot with anger. Her hatred for the Deacons had increased this last year too; though she had never loved them. She could see Thorn's face, closed in cold fury as the Deacons struck him.

The Landmasters of Burgdeeth set little store by the goatherds of Dunoon, yet they must be tolerated or Burgdeeth would have little meat. The people would be living on old hens and an occasional rooster, and a meager few dairy calves tough as string. That, and the garden produce, which was the staple of Cloffi, of course. The Dunoon goat meat, rich and fine-grained, was a delicacy that Zephy suspected went on the Landmaster's table more often than on the tables of the town. She fingered Shanner's soft blanket woven of Dunoon wool and felt suddenly, for no reason, that without the knowledge of Dunoon, of that one free village on the mountain, life would be dull indeed.

When Shanner came up the ladder, ducking his head away from the slanting ceiling, she was sitting very straight in the moonlight. He hated that, hated her to watch him come in late. He *was* drunk. He staggered toward his cot gave her a long resentful stare, slipped out of his pants and jerkin, snatched his blanket from her, and lay down wrapped in it with his hands behind his head. "Why aren't you asleep? Why do you have to sit in that window and spy? Curiosity felled the Farrobb tribes, little sister."

She couldn't help but grin. Even drunk and angry, Shanner could charm the feathers off a river owl. "You'd think," she said slowly, reflecting, "you'd think the Landmaster would wait a day to ride to the hunt, with Nia Skane's burial tomorrow."

"Go to bed," he roared. "You can't help the dead by mourning. Why do you take on so! Why is it always something? Why can't you just leave things the way they are? If he wants to hunt, so let him!" He rolled over, sighed, then growled, "No man wants a wife who doesn't know her place," and was asleep almost at once. The stink of honeyrot filled the room. Zephy stared at him indignantly.

She slid down from the sill at last, satisfyingly chilled, and padded across the cold floor to her own cot. She fell into it, almost dead for sleep, and she slept at once.

THE CRY OF THE VENDOR brought her awake. "*Roasted marrons, hot safron, buy my marrons and brew.*" The rumble of the coal and bittleleaf wagons from Sibot Hill could already he heard and the squeak of water carts coming from the river. She knew, guiltily, that she had dreamed and lay in the darkness wrapped still in a sense of wonder; she wished she could remember the dream, but only a tide of glory remained, slowly deflating as she worried that somehow the Deacons would know she had dreamed.

But that was silly. She rose, lit the candle, glanced at Shanner, still snoring, then washed herself in the icy water from the blue crock. She bound up her hair, dressed in her everyday tunic, and, carrying the candle, started down the ladder to uncover and feed the kitchen fire before Mama should rise.

The sculler opened off the kitchen and was the first room to catch the morning sun. The round wire basket of the mawzee thresher glinted in the brightness. The stone walls of the sculler were lined with shelves that held crocks of mawzee grain, some of yesterday's loaves, a bowl of charp fruit turning golden, and some oddments of tools and jugs and crockery. Zephy knelt by the low stone ice safe, opened its drain and let it drip into a bucket, then took off the lid of the safe itself and settled the bittleleaf packing tighter around yesterday's milk bucket and around the crock of meat. Outside the sculler window, the Trashsinger called and began a tune Zephy loved. She sang it with him softly, "Jajun, Jajun, come to the winter feasting." She longed to reach down her gaylute from where it lay atop the cupboard, but to play it this time of morning when she should be doing her work would only anger Mama, and she guessed she'd done enough of that lately. She got her milk pails from the sculler and went through the kitchen, then the longroom, where one of the chamber girls was setting out plates on the tables. In the entry she passed her mother's room, heard her stirring, then pulled open the heavy outer door.

The street was busy though the sky was barely light. Wagons were unloading at the Storesmaster's and water buckets were being filled. She tried not to think that the Deacons had already buried Nia Skane, in darkness, and were probably, even now, mortaring the stone that would seal her in forever. No one seemed to remember it, the town was far too busy with its morning chores.

By noon she had finished her work in the sculler, hoed the charp bed where weeds seemed to spring overnight, and packed Shanner's noon meal to take to him in the forgeshop. She paused outside the doorway to the shop, for she could hear Shanner and the Kubalese apprentice arguing loudly. She heard the bellows huffing and saw the firelight flare up and saw the shadows of the two facing each other as the Kubalese mocked sarcastically, "What do *I* care what they say in the street! What do *I* care what the old women prattle—Kubalese in the Inn woman's bed!" He laughed harshly.

"Well *I* care, you son of Urdd! I care for my mother's name!" Shanner, usually in charge of a situation, was far from collected now.

The Kubalese's voice was as cold as winter. "Like it or not, what have *you* to say about it? It's none of your affair and none of your sister's, either. If she doesn't stop that nasty tongue, she's going to get more than she bargained for."

"She speaks less pointedly than the gossips on the street, Kubal!"

If it were a Cloffi man their mother was friendly with, people wouldn't talk so. But a Kubalese. Though the men of the town found Kearb-Mattus pleasant enough to drink with, laughing around the longtables at the Inn. And the Kubalese was handsome, Zephy had to admit. He seemed more alive than Cloffi men, somehow, so that women often turned to stare after him. But there was a violence about him, too, something underneath the charm that made Zephy uneasy.

"The girl upsets your mother, boy. She thinks to mind grown-up business." Then he laughed, seemed jovial suddenly—changeable as a junfish, he was. "Needs some ardent boy in her bed, that'd change her view of the world." Zephy's face went hot at his rude talk. "She's not such a bad looking child, fix her up a bit. They're right good before they've had other hands on 'em—shy and goosey as a wild doe on the mountain. And those dark eyes—too bold for a Cloffi man, I'd wager. Eyes like her mother," the Kubalese said and roared with laughter.

Zephy dropped Shanner's dinner basket by the door and fled.

The first time she had been teased about the Kubalese and Mama, she had gone into the sculler in tears, with terrible thoughts about Mama. And she had found Mama waiting, her brown eyes dark with fury, so Zephy knew she had heard the baiting.

Comely, her mother was, and slim, and she could look beautiful. But when she scowled, a storm seemed to crack around her. She had stood blocking the door between sculler and kitchen, her brown hair escaping from its bun and her hands floury from making bread. Zephy had stared back at her, dreadfully ashamed of the gossip—and ashamed of Mama.

"So you believe what they say in the street."

Zephy couldn't answer, could not look at her.

"*Did you ever think they could be wrong!* Did you ever think it could be lies!" There was a long pause, uncomfortable for Zephy. "It's time you thought, Zephyr Eskar." Then, seeing Zephy's chagrin, Mama had taken her in her arms as if she were small again, pushing back her hair as she used to do.

The last time Zephy had heard remarks in the street, she had stormed in through the heavy front doors of the longroom only to face Kearb-Mattus, standing in the shadows, and she had not been able to keep her temper, and flown at him in a rage, screaming childishly, "No one wants you here. Leave my mother alone!"

The Kubalese had stared down at her, his dark eyes expressionless. Then he had caught her by the shoulder so hard that afterward it was bruised. He held her away, his words soft and menacing. "Whatever I do, pretty child, whatever I intend to do, it's none of your affair. Understand me?" The threat in those soft words had chilled Zephy so she hung rigid, gaping at him, a black loathing and fear sweeping her. Wanting to hit him and afraid to and unable to pull away.

"Now come on, pretty little thing"—he had brought his face close to hers, his black beard like a bristling hedge—"Come on, pretty little child—Ha! Temper like a river cat!" He had roared with laughter, spit collecting on his lips.

When at last he let her go, she had whirled away from him and up the stairs to the loft, where she had burst into tears of helpless fury. Her tears were seldom of hurt, but rather of rage at something she was powerless to change.

Mama said once of Kearb-Mattus, "All the children in Burgdeeth follow him. How can you say he's cruel when they all like him so. The children wouldn't—"

"Sweets, Mama! You know his pockets are full of cicaba candy and raisins. He gives them sweets for their attention. Besides, it isn't *all* the children! Nia Skane won't have anything to do with him."

"You're not being fair, Nia is . . ." Mama had stared at Zephy, then finished lamely, "Well most of the children like Kearb-Mattus."

"Nia is what?"

"She . . ." Mama had faltered. Zephy had looked at her evenly. "She . . . oh, Zephy, Nia's different, she's a child that . . . she's just different."

"*Different* because she doesn't run with the other girls her age and do all the stupid things they do? Different because she doesn't giggle all the time? Different, Mama? Different like me and Meatha?"

And now . . . now Nia Skane was dead.

Chapter Three

THORN GLANCED at the yellow ball of sun halfway up the sky. The day was beginning to grow warm. He had been skinning out two wolves; they hung red and naked from the eaves as he began to stretch their thick-furred hides across the hut wall. Behind him the mountain glinted. His stomach rumbled with hunger. He could smell the noon meal cooking; soon enough there would be fried goatmeat and mawzee cakes—his mother fed him up good when he'd been on the pastures all night.

When he finished stretching the hides, he began to strip the meat from the carcasses—they were no longer animals now, writhing in the pain of dying so he gritted his teeth and felt their agony. He had killed them as quickly as he could. Now, with the skins off, he had taught himself to think of them only as hanks of meat. He stripped off the meat in long pieces, sliced it thin, and laid it across the drying rack. It would be salted and cured and mixed with fireberries and otter-herb to make the squares of mountain-meat that would bide the winter nights when he or his father stood watch in the pastures, would bide them all, perhaps, if the winter should be harsh, or if there should be need of food taken hurriedly, without cook fires. He turned to shift the drying rack and saw his father standing silently at the corner of the house examining the hides.

"You got that big dog-wolf!" Oak Dar said, fingering the wide black stripe that decorated the larger hide.

"And his mate, I think," Thorn said sadly.

"Better to go together than parted."

Thorn nodded, feeling warm toward his father. The wolves killed because it was their living, and neither Thorn or the Goatmaster felt animosity toward them. But the wolves killed their herds, and must be taken in turn, that was the way of it.

The Goatmaster examined the striped hide more carefully. "The bucks gored him good."

"Yes. The old wolf put up a battle."

"And you finished him through the neck," he said, putting his finger through Thorn's arrow hole.

Thorn nodded. The older man took out his knife and began to work on the other carcass. Swifter and neater than Thorn he was, taking the meat off the bones clean and quick. Thorn tried to settle to his work, but began to think of Burgdeeth for no reason so the unease within him stirred and rose as it had done again and again since his last trip down, a strong bristling of concern, as if a yeast worked there in Burgdeeth and part of it clung to him when he came away.

The feeling had to do with the Kubalese apprentice to Shanner Eskar. Thorn grinned at the thought of Shanner's bruised face, though he held him no enmity—just that he'd gotten his own back, that was all. Shanner was the best of the Burgdeeth lot, and Thorn had a liking for him. But the Kubalese, Kearb-Mattus, that was another matter. I wish I had the sight really, he thought, instead of these niggling itches. Then I'd know why the Kubalese is there. He turned the carcass and began to strip the other side; the stripping went faster with two working.

He glanced up at the edge of the village once, where the does were being milked, and when he looked back he saw that his father had stopped work and was watching him. Silent, with that studying look. His father's eyes were a rusty brown, and his thatch of hair over that square face as dark as the stripe on the wolf's pelt. His look was unwavering. "You are troubled, son, and I think you do not know why."

"Yes father. Something . . . something . . ."

"Some trouble you carried up with you from Burgdeeth. Is it the Kubalese? Have you heard more about his reasons for being there?"

"Only the story that he was a smith in his own country, and came to Burgdeeth to increase his art."

Oak Dar snorted, unbelieving. "Likely the townspeople of Burgdeeth know no more than that. They believe pretty well as they are bidden. But there is a piece of news. A trader came up the mountain last night, he is staying with Merden's family. He brought news that, if you had not been herding, you would know by now. It is like the rumors that have come, but sounding as if there are more facts to it. The Kubalese are arming heavy, he says, and have stockpiled supplies on the borders. It is thought they plan to work their way silently into Urobb and Farr. If this is true, they will take those two countries as surely as night drowns the sun."

"But that will mean—"

"That Aybil is next. And then Cloffi."

"Will the trader take this word to Burgdeeth? But he has come from there. Did he stop with it?"

"He did not stop, he came through silently under darkness. It is said in Sibot Hill that the Kubalese smith is thick with the Landmaster of Burgdeeth, and the trader thought to warn us first and to seek our advice."

"And that is?"

"He must go to The Landmaster, he can do no less. I fear for him, but there is no other way but the direct one.

To spread the word secretly would only stir fear and leave the men of Burgdeeth open to ridicule, unable to organize anything without their mounts and weapons that are all in the Landmaster's Set. The men of Cloffi are not bold enough, or wilful enough, to plan a good deceit against the Landmaster. They do not value their freedom sufficiently." Oak Dar scratched his head, puzzling. "What good would it do the Landmaster to court collusion with the Kubalese? He would only lose his reign. Four times in the past the Kubalese have begun so, secretly, and each time has ended in conquerings. I can't understand the Landmaster's view of the world if he does not take warning from that.

"Keep your ears open, maybe you'll hear something of value. Market day is soon—meantime we must lay some plans. Our best weapon will be cleverness. Eresu knows the Landmaster would lift no hand to help us, and we are but a small band." He gave Thorn a clear look. "If you had the Rune of Eresu the old man spoke of, would you have the sight?"

"I would have it," Thorn said with sudden conviction.

"It would be a great help to Dunoon. Perhaps to many more." Then Oak Dar grinned. "We would be stoned in Burgdeeth for such talk."

"Stoned, and worse. I have hunted the mountain caves, the old ruins and grottoes for the runestone." Thorn's eyes searched Oak Dar's. "If it is hidden in the north of Cloffi, and if the power is in me to use it, then I mean to have it somehow."

Ever since the old man had spoken his prophecy, Thorn had spent every free moment in the caves of the ancient city Owdneet; he had discovered caves he had not known, had pressed into narrow crevices and seams and searched pools cold as winter. He had tried to send some unbridled sense of seeing out to touch the shard of jade; but such skill had not come on him, had left him as blind.

And while he searched, the runestone lay somewhere in darkness. *Found by the light of one candle,* the old man had said. *Carried in a searching. Lost in terror.* What did it mean? He knew not, but he sensed that the stone would be needed soon, felt it in the very core of his being.

Once, exploring along a cave's high natural ledge, he had been startled to see a clear vision; though it had not to do with the stone. He saw two faces, young girls, very frightened. One of them was crying. He knew her, though not her name. The other, brown eyed, thin faced, was Zephy Eskar. They were kneeling before the winged statue in Burgdeeth; and he knew that this quick, unexplained glimpse was important to him, though he had no clue to help him understand it. It faded quickly, and his feeling of bereavement afterward was strange and powerful.

Chapter Four

ZEPHY DIDN'T KNOW what was the matter, only that Meatha had appeared in the milk line pale as death, and when Zephy asked her in whispers what was wrong, she had burst into tears. Now they knelt at the base of the god-statue, having come for privacy so they could talk; but three older women had pushed through the hedge to kneel in prayer, and they could say nothing; nor could they leave until they had been there an appropriate time. The statue towered above them, the winged god rearing into the sky, his human torso above the horselike body catching the sun, his arms reaching as if, indeed, he lifted on the wind; and beside him the two winged Horses of Eresu thrust skyward; the shadows of their wings swept across the girls' heads and out across the cobbles. Meatha was trying to hide her tears from the women who knelt so near them.

They could not talk until at last they made their way to the housegardens through Burgdeeth's narrow streets, the smells of tannery and candlewax and of baking bread marking the little shops; and the smell of cess from a row of outhouses. The gardens were blessedly empty.

At midday, most women and girls found chores to do in the scullers, coming out again as the hot summer sun lowered. Beside Zephy's vetchpea rows, their two donkeys drowsed in the pen, their ears twitching at the garden flies. The vetchpeas were getting ripe, their long pods dragging the turned earth. The smell of a rotten charp fruit, missed in the last picking, came sickeningly on the breeze.

They sat on the edge of the irrigation ditch. Meatha had stopped crying, but she looked terrified. Her dark hair was dishevelled, and her lavender eyes seemed larger than ever and were bleary from the tears.

Zephy was strung tight with impatience. "Tell me! Whatever is it? Did some boy? . . ."

Meatha shook her head and swallowed. When she spoke at last, her voice was only a whisper. "Not a boy. It—I had a dream. No, it wasn't a dream." She stared at Zephy, shaken. "It was a vision, Zephy. I was awake. I was standing in the sculler. It was a *seeing*. Like Ynell."

Zephy caught her breath, fear rising; fear, and excitement.

"A vision as real as if I were there, the wind was cold and I could smell the mountains. I was awake, Zephy. I didn't see the sculler, I saw . . ." Meatha became silent. Zephy stared at her, waiting, shocked with the sin of it—and with the wonder.

When a dream occurred due to illness, it was supposed to be a gray colorless affair soon wiped clean from the mind with herbs and with sacrificial penances. To have a dream was a sin that could be cured—though Zephy and Meatha had never told anyone of theirs. But to have a true waking vision could only be dealt with through the sacrifice of death.

"At first, before the cold wind came, I was standing by a wagon. The most wonderful wagon, painted with birds and flowers in bright colors. An old, tall man was driving. Lean and sunbrowned, with very white hair. I thought he was a man of great wonder. He didn't say anything, but sat looking down at me while the horses churned and snorted. They were butternut color, not a stroke of white, and beautiful—like Carriol horses. He said—not in words, but in my thoughts and silently—that he must speak with me. There was something happening around us, some activity with many people. He spoke to me in silence, so they never knew. There was someone with him, a boy, but I could not tell who. Then the old man was gone and there was terror all around me, people were pulling at me and jerking at me and at someone else too. It was—they were pulling off our clothes . . ." Meatha caught her breath, her eyes full of such pain that Zephy's own breathing was constricted. "Then it changed and I was alone in a place all barren, with white round boulders humping and a kind of white stone path that climbed the mountain. I was . . ." Meatha's voice shook. "I was tied to the death stone, Zephy."

They had seen children dressed in rags and smeared with dung and filth, strapped across the backs of donkeys like sacks of meal, and taken away to the death stone. Children from Burgdeeth and from Sibot Hill and Quaymus, for only this one road led upward. Always the donkeys were accompanied by red-robed Deacons, and often by the town's Landmaster himself, mounted and austere.

They sat staring at the swirl of water in the ditch. Beyond the green rows of dill and tervil, the misty hills humped along the border between Cloffi and Kubal. To their left, the black towering mountains shadowed the town and fields. Up behind those peaks lay Eresu, where the gods dwelt. *And those who defy the powers of the gods, those who sin as Ynell sinned, shall know death.*

Meatha was a Child of Ynell, they could no longer escape it. If discovered, she would die. Meatha, whose beauty was like the mabin bird, her pale translucent skin and dark hair, her incredibly lavender eyes. If Zephy had ever been jealous of that beauty, she could not be now.

How could the Luff'Eresi be so cruel? What harm could Meatha possibly do?

Meatha roused herself at last. "There's bittleleaf to haul this afternoon; we won't have time to hoe."

"We'll be questioned about why we're out here then. I wish . . . if we'd only be assigned to take a load of bittleleaf to Dunoon . . ." Zephy said hopefully.

"The Deacons would never pick us again, not after last time. My mother said . . ."

"I know. Both our mothers. And the Deacons mad enough to . . ."

"To make a curse-penance on us at worship," Meatha said with shame. But though they had been punished for swimming in the Owdneet, no one had discovered that the seats of their underpants were hairy from the donkey's backs. For in a fit of boldness they had ridden the little beasts along the deserted shore of the Owdneet, galloping wild and crazy with delight, the word *forbidden* shrieking in their heads. No one had thought to look at their underpants, the wet condition of their hair being quite enough to send them, red-faced, to crouch on their knees for most of the seven days afterward, their hands and feet smeared with red clay to symbolize the destruction by fire that the anger of the Luff'Eresi could bring down upon all of Cloffi because of their sinning.

Shanner had shouted with laughter when he heard. "Next time," he had chided, "get the boys to take you, dallying with boys isn't half so bad a sin as girls going by themselves to defy the Covenants. You could always say you fell in the Owdneet by accident in a fit of desire," he had roared.

But there would not be another time. Other girls, dutiful girls or girls clever in hiding their activities, would be sent on the occasional hauling trip. Boys and men did not do such work. If the bittleleaf was delivered from Sibot

Hill and there was no one from Dunoon to take its share up the mountain, then someone from Burgdeeth must. The bittleleaf, used for storing ice, did not keep well. Its replacement was needed often.

For a long time, the shame the village had made them feel about that forbidden swim had been almost more than they could bear.

"Even so, it was worth it," Meatha said now, quietly and passionately. "It was the best day of my whole life. Swimming naked in the Owdneet and galloping in the wind was like—like being someone else, something . . . Oh, I don't know exactly. Something wonderful."

"Yes," Zephy said softly. And she remembered seeing Thorn of Dunoon there, high on the mountain above them guarding the flocks, his red hair catching the sun. She remembered the feeling it had given her of freedom—that one lone figure—remembered all the pleasure of that day, then the sudden weight of hatefulness that had nearly wiped it out when, returning home, they had been confronted by the Deacons. "Why is it that everything that's a pleasure is a sin? When I was little, Mama used to tell me stories to make me forget the Deacons and their horrible meanness. Now I'm too old, I guess." She missed the closeness with Mama, missed Mama's understanding. Was Mama different because of Kearb-Mattus? Or did things just change when you grew up—is it me who's different? She wondered.

Now, the only time Zephy could touch that sense of joy that Mama's stories had created for her was when she and Meatha went secretly to visit Burgdeeth's teacher; and she said now, fearfully, "Are you going to tell Tra. Hoppa about the vision?"

Meatha stared at her. "I don't know. No. It would only put her in more danger. It's enough that she teaches us secretly, tells us more than she teaches the boys, and that she's told us about the tunnel. No one else in Burgdeeth knows about that, not even the Landmaster, and we would all surely be killed if he found out. But now this—I can't tell Tra. Hoppa this, I shouldn't even have told you. Oh, Zephy . . ." Meatha dissolved into tears again, and Zephy, her brown eyes wide with compassion, held her and let her cry.

But Meatha did tell Tra. Hoppa. She had needed desperately to tell someone older, and the little schoolteacher, who shared so many secrets with them, was the only adult they could trust.

Chapter Five

TRA. HOPPA'S HOUSE rose tall and narrow, alone at the edge of the village. Not attached to other houses, it found its own shelter in the ancient grove of twisted plum trees that had been there even before the Herebian Wars, before Burgdeeth was built.

People said Tra. Hoppa was the only woman in Burgdeeth who didn't work for her keep. As if teaching a bunch of fidgeting boys wasn't work! The Landmaster sent only the youngest girls to tend her housegarden, thinking they wouldn't be curious about the history of Ere, wouldn't hunger to learn to read. For no Cloffi woman could read or do more than the simplest ciphering.

Zephy had been only five when she tended Tra. Hoppa's first garden; but Tra. Hoppa had made it easy for her, in her quiet way, to reach out: when the lessons began secretly they were wonderful to Zephy, who had been told all her short life that little girls did not yearn after reading and history, that only boys could attempt such tasks.

But now, it was getting more difficult each day for Zephy and Meatha to make their way to Tra. Hoppa's unseen. The excuses, when they were stopped by a Deacon, had become harder to think up. "What are you doing away from your garden? Why are you not in your sculler, threshing mawzee, baking bread?" There was a limit to how many times you could blame it on a loose donkey or an errand for Mama that might be checked on.

Yet they needed these times with Tra. Hoppa. The Cloffi teachings in Temple were so depressing. Evil and sinning was all the Luff'Eresi seemed concerned about, and humans were weak vessels indeed, if you believed all the Covenants and rituals. Only when they were with Tra. Hoppa did they see, fleetingly, dignity and strength in humankind. Without Tra. Hoppa, they might have grown as sour as the dullest Cloffi woman.

Tra. Hoppa's house had just one room to a floor, the ground floor making the kitchen with a sitting place and a table, the next floor the lesson-room, and the third floor, the loft, Tra. Hoppa's bedroom and study. That a woman should have books and a study was suspect among the other women of Burgdeeth. Perhaps they tolerated it partly because Tra. Hoppa was not a Cloffa but Carriolinian, and those of Carriol had an aura about them that seemed to soften even the staid Cloffi women. Tra. Hoppa had been the only foreigner allowed residence in Burgdeeth—until the Kubalese came. She was the only woman who had ever occupied the position of teacher. But in spite of her sex and her learning, there was a grudging respect for Tra. Hoppa, for she spoke quietly, did not raise her voice in temper, kept her eyes cast down when in public. Only in the loft, where the real books were hidden, did she come truly alive. Then there was nothing docile about her, she was as bright and eager as a child.

The girls stood in her stone kitchen, out of breath as Tra. Hoppa closed the door behind them. Little and thin and wrinkled she was, her white hair tied in the traditional bun. But she moved with quick eagerness, and her deep blue eyes were not the eyes of an aged woman at all. "Come quickly, then. I've such a surprise for you."

The furnishings of the loft were simple. Below the

window was a long floor cushion covered with Zandourian weaving in bright colors and a low chair for Tra. Hoppa. At the other end of the room, Tra. Hoppa's bed was tucked between the bookshelves.

Always in this room Zephy felt freed from Burgdeeth: here she felt she could touch the farthest shores of Ere and touch times long past. Sometimes, here, she could nearly comprehend the vague plane on which the gods dwelt, the plane that came closer only in the years the star Waytheer was close. Here she could give rein to the feelings that made life in Burgdeeth tolerable; feelings which, at the same time, drove her into a passion to leave Burgdeeth behind forever.

The surprise must be a forbidden book; yet that was hard to believe, for it could only have been brought secretly by a trader, and there had been few in the last weeks. Zephy hoped that was it, though: Meatha needed something to take her mind off the vision that had haunted her constantly, turning her pale and silent.

"It is the Book of the Drowning Land," Tra. Hoppa said, drawing forth a frail, leather-bound volume. "I have it from that trader with oil from Sangur—we have . . . mutual friends in Carriol. It tells all the history and the myths of Ere from the point where the Book of Three Cities leaves off, just as it is told in Carriol; tells of the Drowning of Opensa . . ."

When Tra. Hoppa had finished reading to them, Zephy sat staring before her, seeing the island of Opensa, honeycombed with caves that made the ancient city; hearing the earth rumble and seeing it shake as the island began to crack. She could see the gods and their consorts leaping into the sky as the mythical sea god, SkokeDirgOg, sank Opensa in a shower of thunder.

Tra. Hoppa laid the book down and sat quietly studying Meatha. Meatha looked up once, then looked down at her hands again. Zephy started to speak, but the old lady stopped her with a look. "Meatha, you are troubled; will you tell me?"

Meatha fiddled with the fringe on the floor pad, hesitating for a long time. Then, "Do you remember when I had a vision and was too young to know I shouldn't tell? And you stopped me?"

"Of course I do."

"I never told you, Tra. Hoppa, but it happened to me twice after that, when I was old enough to understand. I didn't want you to *have* to know. But now it has happened again, and it was so much stronger, not even like the others. It was as if I was *there*, first here in Burgdeeth and then on the mountain. I could feel the cold wind and smell the mountains, and there was sablevine rusty on the rocks as if it was early winter. I have to tell you, Tra. Hoppa. There's no one else except Zephy, and I'm so afraid."

Tra. Hoppa looked at Meatha for a long moment, then rose to stand staring out the window. When at last she turned back to them, she knelt down on the mat and took Meatha's hands.

"Don't ever be afraid, child. Not for yourself, not for me. Tell me now, you were on the mountain . . ."

Meatha, fragile and trembling, made Zephy want to hit out at something. How could the will of the Luff'Eresi demand that Meatha die at the death stone for something she could no more help than breathing?

When Meatha finished her story, Tra. Hoppa looked as drawn and pale as she. Had Meatha's vision opened some private and uneasy place in Tra. Hoppa's own thoughts?

"What am I to do?" Meatha asked quietly.

"Do, child?" Tra. Hoppa put her arm around Meatha. "You are to do as you have always done. You are to say nothing. You are to act in no way different from any other Cloffi girl, no matter how hard that is. And above all, you are not to be afraid. This is no evil that has visited you, it is something wonderful. You have no cause to be ashamed of it. Only you must be wary that no one learns what you have seen."

Meatha stared back and bit her lip. "Maybe someone else already knows that I—what I am," she said softly. "Maybe the Kubalese knows."

"He couldn't!" Zephy breathed.

"He watches me more than I ever told you, Zephy."

"Yes he does," Tra. Hoppa said. "I have seen him. And he watches the younger children, too. They take his candy, and some of them follow him, but they don't like him much. And some of them, little Elodia Trayd for one, keep out of his way. Haven't you noticed that?"

"Yes," Zephy said. "And something else about Elodia. Yesterday she gave me such a strange look, so—so knowing." She shivered. It had bothered her, she had waked in the night thinking about the child's cool, gray-eyed stare. She had taken Mama's shoes to be sewn, and Elodia was standing with two other little girls in front of the Cobbler's, watching the old men play stones. The frail old men, retired from their masterships, had stood in a semicircle casting the stone across the cobbles in the sun, making bets. Half a dozen little boys had watched them, betting too, while the three girls stood apart as they had been told, silent and docile as sheep.

Except Elodia Trayd. She wasn't docile, she had stared up at Zephy boldly, her gray eyes kindling; and Zephy had seen something in that little face almost like herself there, something crying out wildly. "It was almost as if she felt my anger that the girl children had to be so docile, that they *were* so obedient," Zephy said.

"There's another one like that," Meatha said. "And he stays away from the Kubalese, too. I was watching Kearb-Mattus play with some children, hiding red rags as they do in the Burgdeeth Horse mock hunt in the springtime. He had hidden one rag in a barrel. I could see it, but the children were too short. The little boy, Graged Orden, started for the barrel as if he knew the rag was there, then all at once he went pale. He turned, looked at the Kubalese watching him, and ran away out of the street as if he was terrified. He has avoided the Kubalese since. I've seen him slip around corners to get out of his way."

"I wish the Kubalese had never come to Burgdeeth," Tra. Hoppa said. "That trader brought me more than the forbidden book, he brought rumors that are unsettling. It is said in the south that Kubal is arming for war."

"Against who?" Zephy said, going cold.

"It would not be Carriol," Tra. Hoppa said. "They are too strong."

"Cloffi," Meatha breathed. "Cloffi and Urobb and Farr all lie on the Kubalese border."

"And if they attack one," Zephy said slowly, "they will attack all three."

They stared at each other, the thought of war chilling them. "It is only rumors," Tra. Hoppa said. "But I would wish you two away if such a thing should happen."

Then she smiled. "Come, there's otter-herb tea brewing, and nightberry muffins made with berries from the mountain. Young Thorn of Dunoon brought them down."

Thorn of Dunoon?

But of course, he came to Tra. Hoppa for lessons. In turn, he taught the younger children of Dunoon. And, Zephy wondered suddenly, what kind of lessons did Thorn of Dunoon receive? Ordinary ones, like the boys of Burgdeeth? Or did Thorn come to the loft and read the secret books as she and Meatha did?

She had no reason to suspect such a thing. And she would never ask. Yet—perhaps Thorn of Dunoon was the kind of boy Tra. Hoppa would teach with great interest.

Chapter Six

ERE'S MOONS WAXED to brightness and waned again before the night that, while Cloffi lay sleeping, the Kubalese army rose up, and the little country of Urobb was destroyed.

The attack came down on Urobb on the first night of the Festival of Fish Taking, driving the Urobb tribes back from the river where they had gathered for the fish-rituals, and into the waiting platoons of the Kubalese Horse that had slipped like silent whispers in from the borders of Kubal. A long thin country, Urobb now was squeezed to nothing in the meshing of the two companies of Kubalese warriors, caught and trapped between them just as they themselves had planned to net the breeding shummerfins that swam the River Urobb.

The villages were burned and the women raped and put to labor at food gathering and cooking for the Kubalese bivouacs that remained behind. The hooved animals, horses and donkeys, were taken with the army as bounty, and the meager country, which had only its coal to sell and its fish and mountain crops to sustain it, lay fallen only a few hours after the attack began.

Now that Urobb was taken, Kubal's land extended to the Urobb River. East of the river lay Carriol—Kubal would not attack her—then the sea. But to the west of Kubal lay Farr and Cloffi. Rivers are coveted, they water crops and herds, and they carry gold in their sands. Kubal had the Urobb. Now she eyed the Owdneet that ran down through the center of Cloffi then through Aybil and Farr to the sea.

The escaped and terrified miner who brought the message to Cloffi predicted in a breaking voice Farr's certain demise, and then Aybil's, his eyes red from lack of sleep and from fear and hunger. "And then," he said, almost triumphantly, "and then it will be Cloffi. It will be Cloffi they rape and destroy." His voice was filled with a passion of hatred as he stared up at Thorn—for it was Thorn who found him slipping along in the brush of the river outside Burgdeeth.

The little Urobb miner had come up along the river instead by the road, hiding in the bushes at night and eating of sablevine roots and of berries and morliespongs. When the distraught man saw Thorn, he stared at him as if he stared at death itself, and turned to run but Thorn grabbed him. Thorn saw the man's terror and took him to a sheltered place behind a stand of wild vetchpea. He held out his waterskin, though the river was close, and gave the man his ration of bread and goatsmilk cheese, slicing them on the flat surface of a boulder. The miner ate as if he had not seen proper food for days.

Squally, his name was. When he had told Thorn his story, he wanted to be taken at once up the mountain, before he could be seized and held by the Landmaster. "And I will be, don't doubt you that. I came secretly up the river to give my news freely to the common men of Burgdeeth, not to the Landmaster—there is a Kubal here, is there not, young goatherd?"

Thorn nodded and sat studying the small, wiry miner whose eyes squinted as if the light of common day was too bright after a lifetime in the coal mines.

"It was so in Sibot Hill, a Kubalese has come there.

I had to slip away by night lest they imprison me. The Kubalese have made some bargain with the Landmaster of Sibot Hill. The Landmaster stood before his people and swore there would be no attack from Kubal. He would have sent me to sleep in the Sibot Hill cells, had I not escaped. It will be the same in Burgdeeth. There is no place left save Dunoon where a man can be safe, not this side of the Urobb, boy."

"We'll tell the people of Burgdeeth though," Thorn said shortly. "We'll get away before the Deacons hear of it." If we're quick, he thought. If we're lucky. But he knew they had to try.

They made their way through the high stand of white-barley that separated the river from Burgdeeth and into the back streets and alleys, then to the Inn. But the Kubalese was taking his noon meal there; Thorn could see him through the unshuttered window. He led the Urobb away, to the forgeshop.

Shanner Eskar lay sprawled across a bench, eating charp fruit. Thorn greeted him, then gave his attention to the Forgemaster, who sat at his work table drinking a bowl of broth. Old Yelig honored Thorn with a rare smile, and Thorn went to him and laid his hand on the old man's shoulder. "We have uneasy business to speak of, Yelig. Business the Landmaster won't sanction. Would you rather we went elsewhere?"

"I've not gotten so old and crusty by hiding from the Deacons of Burgdeeth. That is why I am still master of my shop and not playing stones on the street. A bit of serious business isn't going to harm me, lad. Now what is it that brings you here with a face as long as a river-owl's?"

"Urobb has been taken, defeated. This is Squally from Urobb; he brought the news. He feared to bring such to the Landmaster."

Shanner was staring at Thorn, his eyes dark. "He is

right. The Landmaster won't let the news be known. He claims there will be no attack, even though we've been drilling the whole Burgdeeth Horse every day. He's as touchy as a trapped weasel. There's something afoot, and you'd best be out of it, Yelig."

The old man's streaked hair was a bristly thatch across his ears. He stared at Shanner for a long minute, then sat back and motioned the miner to make himself comfortable.

As the story was told, Yelig's expression grew more grim, as did Shanner's, and when it was finished, Squally exhausted with his own emotion, they sat silent. Then at last Shanner glanced up through the window. "The Kubalese will be back after his meal. We'd best spread the word." He looked at Thorn, motioned to the Urobb, and the three of them went out.

ZEPHY WAS SCRUBBING COOKPOTS when she heard shouting in the street. She ran out, leaving the greasy water in the basin, her hands dripping—men had gathered in the street, it looked like all of Burgdeeth.

"Don't let anyone tell you . . ."

"The Landmaster *said* they . . ."

"But it's war!"

"—over the borders of Urobb like hunters taking the stag, the Urobb miner said so!"

"Well *he* got out, didn't he? How do we know—"

"He was the only one. And they were headed for Farr. After that . . ."

She stepped back into the doorway as four red-robed Deacons converged on the group. The crowd drew back at once and stood silent and uneasy before them. The Senior Deacon, Feill Wellick, stood with his staff raised in anger.

Zephy saw Shanner in the crowd. Then she caught her breath, for Thorn of Dunoon was with him, his red hair bright against the stone wall of the Glassmaker's shop. And she thought, He should wear a cap if he wants to go unseen.

What had made her think that? But yes, Thorn and Shanner were slipping away quickly behind the crowd accompanied by a third man: she felt a sick fear for no reason.

There was an ugly sound from the crowd, and when Zephy turned to see, there was Kearb-Mattus standing with the Deacons as self-confident as if he were one of them. No Cloffi man would stand so, head up and eyes brazen, beside Deacons. The Kubalese was going to speak to the crowd! Speak in place of the Deacons? Zephy stood staring.

The Kubalese's voice was deep with confidence. The muttering of the crowd stopped at once. The man's charm and assurance held them. "There will be no war, men of Burgdeeth. Listen to your Deacons. Kubal will not attack Cloffi; the Kubalese and the Landmasters of Cloffi have made a pact of friendship."

"But what of Urobb?" someone shouted.

"Urobb is another matter and not of concern to you."

There was cheering—but some muttering, too. Zephy felt an unease begin to grow in the crowd, and fear crept along her spine. But then another fear touched that one as two of the Deacons stared toward an alley: they started forward suddenly so the crowd drew back; they lunged, caught someone, were struggling to hold him captive, someone who fought them . . .

His red hair flashed as he was pummelled between the Deacons. His arms were pulled behind him, and he was prodded in the direction of the Set between four Deacons. Behind him came the little wizened man, led on a rope like a donkey.

"Might have suspected, a Dunoon goatherd . . ."

"It's the Urobb behind him . . ."

"Why do they take the miner prisoner? Would the Landmaster keep the truth from us?"

"Hush . . ."

"Shanner Eskar was with them, where is Shanner Eskar?"

"It's his mother got him free, I heard the Kubal say . . ."

Zephy stared, stricken, as Thorn of Dunoon was led away. When she could no longer see him, or see the cluster of red robes, she looked stupidly at the crowd, then fled to the sculler.

Shaken and trembling, she stood in the herb scented sculler awash with emotions she could not name. Urobb had been defeated by Kubal. Cloffi might be next. But the spinning terror in the pit of her stomach had nothing to do with war. All she could see was Thorn of Dunoon's face, and the fury in his eyes as he was forced away toward the Set.

When Shanner came home at last, late in the night, she sat up in the darkness of the loft. It would be all right now that Shanner was here. No one had told her anything, no one would speak of what had happened, of Urobb, of war—she had dared not ask about Thorn.

But Shanner was surly to her questions, as unwilling to talk as everyone else. He sat on his cot staring at his feet until she almost screamed with frustration. "What has happened? *Tell* me *something!* And why did they let *you* go and not Thorn?"

"They just let me go," he said dully. "What do you mean, 'and not Thorn'?" She could see he was tired. It took him a minute to realize what she had said. It took her only a second to wish she hadn't said it. He stared at her, surprised. Then he grinned.

"I didn't mean . . ." she began.

"I know what you meant, little sister." He smiled

knowingly. She could have hit him. "Well there's nothing for it now, poor girl." He gave her a look of mock pity. "Well, Zephy, it wasn't *me* brought in the Urobb! What did you want me to do, demand to be taken? By Eresu, this is a blazing damned time to turn into a giddy woman!"

She stared at him, wishing he wouldn't tease. She was awash with uncertainty, confused at her own sudden feelings, and needing him to talk to.

"Why couldn't you just dally around like the other girls? Great flaming Urdd, Zephy, why do you have to make things so serious?"

"What will they do to him?"

"*I* don't know. Lock him up—and the miner, too—for a few days." His eyes were red and tired. She daren't ask anything more.

She held her tears until Shanner was asleep, then she dissolved into a misery she didn't understand and only wanted to be rid of.

Few Cloffa had seen the Landmaster's quarters, except the serving girls who lived there. Though most Burgdeeth men came into the Set to train with the Burgdeeth Horse, their drilling ground was the enclosure itself where the mounts were stabled, not the sumptuous apartments. And Thorn had not seen even the drilling ground, for Dunoon men did not serve in the Horse. He was taken, now, through the parade ground, past the stables, and in through the thick double doors.

The ceiling of the room he entered was as high as the winged statue in the square, as tall as three floors of a common house. Around its upper third ran a balcony with a carved railing, where a fat young girl was standing with a dust cloth in her hand, looking down with curiosity. Below the railing, the walls were wonderfully smooth and were painted with scenes in colors beyond imagining, scenes of the gods, of the Luff'Eresi flying in the clouds. But there was something strange about the pictures, something . . . They were ugly! The Luff'Eresi were not beautiful like the statue in the square: they were heavy, with bold, cruel faces, their wings leathery and thick and their horses' legs common and hairy. Their eyes were cold and cruel, and they held men in their hands, men as small as toys. They were flying with them and tossing them into the sky, they were . . . they were eating them! Apalled, Thorn stood frozen, staring.

A Deacon jerked him rudely, and Thorn tore his gaze from the paintings to see the Landmaster watching him.

"Those are your gods, Thorn of Dunoon," the fat man said sarcastically. He gave the picture a proprietary glance, and his mouth twisted in a caustic smile.

"Why have you brought me here?" Thorn demanded. "What do you want of me?" If he were Oak Dar he would have been more subtle, his father could be very politic, but Thorn could squeeze out nothing but sore anger. "What Covenant have I broken against the Landmaster? What crime have you invented for me, to be dragged here like a trussed pig?"

The Landmaster swelled at Thorn's insolence, his bald head and round stomach seeming to grow tighter; he motioned to the Deacons, who lined up on either side of Thorn. Thorn wished he could laugh in the crude ruler's face, but his sullen fury was too great.

"You have defied the Covenant of Primacy. Or are you so ignorant you don't know the Covenant of Primacy, goatherd?"

"*Primacy!* What has primacy to do with letting a poor Urobb miner say his piece?"

"Primacy entails that all news of Ere come first to the Landmaster, Cherban! *You* had no right . . ." Thorn stared at him with interest. The man's cold demeanor was pretty thin. "*You* had no right to bring *any* news of Ere to the people of Burgdeeth! False news it was, and upset them unduly, goatherd! Take him away. Lock him where the Urobb was; we'll see how the whelp likes cow dung and gutter-water for supper."

Fury blinded Thorn. As he was forced at sword point through the Set, even the beauty of the inner gardens and fountains could not cut through his anger.

The cellhouse stood alone on the opposite side of the Set. As Thorn was thrust through the door, he spun around to see the Urobb miner coming toward him across the parade yard, led on a long rope by the Kubalese on his dark war horse. Kearb-Mattus's crude laugh rang across the Set. "I'm taking your friend to Urobb, Cherban, as fast as my horse can gallop. If he can run faster, he might be alive when he reaches his homeland."

Thorn gripped the door bolt helplessly as the Kubalese trotted off, Squally running behind.

It was five days that Thorn languished in the Landmaster's jail; the floor was deep in filth, water was brought only once a day and that little enough, and the food was cold mawzee mush gone sour, not fit even for pigs. For two days he did not eat at all, then when he did eat, the food came up again. But on the third day, before dawn, he woke in the near darkness to see a silent figure standing outside the bars. Fear gripped him; but it was a small figure. He rose and went toward it, and could sense a quiet urgency beneath her stillness. *Was* it a girl? Or a young boy? The light was better on the basket: and the smell of food made his mouth water. But the hands holding the basket—yes, a girl's hands.

He could barely see her face as she handed the basket and waterskin through the bars: dark eyes, dark hair pulled down inside her collar, and wearing something baggy and shapeless. "I can't leave the waterskin or the basket," she whispered. "They'll find them. Take the food out, it's in a napkin. Hurry!"

He reached out to do as she told him, felt her hand brush his. He glanced around the courtyard, but could see nothing else in the darkness. "How did you get in?" He put the basket down. "Zephy? Is it Zephy?" She was trembling.

"I slipped through behind the men coming to drill for the Horse. I put on Shanner's clothes and walked behind him. He didn't know, no one noticed. I—I have to go back so I can get out when the horses go through. I tried to come yesterday but there were Deacons by the gate."

He took the napkin, drank deep of the fresh water then emptied the rest into the crock the guard had left. As he finished he reached through again and took her hand, and a strange, quick feeling touched him; he felt her sigh rather than heard her, and the only thing he could think to say was, "Why? Why did you come?"

"It's going to be light soon, the drill is making up, the torches are already lit." She reached hastily for the waterskin and basket. He touched her hair once, then she was gone into the shadows along the wall.

He stood staring after her, then put his strange feeling down to hunger, and turned eagerly to the meat rolls and mawzee cakes and bread. Why had she bothered about him? If she were caught . . . He had felt she was trembling almost before he touched her. Fear, he guessed. Fear . . .

He was unwilling to leave any food judiciously for later, afraid it would be found. He drank the rest of the water, too, and when the Deacon came with his sour gruel at midmorning, Thorn threw the bowl in his face.

She came the next morning. He was awake and waiting for her, though he had supposed she would not come again. He heard the early morning grumbling of Burgdeeth's men, then saw her dark shadow slipping along the wall. He heard the horses nicker and the sound of hooves on the cobbles, but he was aware only of her, close to him. "There's only salt cow meat," she whispered. "The goat meat is gone." He knew, again, that she was trembling. The torches flared on the other side of the Set. He took the napkin and waterskin from her, then held her by her thin elbows so she stepped closer and stood looking at him. In the near-dark the sense of her was strange and heady. He couldn't ask, today, why she had come.

When she did not come the next morning, he tried to feign sickness so the Deacon with the key would come and open the cell—surely he could overpower one Deacon. But it didn't work; they didn't care if he was sick; they didn't care if he died there. He was ashamed he could not devise a way to escape. He thought of Zephy again and hoped she was all right. Then on the fifth day when she had not appeared and his hunger was worse than before, he looked up to see Oak Dar striding across the Set. Like a conquering lord came the Goatmaster, with the Deacons trailing sullenly behind.

It all happened in an instant. The lock slid back, Thorn stepped out of the cell. By Oak Dar's eyes he knew to say no word. He strode off by his father's side in silence, and only when they were through the gate and free at last did Thorn turn to stare at him. "What did you have to do? You didn't bargain for me?"

"I bargained," Oak Dar said shortly. "I bargained all of Dunoon for you."

"You did what?" Then he saw the laughter behind his father's eyes. "You bargained what?"

"I bargained all of Dunoon. I told him if I did not take you home with me, there would be not a goat carcass nor a hide come to Burgdeeth and not a man or animal on the mountain in any place where Burgdeeth would ever find them. I told him they'd be living on their milk cows, for all Dunoon would furnish their meat."

Thorn roared with laughter. "But how did you know I was there?"

"A little Urobb miner slipped into Dunoon bruised and bleeding, with a rope still around his waist.

"Squally! How did he get away? He must have cut the rope."

"He did just that—after killing the Kubal's horse with a stone and slipping the Kubal's knife out."

"He didn't kill the Kubal?"

"No, the fool."

"Squally had better make himself scarce. If that Kubalese finds him . . ."

"He's gone up over the Rim into Karra; no Kubal would be fool enough to hunt a man there."

No sensible man would hide in the high barren deserts, either. And behind Karra the mountains were utterly unknown. Thorn felt a wave of sadness for Squally.

They made their way quickly through the whitebarley field to the river. Above them the mountain was washed with low rain clouds; Thorn thought he had never seen anything so welcome or smelled such a scent as the tang of damp sablevine that blew down to them. Cloud shadows lay dark against the bright pastures on the slope, and to his left over the highest peaks, something in the heavy clouds moved so he caught his breath—but then it was gone. He stood willing it back but it did not come, and at last he caught up with Oak Dar, eager to be home. As they climbed above Burgdeeth he glanced back once, feeling some disquiet; the clouds were very low so that even Dunoon was covered; and they lay down over Burgdeeth's fields behind him.

ZEPHY KNEW WHEN THORN was released because Meatha saw Oak Dar striding into the Set and ran to tell her. By the time Zephy got to the square, Thorn and his father were going up through the whitebarley field toward the river, sun and shadow striking them. Thorn didn't look back, he didn't turn to see her standing there.

"It doesn't matter," she said fiercely, turning away from Meatha's sympathetic gaze. She went back to her field alone, picked up her abandoned hoe, and set to work. Had Thorn felt nothing for her, then? Had the way he looked at her meant only that he was glad to be fed? Her angry hoeing made the dry mawzee leaves rattle, and she knocked a grain pod to the ground so it split open to scatter its precious store. She looked up the mountain and saw the two figures, dark against a patch of sun. Thorn did not pause, and her longing was terrible. Was he looking back in her direction? Well he couldn't see her anyway here among the crops in the cloud shadow.

Here in the cloud shadow?

The shadow was moving! Not drifting, moving! It was alive! She stared upward, reached upward as the wings swept above her surging against cloud and sun, wings lifting—the beautiful Horses of Eresu, their necks stretched in flight, their wings knifing and turning the wind. She reached, loving them, searching for a god among them . . .

But they were gone in a cloud so suddenly, in the rising wind. Gone.

She saw them once more, a darkness surging over the Kubalese hills and vanishing quickly. She stood staring, her pulse pounding, her whole being enflamed.

And on the mountain, Thorn and Oak Dar stood frozen with the wonder of the flight as the dark cloud moved over Burgdeeth and receded beyond the Kubalese hills.

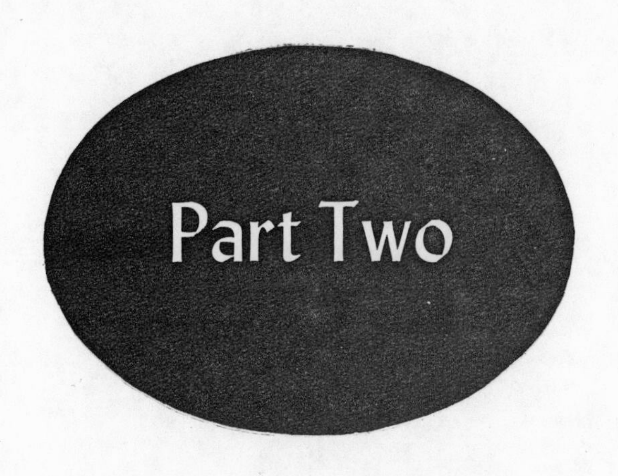

The Runestone

In the beginning there was order upon the land and men were obedient. But mortals grew covetous: they lusted after the powers of the gods, and their blasphemy spread to infect many. They rose in violence against the gods; and they laid siege to the holy city Owdneet and all was evil upon Ere.

So the Luff'Eresi made the earth to tremble. They made fires to spew from the mountains and rivers of fire to cover the land.

Few men survived the Fire Scourge, and those few went in fear to the south. This was a time of shadow when cinders fell from the sky, and the sun shone only dimly, and the minds of men were dark. There were few flocks and few seed and few women to husband. But still men made further evil; men sinned, and in sin the women conceived Children of Ynell; and these changelings could speak with closed mouths, and they could see visions invisible to men. The gods' powers were usurped; and the gods were sore angered. And to appease the gods, men burned the Children of Ynell in sacrifice.

Then on the Eve of Harvest, when men were standing in their cut fields, one black cloud came covering the sky. And a voice cried out, "You have sinned. Kneel down." And the men knelt in their fields. And the voice said, "You have taken what is ours. You have incurred the wrath of the Luff'Eresi. Your fields will die, and you will be hungry. You must bring a tithing of your crops: and you must burn your fields after harvest to propitiate the Fire: and nevermore will you sacrifice what is ours to sacrifice. Henceforth you will bring the Children of Ynell to the Death Stone, for the Luff'Eresi to kill as we see fit."

From *The Book of Fire*, Cloffi.

Chapter Seven

BURGDEETH DID NOT TALK of war at first, but then people began to whisper. Even when Zephy had slipped into the Set with food for Thorn, her danger had not seemed so great, her possible discovery so shattering, with the thought of real danger raw in her mind. And she could tell Mama was worried and upset. Though in spite of it, Mama was as friendly with Kearb-Mattus as ever.

No one ever expected war, she guessed. Certainly the men of Urobb hadn't expected it as they spread their nets; how could they know they would be dead in the morning? Everything we do is hinged on war, she thought. *If* we're not attacked; *if* there's no war in Cloffi; if life goes on at all.

Would the prayers at Fire Scourge help? Could they help, as the Covenants taught? Would the gods intervene? Zephy didn't know, she felt she didn't know anything. But Fire Scourge, the most dramatic supplication of the year, when the cut fields were lit with the long line of torches and the gods propitiated with fire, would such a strong supplication help Cloffi?

The volcanoes had stopped war twice in Ere's history. But then it was the sacred cities themselves that had been attacked; no wonder the fires spilled forth.

Do I believe that? She thought suddenly. Do I really

believe the gods made the volcanoes erupt to stop the attacks on their cities? Do I believe the gods *can* do such a thing?

If the gods are real, why do they let war come at all? And why did they let their own cities be attacked in the first place?

After Fire Scourge the fields would lie black and burned-smelling until the snows came to cover them. She felt so unsettled—as if life were taking a turning she could not prevent, nor yet hurry, and the waiting was unbearable; yet the finality would be worse. She remained edgy and cross even when she and Meatha managed to slip into Tra. Hoppa's kitchen. All three felt too oppressed by the fate of Urobb to have lessons. Tra. Hoppa looked very tired.

Meatha clung to the old lady, fearful and wan. "It makes you feel so trapped, Tra. Hoppa. How *could* we escape, really? If the attack comes so suddenly, from all sides, the way it did in Urobb . . ."

"You could go to the mountain," Tra. Hoppa said sternly. "You don't think they'd search all the caves. Those mountains are honeycombed with caves."

"But you—"

"Never mind about me. I'm a wiley old thing. And if you can't get to the caves, slip into the tunnel until you can get away." She grinned at them. "You two can outsmart a few clumsy Kubalese soldiers if you keep your wits about you. Though we may be in for some difficult times. If Urobb had had the strength and determination of Carriol, Kubal would never have attacked her. Nor would Kubal threaten Cloffi now, if Cloffi were strong. But strength can only begin inside, with its people, and with Cloffi as she is now . . ."

"How could anything *ever* begin with Cloffi's people?" Meatha said bitterly.

"It would take those who truly cared."

"No one cares!"

It won't happen, Zephy thought desperately. War can't happen to us. The light from the window cut across Tra. Hoppa's gray hair and made her wrinkles, as she turned, show plainly. It was strange to think of Tra. Hoppa as old, for she was nothing like the old ladies of Burgdeeth. It was as if all Tra. Hoppa's life lay in stages there inside, still to be seen and touched. The other old women of Burgdeeth seemed to have retained nothing of their pasts but the bitterness.

When they left Tra. Hoppa, it was quickly, for the Horse had begun to drill on the road beyond the grove. Such a drill outside the Set was most unusual. "I suppose the Landmaster has taken *some* heed of the defeat of Urobb," Tra. Hoppa said bitterly. "At least the Horse is doing more than their usual playful sparring. You must go by the tunnel, they can see all over the housegardens from that road."

The tunnel was as old as Burgdeeth. It began in the plum grove where the old prison had stood, and ended beneath the sacred statue. It had been the means of escape for the Children of Ynell who had, as slaves, built much of the original town of Burgdeeth. They had dug the tunnel secretly at night and, when they cast and erected the statue, had made a hollow opening in its base to join the tunnel opening. Only Tra. Hoppa knew of the tunnel, and she had learned of it in Carriol: the secret had been well kept from the landmasters of Burgdeeth. "It will be wanted one day," she had said once, "as it was wanted before. It might be needed several times before Burgdeeth is free."

Tra. Hoppa had them out the door before they could catch their breaths, the candle flame nearly invisible in the daylight. "Quick, Zephy, pivot the stone back. Hurry!"

The stone, a small pivoting boulder surrounded by

humped gray rocks, moved with the pressure of Zephy's shoulder. The tunnel would lead them, as it had those others, beneath Burgdeeth into the hollow base of the statue. When darkness had come, those Children had pushed back the bronze panel and fled Burgdeeth forever. Now Zephy and Meatha slipped down into darkness as, above them, Tra. Hoppa shouldered the stone back into place.

Beyond the light that the candle threw on dirt-mortared walls, the tunnel was utterly black. It smelled damp. They could just see the first supporting timber, a thick tree trunk sunk between the stones.

The weight of the earth above them seemed to press down intolerably as they made their way in the darkness, the candlelight dodging and shifting.

"I never liked it," Meatha whispered.

"It's better than getting caught."

Why did they whisper? The tunnel made them do it. As if, if they spoke aloud, they might—what? Stir awake something alive in the tunnel walls themselves? Zephy snorted at herself and tried to concentrate on the little sphere of candlelight as Meatha pressed close behind, bumping her now and then in her impatience to get on.

The ceiling curved down into the walls, making the head room higher in the middle; but too low, still, to be pleasant. The candle guttered once, as if a breath had touched it—maybe Zephy's own, though. Then it steadied, picking out the niche where the relics of Owdneet had once lain. The niche was empty, of course; they had long since ceased to explore it. But now suddenly Zephy wanted to reach in. She held the light up and felt into the hollow. The first Children of Ynell had put their hands in just so, had felt the rough dirt walls, had . . . she found herself scraping and working at something, some protrusion in the hard dirt . . . something smooth . . . something . . . It came away suddenly and fell into her hand, so heavy she dropped it. She fished it out and held it to the light.

It was a bit of green stone as long as her finger, sharp-pointed at one end and rounded at the other, with jagged sides. It looked like jade. On the round end were carvings—runes! The girls stood staring. The stone gleamed, stirring Zephy in a way she could not understand. It looked as if perhaps it had been part of a round and much larger stone that had somehow shattered. It had been completely buried in the dirt of the niche, though now it seemed to be shining more brightly, as if . . . Zephy looked up toward the end of the tunnel, where a cold light burned suddenly . . .

Where no light should have been!

The light reflected on the green stone: a light where a moment before there had been only blackness, a light that was growing brighter still, had grown into a brilliance so penetrating Zephy could hardly look. The tunnel walls had disappeared; the light glowed in an immense space ahead of them, an unbounded space.

They stepped forward into the vastness with no thought that they should not.

It was like a cavern of light, a cavern without walls, if such a thing could be imagined. The space seemed to cant and tilt to create the *feeling* of walls across the emptiness. There was no sound, no stir of air.

Then gradually they became aware of something else.

The space seemed to be expanding. It was growing lighter and rising; it was luminous, as if mists drifted; and though there was no color, all colors seemed to swirl around them as if colors had voices that could penetrate the soul. The spaces pulled at them, beckoned to them until at last Zephy thought she could see far distant walls. Then she realized they were mountains, mountains rising in a space that was larger than the world she knew, larger than the sky, as if the sky had swelled suddenly higher and everything was farther off. The sense of light behind the mists was of a terrible brilliance; she could feel the shadows moving, and yet they were not shadows, they were . . . Oh! the figures moving toward them had great, spreading wings; figures that hovered above them, around them—half-horse, half-man, with shining wings. *You are come,* they seemed to whisper, and laughed with voices filled with joy. *You must reach out, you will reach outward—if you are the chosen, you must extend yourselves, you three—and three—and more. You will reach out . . .*

Then they were gone; there was only blackness; and Zephy had dropped the stone.

If she found it and picked it up, the vision would return, and she wanted that desperately—yet she trembled with fear as she knelt and began to feel for the stone in the darkness. The candle, its light strangely snuffed, lay abandoned.

After a long while she had almost given up. Had the stone rolled completely away? She was frantic to find it now; then when she did at last, it was far from where it had fallen. She touched it and light flared around her so she drew her hand away as if it had been burned. She longed for the vision—and she was terrified of it.

Finally she took the stone up in her handkerchief. Again she was surprised at its weight. She felt along the wall for the niche and laid it quickly inside.

Meatha said nothing. If she wanted the vision to return, she did not ask for it. They groped ahead, the walls pressing close around them; they did not talk, the vision still held them utterly. They were quenched with it, as if one moment of wonder, of such brilliance, was all they could manage without blinding themselves. It encompassed them completely.

When they reached the lighter hollow beneath the statue, Zephy felt she had come back from an infinite distance. Tiny points of light like little stars shone through the peepholes in the bronze base of the statue. Zephy peered out on one side, Meatha on the other, but they were reluctant to go. They stood silently holding the vision, yearning for it, nearly turning back into the tunnel. What had Zephy held; what was the stone? *Had* they seen a vision, or had they touched a reality they could not comprehend?

At last Meatha pushed open the bronze door in the base, and they slipped through. Voices brought them up short; they pushed the door back under cover of their bodies then knelt hastily before the statue, their arms crossed over their chests in servility, heads bowed, as two men came across the square.

Zephy stared at the ground and moved her lips in prayer. The shadow of a hoof cut across her hand as if the Luff'Eresi touched her in benediction; and it was in true prayer that she knelt, for she had stood on the brink of a world whose dimensions made her own world flat and colorless, a world outside of everything she knew, where the gods had drifted the way sunlight drifts through water—yet had been real beyond anything she had ever known.

When at last they rose to go, they walked close together, shivering. And once they looked back at the bronze Luff'Eresi sweeping above the square with his consorts leaping beside him. I have seen them, Zephy thought. I have seen the true gods. Then she thought suddenly, numb with surprise, and frightened: I am like Ynell. I, too, am a Child of Ynell.

For days afterward she would wake in the darkness of the loft knowing this and feeling terrified. Then she would come fully awake and remember the vision vividly, would lie staring out at the changing sky and seeing that other world instead. Ephemeral as gauze it had been, yet as real as stone. I am like Ynell, she would think again, amazed. I am a Child of Ynell.

Then one morning two small boys were drowned, and everything else was driven from Zephy's head.

An older boy found them and ran at once to the Deacons. The two little bodies had been washed onto the bank of the river, and were mud-covered and icy cold. Zephy did not run with the crowd to see, and when she heard how the children had looked, she was glad she hadn't. The horror of the ceremonial viewing was quite enough to turn her sick; sick at the deaths, sick with a fear she could not even name. And one of the boys was little Graged Orden. She and Meatha could only think of the game of search-and-seek and of the barrel with the red rag hidden and little Graged Orden running from Kearb-Mattus in terror. They sat together in Temple while the red robed Deacons said the Prayers and Covenants and the Ritual Mournings and held the burning chalice above the little coffins; while the citizens of Cloffi bent, one by one, before the coffins with their hands crossed over their shoulders and their heads lowered in submission to the will of the Luff'Eresi.

The coffins would be placed in the burial wall and covered with sacred mortar and stone. This funeral, so soon after Nia's, was horrible.

Late on the night of the funeral, Zephy heard hoofbeats in the street, but when she rose to look there was nothing. She sat in the window for a long time, the fear of death clinging to her.

Chapter Eight

"SHANNER, WAKE UP. *Shanner!*" Zephy shook his shoulder, jostled him, but he continued to snore. She lit the candle and held it close to his face. "Shanner! It's Market Day!"

"Mphh."

"Come on! You know I can't lift the barrels myself." He *would* snore like a lump. She snatched the covers back and jerked his shoulder, pummeling him until he opened his eyes.

"Market Day," she repeated.

"Last night. Could have done it last night Zephy . . ."

"You weren't *here.*" She glowered until he sat up. The nearly full moons had gone, the only light was the sputtering glow from the candle. Even Waytheer could not be seen. The wind came in, and Shanner shivered. She pulled the shutters closed and latched them. "That'll be warmer, it'll be light soon."

"It'll never be light." He reached for his pants and boots. "Cold!"

She snorted with disgust.

On the street they walked beneath the sound of banners snapping on the dark wind, Fire Scourge banners hung out last night from the windows and rooftops of Burgdeeth, flapping in the fitful gusts to mark the beginning of the five day celebration. And special banners, too, to mark this year of Waytheer. The star would not be so close again for ten years; the Luff'Eresi would not come again so strong or speak so clearly to man for ten years. Every prayer, every supplication put forth now would have more meaning.

They went in darkness to get Nida and her creaking wagon. Zephy could tell Nida from Dess only when Dess kicked her absently as she tried to pull the bridle on. Nida never would. She cursed Dess and let her loose, smarting and cross and cold; almost wishing she were back in bed and Market Day was past.

"Brewmaster'll be livid," Shanner said. "Couldn't you have remembered last night?"

"I couldn't find you. You were off with a girl, I suppose." The whole town had been seething with wagons last night, waiting to get settled in the square. The Inn had been packed full. She had looked for Shanner everywhere when she should have been cleaning up in the late hours, washing mugs. "They emptied every barrel. You might have remembered; you might have known they would!"

He grumbled something unintelligible as they rounded the corner by the Brewmaster's. A tiny light burned in the window. "He's up," Zephy breathed thankfully.

But the old man growled worse than Shanner and heaved the honeyrot casks onto the wagon so brutally that Zephy thought they would have it all spilled, the casks caved in, and honeyrot flowing in the street.

The sky had begun to gray above the rooftops. At the sculler, Zephy held the door while Shanner hoisted the barrels through, seven barrels of honeyrot to set side by side for the noon meal. When she took Nida back to the fields, the sky was as yellow as mawzee mush, and the banners bright and blowing so Nida flicked her ears at them and snorted against Zephy's cheek. In the shed, as

Zephy hung up the harness, she paused to examine the rent in Nida's packsaddle where the donkey had shied stupidly against a building. The straw was coming out. It should be mended. Zephy couldn't get her mind properly on mending with Market Day at hand.

Thorn would be coming down the mountain this morning to trade hides and blankets at Market. Well at least he always had. She glanced up at the mountain. Will he come to find me? Will he want to?

Will he even think of it?

Would she be bold enough to search him out? What, and stand staring like a sick calf? Wait for him to thank her for risking her stupid neck in the Set? Oh, Great Eresu, she thought. What's the matter with me?

And, would Thorn stay for the Singing?

In Burgdeeth, public singing was sanctioned only at festival time, at Fire Scourge and Planting and Solstace. She glanced in the direction of the river where the road came down from Dunoon and felt her spirits lift. Thorn always stayed for the Singing. Later in the sculler, she reached down her gaylute from atop the cupboard, and stood carefully polishing it.

It was well before dawn when Thorn and Loke finished packing their hides and blankets across the backs of their four best bucks. The moons had already set. They worked by the light of the cookfire from the open door, for their mother had risen to lay a hot meal for them. The bucks were restless, wanting to be off but looking over their shoulders, too, toward their herds, nervy and light-footed and shifting about as they were saddled. The bucks stood as tall as Thorn when their heads were raised. Their spiralling horns were ridged intricately and sharp pointed as spears, rising as high as Thorn could reach; deadly if they pierced a man. Thorn glanced at Loke as the younger boy fastened a basket of cheese and mountain meat on top a pack, then looked up one last time at the mountain: they had patrolled it constantly since Urobb fell. Thorn spoke to the bucks at last, and they started down the dark slope.

Not until the morning sky began to grow light, so the boulders loomed clearly around them, did they feel easier. As the sky began to yellow, they sang a little, the old marching songs—songs of the Herebian tribes, songs forbidden in Cloffi. And well they might be, for the Herebian were father to the Kubal. But lusty songs and bold they were, and the two sang them now with changed words, in rude defiance of Kubalese might.

"What would they do to us?" Loke asked suddenly. "What would the Kubalese do if they conquered Cloffi?" The boy gazed at Thorn with trust. The talk of attack must have upset Loke more than he had shown. Thorn studied his brother's freckled face with a feeling of tenderness —and of fear. It was not for nothing that Tra. Hoppa had taught him Ere's history; he knew what could happen to them. But there was something else, too, something on the side of Dunoon. "They could kill us all," he said evenly. "Except for one thing." He looked into Loke's eyes and saw his own fears there. "We're too valuable to destroy. The Kubalese could never herd our goats and make them produce, and they're the only decent meat in Cloffi. Crude as the Kubalese are, I expect they are not foolish. They would likely keep Dunoon as slave, for food, for goat meat and milk and wool. They would keep us slave, Loke, slave to tend our own herds."

"But we never would! I'd kill my herd first, before I'd be slave to Kubal!"

Thorn said no more. The plans he had made with the Goatmaster were best kept just to the two of them. The more who knew, even his little brother, the more who could be forced to talk.

"Is that why . . ." Loke looked at him steadily. "Is that why Burgdeeth has tolerated us all these generations? Because of the meat and the wool?

"What else? You know the Landmasters have always hated us. But even they know our herds would die under the bungling hands of Burgdeeth. Our mountain goats are not like the donkeys and the poor steeds of Cloffi, to be rough handled or to tolerate cruelty and indifference. You know as well as I they were never meant to be fenced or to live in the confines of the valley. And no Landmaster would permit his people to live on the mountain to herd them; there is too much of freedom there, too much of space, too much of sky to woo away Burgdeeth's fettered manhood."

"Tolerated for our goat meat!" Loke said furiously.

"Well, we don't have to stay on these pastures; though they are by far the richest. Maybe the Landmaster dreams that one day we'll be brought to our knees and made as docile as the Cloffa. Anyhow, it all may come to nothing, this talk of attack." He cuffed Loke across the shoulders. "It's Market Day, boy! Good food and new sights, and a pocket full of silver."

They stopped to water the bucks before leaving the river, the goats sloshing playfully, then took the narrow trail that crossed the lower whitebarley field and came into Burgdeeth by a side street. They could see the square ahead overflowing with bright wagons and banners, with horses and men milling about underneath the great bronze statue. Did the Landmaster ever really look at the grandeur and gentleness of the god towering there? What kind of twisted spirit could live with the pictures that were painted on the Landmaster's walls?

Thorn took the black goat's halter and led him forward to where Loke had found a spot to his liking just beside the hedge. The younger boy had already begun to spread out his wares on an old blanket, brown hides and rust, cream and black, and the blankets woven in the same tones, their patterns of song and myth catching a slash of light from between the feet of the statue. Thorn grinned at Loke; the boy could hardly wait to begin trading. Thorn left him to it, as his brother preferred, and began to walk among the wagons, wondering at the richness of the wares. He moved alternately in sun and in shadow, where canvas roofs had been spread to shelter the displays of silks and linens and copper pots, of enamelled brasswear and carved chairs and fancy harness and bright-dyed leather goods, and of sweets—soursugar and saffron drops, bars of honeywax from Doonas, and even dates and onyrood pods from Moramia, dipped in crystalized sugar. Thorn's mouth watered at the sight of them; he slipped two coins from his belt and bought soursugar and onyrood and took them to share with Loke, coming away again to prowl at more length among the crowds—a rare holiday, this, and the sun warm on his back. He felt an unaccustomed satisfaction with the color and the noise and the crowds, he who was usually happiest alone.

But there was a disquiet in him, too. He kept remembering the small figure standing in the darkness beside his prison bars. He watched for her in the crowd and thought of the line of her chin and the way her brown hair fell over her shoulders.

He remembered last year's Singing, the way she had played her gaylute, and had sung "Jajun Jajun" and "Smallsinger Tell Me." He remembered her dancing wildly while Shanner played for her.

She had changed a lot, he thought. She had been a child then.

He thought of her dark eyes, and wanted to ask her—ask her what? He looked up and searched the crowd as if he would see her suddenly then stepped aside as two Kubalese on great heavy horses came around from behind a wagon. How could they show their faces, with Urobb so lately slaughtered? Why did the Landmaster allow them in Burgdeeth? He stared after them coldly.

There was a Sangurian ballad troop in one wagon, and Thorn stood for a while listening to the man and his three women singing softly the stories of Bede Thostle and the Goosetree of Madoc, and of the Demon of Sangur Neck. Then when he turned away to wander once more, he came around a little tent with brass wares from Pelli, and he stopped suddenly, to stare.

The man was turned away from Thorn, but the set of his shoulders was familiar as he adjusted the harness of a fine butternut mare. His white hair caught the light. His tall thin frame seemed taut and hard as a sapling. The wagon the mare pulled was brighter than any on the square, painted with birds and flowers in every color you could name. And across its side, in letters lined with gold, were the words, JUGGLER AND MASTER OF TRICKS. As Thorn stood staring, the man turned; one quick motion, and he was looking into Thorn's eyes; and Thorn knew at once he must not speak or recognize him in any way.

"Fancy my wagon, do you, boy?" the old man said lightly in a manner of speech that was certainly not his own and loud enough for people to hear. "Fancy a trick or two? Silver, boy!" The old man's voice was loud and beguiling. "Silver will get you a trick . . ." But Thorn grumbled something rude and turned away as if he were not interested. He could feel Anchorstar's satisfaction, feel his warm and silent greeting so his own pulse raced as he turned indifferently to examine a display of tin. The old man took the team's heads and backed the wagon into an alley. Thorn turned in time to see the two horses' noses bobbing as they guided their burden out of the way. He knew Anchorstar would speak to him later, speak privately.

It was not a snake's breath later that he rounded the

square and heard Loke's voice raised in anger, heard one of the bucks bellow a challenge. Alarmed, he leaped across a wagon tongue and some barrels to come around the statue's hedge.

A group of children had gathered around the bucks as children usually did, to admire them and to push their hands into the thick wool coats and grin at their warmth and silkiness, to pull a head down and feel the spiraling horns; the bucks could be bad-tempered with an adult, but were patient enough with children.

But it was not the children, laughing with delight, that had caused Loke's shout and the angry bellow. The cream buck stood apart with his head lowered and his ears back, ready to charge. His quarry was the dark Kubalese, Kearb-Mattus. The man cowered, now, against a wagon. Had he been teasing the animal? The cream buck, the worst tempered of the lot, did not take to strangers. Thorn took his halter and settled him. Loke's face was red with anger. "He was feeling in the pack, he *said* it was a game."

Thorn gave Loke a restraining look and turned to face the Kubalese. "What were you doing?"

Kearb-Mattus smiled, his body relaxing now. "It was a game, friend. A game for the children—a game of hide-and-search. Come, let us have a game, it's innocent enough. What say you, goatman?" A curious crowd had gathered. Thorn studied the Kubalese closely; then he caught a glimpse of Anchorstar moving in through the crowd, and the sudden command of Anchorstar's thoughts was plain. Thorn swallowed his temper and stepped back.

"Play your game then, Kubal. One game."

The Kubalese looked mildly surprised. Loke went pale with fury.

"Play your game," Thorn repeated, at Anchorstar's silent command. The Kubalese held up his hand and a goldpiece flashed bright between his fingers; the crowd caught its breath; the children stepped forward with a sigh of longing. Such a coin would buy sweets they could not count. Kearb-Mattus smiled, turned his back, and began to rummage among the packs and into the bucks' thick coats. You couldn't tell where he hid the coin. Or did he still have it? The bucks shifted their feet and twitched their ears nervously, but Thorn spoke to them and they quieted. The children watched the Kubalese without blinking. When he was finished, he made a signal and they scattered at once, searching frantically.

All but three. Three children held back, stood close together to stare up at the Kubalese. Kearb-Mattus pretended not to see them, but Thorn thought his interest was keen. One of them, the smallest boy, darted a quick glance at the black buck then looked away at once; the other two followed his gaze. Kearb-Mattus' voice rose, "Sweets it will buy, sweets and wonders . . ." The little boy—Toca, Thorn thought, Toca Dreeb—had a hot pink look about him as if he could hardly contain himself. Then suddenly for no apparent reason he turned and melted into the crowd. The other two followed him.

Kearb-Mattus scowled, stood for a moment uncertain, then clapped his hands. "Hunt's over, children! Time's up! No one found the gold piece." He walked to the black buck and drew the coin from deep beneath its saddle. "Game's over," he roared, "No one was quick enough this time." He turned to go, but Thorn stepped into his path.

The Kubalese raised his hand to push past, making Thorn's temper flare. He grabbed the man's wrist and twisted the coin from his fingers. He felt Anchorstar's distress too late, ignored it in his fury.

"It's not over, Kubal! You said the finder would keep the coin, and that implies a finder. They had too little time. Hide the coin again. *Or shall I?*"

The Kubalese's look was black. He raised his fist—it was like a ham . . .

But before he could swing, his arm was grabbed from

behind and twisted until he knelt. Anchorstar stood over him; he scowled down at the Kubalese, then nodded to Thorn to continue speaking.

"Hide it," Thorn said.

"Why should I?" The Kubalese was furious.

"Because you promised them. And because if you don't, this trickster and I will break both your arms for you."

The Kubalese accepted the coin with a look of hatred and flicked it carelessly into the air so it lit among the bucks' feet; at once the children were on it, surging and scrambling—a big boy screamed his success and disappeared, running.

Zephy couldn't see all that happened, the crowd was too thick, people too tall in front of her. She pushed and stretched, saw Kearb-Mattus raise his fist, saw Thorn's red thatch, saw the white-haired man move quickly through the crowd, heard the voices raised in anger. Beside her Meatha was pale as milk, staring; but Zephy paid her little attention, until Meatha shook her arm and breathed, "Anchorstar. It's Anchorstar! It's the man I saw—on the wagon . . ."

Zephy turned. She stared at Meatha, uncomprehending. Then she understood what Meatha was saying. But Meatha must be mistaken: This was not the way Meatha's vision had been. Where was the bright wagon, the horses? Then Meatha's urgency was forgotten as Thorn's voice rose in anger. Zephy pushed through the crowd frantically, trying to see, trying to understand what was taking place.

When the crowd dispersed at last, wandering off, she was little the wiser about what had happened, except that Thorn and the tall white-haired man had stood facing the Kubalese together. She turned shy and uncomfortable then and pulled Meatha away. She didn't want to talk to Thorn; she didn't know what to say to him.

Meatha seemed glad enough to go. Had she been wrong, then, about the tall man? They made their way to the other side of the square and occupied themselves among the wonders of leather and tin and weavings; and neither spoke for a long time. The colors of the wagons were like fire; indigo and saffron and crimson spilled upon the day. There was a display of sugar spinning and a wagon of glinting pearls and sprika shells from the Bay of Pelli. And an old woman wizened as a dried fig laid out wonderful needlework with her brown, trembling hands. There were ginger pies filled with clotted cream, to eat in the shade of a Sangurian wagon, and all the time Zephy was silent and preoccupied. Wanting to be with Thorn but too shy and making herself miserable.

Then it was noon suddenly, the sun overhead. Mama would be furious, serving up the meal without her. She fled through the crowded streets guiltily, tripped over a clutter of bright brooms, and burst in through the sculler to meet her mother's hot, angry frown.

Chapter Nine

THE KITCHEN was unbearably hot. Mawzee cakes and side meat were sizzling on the great black stove. Mama flipped half a dozen cakes onto the platter before she looked at Zephy. Her face was flushed from the heat. She pushed back a wisp of hair with that quick, angry motion Zephy dreaded. "The honeyrot, Zephy. Pour it out. Where have you been! Put some charp fruit in a basket and cut the bread."

Zephy fled gladly to the sculler, grabbed up a basket, filled it with charp fruit, and laid six loaves on top. She hurried through the kitchen with her attention fully on the basket and pushed through the door into the longroom.

The clatter of voices and plates hit her like a blow. The two chamber girls were hurrying between the crowded tables with steaming platters, Sulka's pale hair fallen around her shoulders, and Thara having trouble getting her bulk through the narrow aisles between the backs of the seated men, her platter held high. Zephy dropped her basket on the serving table and began to cut the bread, then stopped to pour out honeyrot as the men around her clambered for drink. The noise, trapped under the low rafters, churned so the voices came in scraps of shouting that seemed to explode around her. She loaded a tray with bread and brimming mugs and started down between the aisles.

The food and drink were grabbed away by great hands with seldom a thank you or a notice of whether anyone carried the tray or whether it walked by itself. There were four Kubalese sitting with Kearb-Mattus. Where had they come from? How could they show their faces after sacking Urobb! Kearb-Mattus's voice drowned out his neighbors. She watched them with hatred, listening in spite of herself.

"—of Fire Scourge, it should be a sight, all the pomp and fuss. You've never seen such a—" She lost some of it in the ruckus, then, "Five days of praying on their knees and wouldn't you know—" She held her breath, straining to listen, her fury growing. "—on the last night!" Kearb-Mattus shouted, and the men laughed fit to kill. Zephy turned away, toward the serving table.

The Trashsinger and the Vendor were sitting on a bench out of the way, their backs to the wall, making themselves a part of the hubub of market day; remembering, she thought, when they, too, were shouting young men strong in their bodies and boisterous in their ways. She smiled down at them and handed them honeyrot and bread.

And when she turned to look back at the room, Elij Cooth had joined the Kubalese. He sat among them laughing. She stared at him, her anger rising anew. Elij was as much a traitor as his father if he could pander to the Kubalese so. What was the pact that Kubal and Cloffi were supposed to have made, anyway? Did the Landmaster believe the Kubalese would honor any pact? She stacked dirty plates onto her tray, pressing through between the crowded rows. Elij was leaning over the table, reaching for bread. Zephy gave him a look of hatred as she passed—and suddenly she was jerked back and pulled around so she lost her balance and fell, groping, across Elij's lap.

She kicked at him and struggled; the tray fell, the dishes clattering. Elij's grip was like steel. He was drunk, drunk and pawing her. She twisted, kicked again; there was laughter all around her—then Elij had his hand under her tunic. She snatched up the tray and jammed it into his stomach, felt his grip loosen, then was on her feet, shoving the greasy tray in his face.

She stood in the sculler seething with rage, hating Elij Cooth, hating everything; hating a system where a girl could be pawed and everyone laughed. Hating, most of all, her own weakness for not being able to fight back.

At last, her rage hard and cold inside her, she straightened her tunic and went back into the kitchen.

Mama had left the pans soaking. Zephy began to scrub them, her anger driving her so she broke a nail at the quick and swore like a man. Thara came to help her, then Sulka with another load. They glanced at her and grinned, but she didn't acknowledge their looks. Her anger was so great it kept even those two silent, and at last she escaped toward the square.

The sun was warm on the empty streets. Burgdeeth seemed utterly deserted; only the myriad smells—tannery, baking, tammi drying, outhouses—would tell you anyone lived there. The cobbles glinted in the sunlight, and ahead of her the colors in the square were as brilliant as Zandourian silk. She came around a wagon into the square —and stopped.

Coming down the street she had heard no sound from the square. Now she could only stand staring at the people who were crowded there utterly silent: the square overflowed with wagons and animals, and with people still as death, everyone staring in one direction.

They were watching a bright wagon, and *Anchorstar*, she thought wildly, her mind exploding with the word; for the man of Meatha's vision stood tall in the open back.

She drew closer and could see flowers and birds painted on the sides of the wagon, and the words, JUGGLER AND MASTER OF TRICKS. The two Carriolinian horses were just as Meatha had described them: butternut, all butternut, not a stroke of white.

The back of the closed wagon had been opened out like a stage, and there above the crowd, the tall imposing man held the throng silent by his still presence, his hands raised. The sunlight slashed across his satin cloak so it shone with every shade of red; the gravity of his face seemed to hold the crowd in awe . . .

Then suddenly he was juggling. She didn't see him start, one minute he was still, and the next he was tossing a dozen glinting spinning objects high in the air. His expression and stance had not changed. Most jugglers—though they had few enough in Burgdeeth where the Landmaster hardly tolerated them—would be grimacing and frowning now, dancing around to keep their wares balanced, smiling and scowling as they performed their simple tricks. Anchorstar's face was quiet, his eyes vivid and cool. His hands seemed hardly to move as the objects flew and twisted and fell to be tossed again, twelve tumbling golden cages glinting and winking in the sunlight. And in the cages—birds! Bright little birds, each one lifting to the rise and fall of the golden cages with little lithe movements as if they had done this trick a hundred times and in truth were enjoying it. There was no frantic fluttering, only the graceful, delicate balancing as the cages tumbled and gleamed.

And then she saw Meatha, standing farther along the edge of the square. She was staring up at Anchorstar as if she had been turned to stone. And, though Anchorstar seemed to be looking beyond her across the crowd, Zephy felt sure it was Meatha on whom his attention really dwelt.

Meatha, pale as whitebarley flour. Meatha, caught in something—caught . . . And then Zephy knew: they were speaking. Like Ynell, silently speaking across the heads of the crowd. *This* was the vision Meatha had seen: the old man, the wagon, the silent communication.

When Anchorstar had finished juggling, the crowd remained quiet, as if it had been mesmerized with the flirting circle of motion and light; and then their silence broke, they roared with applause, stamping and shouting and pressing closer around the wagon.

Where the back of the wagon had been dropped to make the stage, and the sides folded back, you could see that the inside was painted in small intricate patterns of red and gold. The tailgate was supported on carven legs. And there around the juggler's feet was the paraphernalia he used to entertain, cages and boxes and jars, and a brightly painted barrel, which he now held up, pouring water out into three cups and passing them down into the crowd. He had ceased to look at Meatha; and Meatha herself seemed dazed, shrinking into the crowd as if she wished not to be touched or disturbed. The banners in the square hung slack in the windless afternoon; the statue of the Luff'Eresi shone blindingly in the harsh sun, a small pool of shadow dark around its feet. Now the juggler was holding up the cask, and the liquid he poured was red wine; it was tasted, was passed around, and a sigh of wonder escaped the crowd. Zephy learned later that he had made an egg jump in the air from one hat to another, and then had put it into a yellow silk bag, handed it to a trader and, when the trader opened the bag, a full-grown rooster had flown out. He had made divvot cards appear in the hats and pockets of the crowd; and he had pointed out silver coins in empty pails presented to him, pails which he never touched. But the juggling—the juggling of the cages was the most wonderful.

He held up a silver staff now, and the noise of the crowd died as sharp and quick as if a knife had sliced it.

And there . . . Oh, but the Deacons had ridden into

the square. They paused as one, silent and ominous, their swords across their saddles and the purple flag of Burgdeeth hanging limp but commanding atop the color-bearer's staff. The crowd began to shift and mutter, to glance around, some to leave the square.

And Zephy saw that in the opposite corner the Landmaster waited, his gray stallion pawing. The Landmaster's girth and height were impressive; his uniform shone. The people glanced at him and shrank more quickly from the painted wagon, pushing and shouldering each other.

The space around the wagon widened. Soon the juggler stood alone.

Zephy pushed through the crowd to the hedge where Meatha stood staring in frozen panic. The shadow of wings darkened her face.

The Deacons surrounded the wagon. The girls watched as Anchorstar descended and began to tighten his harness, and to close up the tailgate and the sides. There were no harsh words, hardly any words. They seemed unnecessary. The Deacons' intent was clear.

When Anchorstar climbed into the wagon at last, he looked terrifying in his calmness. He lifted the reins without comment, backed the horses, and turned them toward the south as the Deacons were directing—there was nowhere else to go. To the north lay only Dunoon. And that, of course, would be forbidden to him.

When Anchorstar had gone, when the wagon could no longer be seen down the road and people had at last begun to return to the square, Zephy and Meatha slipped out through the housegardens, past the plum grove, and into the Landmaster's southern whitebarley field. The grain was tall and heavy-headed, ready for harvest, and they would be dealt with harshly if they were caught there, knocking heads off the stalks as they crept through. They slipped along as gently as they could, trying not to shake the stalks, planning that when they came out onto the road at the end of the field they would run to catch up with the wagon.

But three mounted Deacons guarded the road; Zephy's blood went cold as she stared up at their closed, stern faces. "A donkey," she cried, desperate for any excuse. "Have you seen a brown donkey? Dragging her halter rope . . ."

The Deacons did not comment. They stared back toward the village in clear command as to the direction the girls should take. There was nothing you could do, there was no way to battle Deacons. Defeated, they turned around and started back up the road.

"I hate them!" Meatha whispered vehemently.

"They don't have to be so overbearing just because—just because . . . Oh, to Urdd with the flaming Deacons!"

Meatha seemed utterly destroyed. Zephy watched her, concerned. Sometimes you couldn't tell with Meatha; there was something about her, a kind of delicate, tight-strung stubbornness that . . . Then Zephy caught her breath as Meatha dissolved into sudden shaking sobs. Alarmed, Zephy shoved her into the whitebarley where she would not be seen, and put her arms around her. She could feel the wracking sobs, could feel Meatha's heart pounding. She looked down the road, terrified that the Deacons would come, then pushed Meatha deeper into the field, propelling her away from the road until they were well out in the middle of the tall stand of grain.

Never in her life had she seen Meatha so out of control. She had seen her cry silent tears when she was hurt by someone, but never tears like this, crying as if her very soul was lost.

When it seemed Meatha could cry no longer, she stared up at Zephy, her face blotched, her eyes swollen. "He spoke to me, Zephy. Anchorstar spoke to me. He couldn't tell me all of it, and now they've driven him away.

There was something . . ." She pressed her fist to her mouth, then at last began again, "It was like a fog, when you know things are in it but you can't see them. He said we must talk together. There is something I must do. For Anchorstar, something I must do for him," she said with awe. And then the hopelessness of her defeat seemed to fill her and shake her utterly, and she dissolved into tears again, her face growing so white Zephy was frightened for her. "He said that the Children . . . that the Children . . . Oh I wish I understood . . .

"It wasn't anything in words, just in knowing. Then he made me go away from him in my mind. He wanted his mind free because he could feel the Deacons coming.

"And when he drove away I tried to speak with him, but I couldn't. There was nothing. And now it's too late." She sat staring miserably at the whitebarley that made a wall around them.

"It's *not* too late. We'll think of something." Zephy's anger surged at the Deacons, at her own helplessness. "Don't cry! It doesn't help to *cry!*"

Only a faint rustle of the whitebarley told Zephy they were not alone; she blanched with fear as they crouched, frozen; it would do no good to run.

The heavy sheaves parted.

And Thorn of Dunoon stood looking down at them, his red hair catching the sun, his eyes quiet and concerned.

"It's all right, the Deacons have gone back. You can come out now. Here . . ." He knelt and lifted Meatha as easily as he might lift a new fawn and began to make his way back through the whitebarley toward the road. Zephy followed him in silent confusion.

Then in a flash of memory she saw a picture of Thorn and Anchorstar beside the goats, facing Kearb-Mattus together. Thorn of Dunoon—and Anchorstar!

They went up the road quickly and through the plum

grove to a vetchpea patch on the other side, pausing to talk only when they were at last sheltered.

And there in the shade of the heavy vines Thorn told them about Anchorstar and about how the old man had come to him at night on the mountain. If he paused sometimes, perhaps it was to remember.

He told them how Anchorstar had appeared suddenly, coming so silently in the night that even the guardbucks didn't hear him, and had spoken to him about the Children of Ynell. He told how Anchorstar had known about the spark in Thorn's own being that made him like Ynell. *Did* Thorn leave something out, hold something back, or did Zephy only imagine that? Yet why would he? He had given them his trust implicitly: for Thorn's confession to them of his own skills put his very life in their hands.

He told them how he had slipped into Anchorstar's wagon before Anchorstar started his act, had been there inside all the time the juggler was doing his tricks, then had ridden out with him, the two of them laying a plan to get Anchorstar to Dunoon. "For he would speak with you two," he said matter-of-factly, brushing a gnat from his face—a flock of them buzzed among the vetchpea vines, annoying in the late afternoon heat. "He would speak with you both," he repeated in answer to Zephy's surprised look. "For you are the only two older ones in Burgdeeth."

"The only two older *what?*" Zephy whispered, going cold.

"The only two . . ." He studied her as he waited for her to understand. But she refused to understand and only stared at him blankly.

"The only two Children of Ynell," Meatha breathed at last, her eyes never leaving Thorn's.

"I'm not . . ." Zephy began. But she could not say more, she could not deny it, not after the vision in the tunnel. "I'm not . . ." she tried again, almost inaudibly.

Then she gave it up and sat staring at Thorn. She did not speak of the tunnel. Nor did Meatha.

"I have a trace of the gift," Thorn said. "But only a trace. Anchorstar will need all three of us." He would say nothing more. He bent the talk instead to laying out the plan he had discussed with Anchorstar. It sounded simple enough, to bring the wagon through Burgdeeth after midnight, after the Singing was finished and people had gone to bed. Simple, and dangerous. For if Anchorstar were caught, Thorn felt he would be killed.

"Couldn't he leave his horses and wagon somewhere and go on foot?" Zephy asked. "It would be safer."

"But how?" Thorn said. "Near Burgdeeth they would be seen, and anywhere off in the hills there would be no one to care for the horses. Tied animals run out of grazing, loose animals stray . . ." he gazed at her, questioning, and she realized what a silly question it had been. His eyes were such a dark green, like the river where it ran deep and still. And direct, so direct they made her self-conscious—yet they made her trust him, too. She felt that the three of them were bound together suddenly in something as bizarre and terrifying as anything she could imagine. The three of them . . . *You three—and three—* the words seemed to echo from a long way off. *You three—you will reach out—if you are the chosen;* she stared at Thorn and felt her spirit twist in sudden confusion.

It was Meatha who seemed transported into a joy of spirit so absolute that Zephy was sobered by it, for Meatha was lifted into a passion that encompassed her utterly. Was this what Anchorstar was capable of? And then she thought, could he be other than what they believed, could he be leading them into something evil?

But Thorn—Thorn would not deceive them.

And when she thought of the stone in the tunnel she knew that an aura of otherness, of mystery and wonder, truly did exist. She thought of telling Thorn about the stone.

But she would wait. If Anchorstar had tricked them, tricked Thorn, then it would be too late; and she vowed to keep the thought of it hidden when at last she faced Anchorstar.

It was nearly evening when they left the housegardens and went to fetch Loke and the bucks. They took the bucks to be bedded down with Nida and Dess, watered and fed them, then stood leaning silently on the rail. "The Singing will begin soon," Thorn said. "We'd best make a spectacle of it. More eyes than mine saw you two staring at Anchorstar in the square when everyone else had gone. And saw you leave it, too. We'd best make it appear that Anchorstar is well out of our thoughts, that we're wild with the pleasure of Market Night. Do you remember last year, Zephy, when you danced 'Jajun Jajun' alone atop the Storemaster's wagon, with Shanner and half a dozen clapping and playing for you?"

Did he remember that? She flushed, feeling as simple and hot-faced as any Burgdeeth girl. "Tonight," he said lightly, "we'll dance 'Jajun Jajun' as it's never been danced before." His smile was so full of easy friendliness that she couldn't help but smile back. But she thought later, I'm not so shy with other boys. What's the matter with me?

Well you couldn't be shy with the music playing; you couldn't be shy when you were singing. Caught up in the rhythm of the music and the blaze of lantern light that drove back the darkness, they danced and sang and forgot everything else. Zephy forgot her shyness in the laughter of Thorn's eyes, in his voice as they sang the old songs.

She played her gaylute for the singing but quickly handed it to Meatha when Thorn swept her into a Sangurian reel that lifted her, made her forget the danger that lay ahead of them—the music was a river that carried them churning wildly down its length so no other thought was possible.

Again and again she saw Mama dancing with Kearb-Mattus. She was embarassed when Mama danced the wild, clapping Rondingly with him, for he did not know the steps and stumped clumsily beside her. In spite of his strange appeal, the Kubalese was not made for dancing. And Mama made a spectacle of herself, clapping and whirling like a girl. It was embarrassing to see her own mother behaving with such abandon.

Late in the night Elij presented Thorn with a sheaf of whitebarley and claimed Zephy as partner. He was so drunk he could hardly keep his feet. Zephy tried to stay out of his way, but she was well-trodden on before the music stopped and she turned away from him—only to be pulled back to face him.

"What's th' matter, Zephy? One more dance—one dance . . ." His arm went around her too tight, and when he saw Thorn approaching, his grip tightened further and his voice came loud and slurred. "How c'n you lower yourself to dance w'th a—w'th a *goatherd!*"

She stared at Elij, then pushed him away and went boldly to Thorn. Elij's gaze followed her, his eyes like ice.

When the music stopped again, Elij was beside them, his voice carrying across the square, "A girl pregnant by a goatherd—a Cherban goatherd—would be driven from Cloffi in rags."

Zephy's face flamed. Someone snickered. She could not look at Thorn. Someone else hooted, and several boys began to laugh. When she did glance sideways at Thorn, she saw his fists clenched as if he were trying to hold his temper.

"C'me here, Zephy Eskar. Come over here and let's see what the young goatherd finds so appealing. C'm on—let's pass it around a little . . ."

Thorn had him down, pounding him, and Elij so drunk he could hardly fight back. Thorn's fury made Zephy go cold as she grabbed his arm, dragged at him. "He's drunk, Thorn, he's too drunk . . ." And Thorn, comprehending finally, pulled back and stood up, ashamed, Elij crouching before him in the street. The catcalls and laughter were ugly, were all directed at Thorn; though no one made a move toward him. "Come on," Zephy whispered. He stood belligerently, furious. Then he seemed to collect himself, and took her arm at last, and led her away from the street. She wondered if his fury would spill over and lash out at her, too. It was strange that the Deacons, who had watched from their elevated seats at the side of the square, had not come forward to beat Thorn. What devious punishment did they have in their minds for later?

Fog had begun to drift in from the river and settle between the buildings as they stood together in a side street. "I'm sorry," Thorn said, "to cause talk like that about you. Goatherd. It's not a nice word in Burgdeeth."

"It wasn't you that caused Elij's rudeness. If I'd been nice to him, if I'd danced with him—he stepped all over my feet," she said, trying to make light of it.

"Does he—does he court you?"

"Me?" She didn't know whether to laugh or to scream at him. "Me and Elij Cooth? Oh no, Thorn. I wouldn't have him."

"That shows good taste," Thorn said, grinning. "I never thought you'd have him. But sometimes . . ." he paused and studied her. "Usually a girl has little choice."

She grinned back. "I'd feed him painon bark and ashes and make him so sick he'd be sorry he ever knew me."

Thorn smiled. He was so close she trembled. Surely he would kiss her. She was terrified. Then when he didn't, when he took her hand instead and turned back toward the square, there was an emptiness like lead inside.

Chapter Nine

In the square, the music was quieter. Elij had gone and interest in the fight had died away. Other couples had drifted off, and the crowd was smaller. Soon four of the Deacons retired. The fog settled down thicker, fuzzing the lantern light to a glistening haze, then growing brighter as the moons rose behind it.

When the music was stilled and the square empty at last, Zephy and Thorn and Meatha met in the housegardens, each going separately through back ways. There they woke Loke where he slept wrapped in blankets by the donkey pen.

Chapter Ten

THE THIN RADIANCE of moonlight through fog made the street much too light, a diffused brightness. One couldn't be sure whether there was clarity of vision or only the glittering haze masking things unseen. Zephy peered out of the alley. "Why couldn't it be dark."

"It wouldn't be dark so close to Fire Scourge," Meatha whispered reasonably. The full moons behind the fog were like two lamps in their brilliance. Meatha shifted deeper into the shoulder-narrow alley, pressing against Zephy who was, in turn, pressed against the damp stone.

The bright fog would surely set the wagon off too plainly; though Zephy guessed it was better than the bare full moons shining down. The night was utterly silent; strange, after so much music. She felt as if an echo of music still vibrated, unheard. Meatha sighed, nervy with apprehension, then slipped out of the alley and away, a dark shape beside the wall disappearing at once into the fog. She would stand watch between Zephy and the square, prepared to whistle softly if anyone appeared in the street. It had taken Thorn a long time to teach them the whistle of the river-owl. Thorn would be in the square now. And Loke, with the bucks, would be watching from the north end of town. Even in the silence the wagon should not be heard, for the wheels and the horse's hooves would be wrapped with rags.

Alone, Zephy felt very exposed, even in the narrow alley. She hardly dared breathe for listening. Once she thought she heard a door open softly. But it could have been inside a house. She tried to see deeper into the mist. If someone were standing across the street, would she see them? But of course there was no one; all Burgdeeth slept after the night of dancing. The dampness of the stone against which she was pressed chilled her. She stood away from the wall shivering, disliking the fog suddenly.

Among the coastal countries, Aybil and Farr, Pelli and Sangur, fog was said to be the breath of SkokeDirgOg, and men kept to their closed houses. How much superstition men lived by. If it were not for Tra. Hoppa, would she and Meatha be the same? Were they being as foolish now, just as believing of falsehood when they put their trust in Anchorstar as they were doing?

But to speak to Anchorstar, to speak without words, that was not superstition. That was real, something they had done themselves—or, Meatha had.

And did Meatha see truly? Or was her vision as warped as the Cloffi history of Ere? Was what she thought *truth* just another falsehood?

A faint hollow sound shook her, a ghost of a sound. Then almost at once the wagon was looming out of the fog, its muffled hoofbeats like blunt whispers, the horses warm-smelling; the wagon was nearly on top of her, the muffled wheels and rag-shod hooves sucking strangely at the damp street. For an instant Anchorstar's face was above her, his eyes looking into hers, speaking a message she could not doubt; how could she ever have doubted him, the direct, honest warmth of his gaze that seemed to see right into her, to bare his own soul for her. Then he was gone, swallowed up. From the back of the wagon Thorn reached down to touch her cheek, then he too was gone; the wagon had disappeared, gone as if it had never been. No sound remained. Ahead in the fog, had Loke joined them? They must meet the river high above the last fields where the path was rough and stony; to use the lower road would have been foolish. She shivered at what tomorrow would bring. It seemed a wild plan, to slip out of Burgdeeth during the reaping. To stand before Anchorstar in a meeting that, Zephy felt, would change her life in ways that terrified her.

She slipped out into the street. Meatha would be finding her way home now. The fog made distances seem different; she quailed as something moved close by, then saw it was her own fog-distorted shadow against a door. She found her stairway and climbed it, lifting the door with all her strength to keep it from creaking. She climbed the two flights and the ladder, undressed in darkness, and was in bed at last. But she couldn't sleep. She thought of Thorn's green-eyed gaze, and Anchorstar's dark, penetrating look, that were in some way alike. Both challenged and both comforted her. Then she dropped into sleep as suddenly as a stone drops into water.

THE CHANTING of Prayer Morning woke her. She tried to slip back into sleep, felt as exhausted as if she had not slept at all. She pulled the covers up, but the Deacons' voices raised in unison were so insistent that at last she rose. She washed and dressed in a stupor with the chanting annoying her. The demanding voices seemed to destroy what little privacy she had. Outside, the fog still shrouded Burgdeeth, veiling the houses below her. She scowled down at the fog-muffled street and thought about dumping her dirty washwater down on the Deacons' righteous heads; and that shocking idea made her feel a good deal better.

At least she wouldn't have to start breakfast, for Prayer Mornings meant fasting. Her stomach rumbled in protest and she was at once ravenous. She pulled on her cloak and went down; maybe she could slip a little bread from the sculler.

But Kearb-Mattus was there before her, rummaging. *He* didn't fast; *he* didn't go to services. She went out again, feeling irritable.

In the street the banners hung limp and pale as if the fog had robbed them of their colors. The wet cobbles were slippery; and people, coming out of their houses, paused and stared at the cloistered morning in annoyance. Zephy shivered and pulled her cloak tighter. She glanced back to see Mama coming out behind her, joining the Cobbler's wife. She went on ahead, not wanting to talk to Mama.

The six red-robed Deacons, marching at the head of the straggling procession, had backs as straight as painon trees. Zephy tried to walk straighter and more in time with them, as was expected. As the procession entered the square, the fog shifted so the fog-veiled god seemed to lift, turning; seemed airborne then disappeared behind a heavy wash of mist.

It was strange that the Horses of Eresu were tolerated there with the gods. But what an odd question; why wouldn't they be? They were the gods' own consorts. Yet the Horses of Eresu were only mortal, as man was. They were truly of Ere, and the gods were not. What were the gods, then? Did they become fully visible only at Waytheer as the Covenants taught? *Was* Eresu a place of two worlds, the heavenly one and the earthly one overlapping? She could never understand how that could be. She felt half-asleep, yet questions were crowding into her head with sudden surprising strength. As if, while she slept, questions had been pulled forth from the very depths of herself, those questions that troubled her most.

The Deacons had knelt before the Temple steps; behind them the procession knelt, too, as the Landmaster, broad under his swirl of red silk, made the entry signs across the door. Zephy bowed her head in quick submission. But she felt as rebellious at the ceremony as she had ever been in her life.

The red robes were bright against the white stone as the Deacons rose and climbed the stair. Four Deacons entered the Temple behind the Landmaster. The two youngest stood beside the entryway, their sheafs of whitebarley raised, and began to say the blessing in monotonous tones as the citizens of Burgdeeth filed by to enter the holy place.

Inside, the women and girls turned to one side, and the men and boys to the other. The six Deacons knelt before the carven stone dais on which the Landmaster stood with his hands crossed over his shoulders to represent his nakedness without wings. The citizens of Burgdeeth bent their heads in holy submission. The candles, placed in niches along the wall, sent long shadows of the Landmaster and Deacons across the heads of the kneeling people. Zephy peered up under her lashes, searching for Meatha, but she could not see her, and became uneasy. Had Meatha gotten home unseen last night?

This Worship of the First Dawn, just as the Worship of the Last Day, laid upon Burgdeeth protection against the wrath of the Luff'Eresi for all the following year. It began the five days of ceremonies that insured good crops and fertility and protected all who were sincere against hunger and against the evils of avarice and pride and curiosity.

The prayers were rising now, "Oh bless us, humble we are. Bless us, weak we are and afraid." She intoned the words without feeling—yet with a real prayer deep in her heart: *Let them be safe, let Thorn and Anchorstar be safe . . .* "And we bow our heads in submission, we kneel to the ground before you our gods who are not earthbound"—*Let them be safe*—"and we worship your sky and your land on which we are suffered to dwell . . ."

The grain and fruit were being offered now, lifted into

the flame. Their burning smell began to fill the Temple. Zephy choked with its bitter sweetness, tried not to cough, and knew the eyes of the Deacons were on her. She felt her face go red with humiliation as people glanced sideways.

Across the aisle the men of Burgdeeth, row after row of grown men, were bowing and kneeling submissively, their lips moving in prayer. Zephy could not picture Anchorstar behaving so. And the few times she had seen Thorn and Loke come to Temple their heads had bent very slightly, and their backs, when they knelt, were straight as zayn trees so you could see no hint of submission.

As if something in her head had saved forgotten memories to fling at her now, a dozen scenes came back to Zephy suddenly and sharply. She was standing in the Candler's watching him pour hot wax into molds all the same shape, the same size. Couldn't they be different sizes, she asked him. Could you make a square candle? If you put in berry juice would it make the wax red?

"Candles've always been made this way; why'd you want any other? When one burns down you just pluck another on top. If you had all different sizes and shapes, how'd they fit the holders? And who ever heard of square candles? Talk like that don't please the Deacons none." He had stared down at her coldly from behind his work table.

And the Shoemaker. All Burgdeeth's shoes were the same. Men's. Women's. Children's. Boots the same only taller. There must be some other way for shoes to look.

"What way would you have 'em? Soles on the top and the lacing underneath?" The Shoemaker had guffawed and Zephy had turned away rigid with anger. Couldn't anyone see what she meant?

She thought of last night, so the memory of the music caught her up, came into her head more real than the Temple prayers; she closed her eyes and felt the warmth of Thorn's closeness, felt his hands holding hers.

The offering was flaming to blackness. The Deacons knelt and bent their heads until their foreheads touched the dais. Behind them, the citizens of Burgdeeth knelt as one.

At last the offering was ashes, the flame dead, the Temple gray with smoke. The Deacon's voices rose in a cry like ferret-dogs as the Seven Prayers of the First Day began. This depressed Zephy, all the Five Days of Worship depressed her—until the Prayers of the Last Night. She could suffer the rest for that.

On the Last Night, after the kneeling, after the terrible shrill whining of the Deacons, the worshippers would rise and march out of the Temple, each carrying a torch lit from the blessed vessel, would march into the town square and around the great statue. Their faces would be turned upward toward the night sky and the stars, toward Waytheer and the full moons. Toward the gods. The Deacons would raise their voices in a gentler litany then, in a song of true prayer. And maybe, in the sky, dark shapes might move, windborne, across the faces of the moons.

Now, the sudden stirring around her brought Zephy back to the present as the worshippers rose. As they turned toward the door, she saw Meatha where she had been sitting behind her; and Burgdeeth's citizens filed out into the bright morning and headed directly for the fields.

"Do you think the wagon got through all right?" Zephy breathed faintly as she caught up with Meatha.

"They are safe in Dunoon," Meatha whispered without hesitation. Then she would say no more, nor look at Zephy, as if she were wrapped in some private cocoon of emotion she did not want to share.

The fog had burned away and the sun was coming as they took up their scythes and began to cut the heavy whitebarley stalks, swinging in loose rhythm with the other women and girls who formed a long line on either side of them. Then, as the slower reapers dropped back the line began to waver. Behind them came the wagon pulled by six donkeys and driven by a young girl, accompanied by two loaders: older women with strong backs who could throw the sheaves in such a skilled way that the grain was not disturbed.

The sun was well above the hills before there were changes in the harvest line, a girl dropping out because of illness, three coming late to join them after nursing babies—now two more missing might not be noticed by the patrolling Deacons. After all, three fields were being cut besides the main field where the men were working. As the harvesters cut to the edge of the woods that bordered the river, then turned back upon a new row, straggling, one or two stopping to rest, Zephy and Meatha were there one moment and gone the next, slipping through the underbrush, their hearts pounding.

They lay for a long time on the riverbank, and once a Deacon's horse passed so close they didn't dare breathe. But if they were discovered here, it would only be a matter of idling, of cooling off. Chastisement, a beating. At last, when they heard no other sound, no breaking branches, no voice calling out, they rose and started up the river.

They kept as well hidden as they could, staying close to the painon trees that lined the fields on their right, then to the cicaba grove, almost overpowered by the honey scent of the cicaba. At the end of the grove, Burgdeeth would end too, and the wild fields begin, the forbidden fields where no one was allowed save those on sanctioned business for Burgdeeth: the meat cart, the ice wagons, the loads of bitleaf. They could still hear, faintly, the sounds of the threshing, the hush, hush of the scythes and the muttering of women's voices, the occasional calls or laughter. They walked hunched over instinctively, though the cicaba trees were dense and shielding.

Thorn won't be there, Zephy thought. He won't be waiting.

But when they reached the end of the cicaba grove he was there, leaning idly against a tree trunk, a pile of forbidden cicaba gleaming red at his feet. His trousers were rolled to his knees, and his damp clothes clung to him as if he had pulled them on hastily after swimming. "Took you long enough," he said lightly.

"Temple . . ." Zephy began, and felt herself go weak at his presence.

He grinned, and handed Zephy a cicaba, and one to Meatha. They sat eating the fruit messily, as casual about it—though Zephy and Meatha had never tasted cicaba—as if they had been the Landmaster's own family. The rind was sharp-tasting, and the fruit inside as sweet as honey. It stained their mouths red so they would be hard put to deny their thievery, were they caught. We won't be, Zephy thought. Not now, not with Thorn, we won't.

Across the river, some vetchpea vines had gone wild and grown into tangles that climbed the painon trees and hung down in green curtains. Zephy stared, thinking someone might be watching from there, but Thorn shook his head. "I looked, there's no one." And when they went on at last, the hanging vetchpeas vanished quite soon as the river and path turned left.

Burgdeeth and the Landmaster's fields were behind them now; the wild steep fields and black boulders rose toward the mountain, the river cutting swiftly down to pass them noisily. They were at the foot of the Ring of Fire; Zephy felt the strength of the land around her, felt its weight as it rose above her, the solidity of stone that seemed to have its roots deep in the world's core. She turned and saw Burgdeeth, so small; then followed Thorn hastily as they slipped from boulder to boulder, staying in shadow. She remembered how stark a small figure, set against the pale grass of the mountain, could appear from below.

Last night at the Singing with the blackness driven back to the edges of the square, with the lamps and candles casting wildly dancing shadows across the stone houses and across the winged statue, with the fiddles and gaylutes and calmets making such a racket, she had felt that nothing could happen to Burgdeeth—or to them. Just as the blackness of night had been destroyed, so the fear of danger, the fear of war, had been put aside as if no harm could come as long as the music lasted. Now in the daylight she felt the reality of their danger once more, the reality of the Kubalese intent.

But such a mood could not last, for the lifting sun sent a clear light onto the mountain, picking out the silver river and, sharply, the black boulders that had been strewn over the land by the eruption of the volcanoes. When she thought of the volcanoes she felt the excitement that she felt in Temple sometimes, as if her thoughts were trying to break free, could almost free themselves. Had the river boiled dry in that terrible erupting heat? If it happened now, this minute, could they escape? She could imagine the lava pouring red and smoking over the little stone huts of Dunoon that perched far above them.

Thorn stared at her. "You're frightened. Does the mountain do that?"

"Not the mountain. I was thinking of the volcanoes. *Why* did it happen? *Really* why?"

"Because there was fire in the mountain," Thorn said, "a fire that had to come out just as surely as a boiling pot will shake off its lid."

"But why *then*, just when Owdneet was attacked?"

He smiled. "Are you asking me if I believe in the Cloffi Books of Ere? Or are you asking if *you* do?"

"I don't know. I don't know what I'm asking."

He looked at her, and she felt a weakness take her

suddenly, a power between them that she could not resist, so that there was nothing real in all the world but Thorn and herself. His eyes darkened, he looked, and touched her hand—and then he turned away.

When they reached Dunoon, the stone huts were washed with sun, casting sharp shadows up the mountain. Zephy looked down to the valley, and it was as if she stood on the edge of the sky, so falling away was the land. The countries beyond Cloffi dropped until they merged into the far-off haze; space, infinite space fell away beneath her feet, and the wonder of it held her utterly so she stood staring until Meatha pulled her away, impatient to get on.

There were three orphaned fawns in the village tended by a small boy, and some women were grinding mawzee and wild grains while a young couple laid stone for a house. High behind Dunoon the herds of goats could be seen, and to the left a black cleft between two crags. It was into this cleft that Thorn would guide them. He led them across the village and up beside the river that had grown deeper and narrower as it flowed out from the cleft. The air was cold here. Small fish flashed in the cascading water, and once Meatha stopped and pointed, picking out a gray shape high above on the rocks.

"Wolves. They won't bother in the daylight," Thorn said. "There aren't so many left now, not as there were when my father was young. Then they roamed the mountains in packs of fifty and more."

"But how do you keep them away?" Meatha, like Zephy, felt a deep fear of the wolves of Dunoon.

"The bucks," Thorn said. "Did you ever see a big buck goat charge a wolf? With five or six together, a pack doesn't have a chance. That's why we have several bucks to a herd. It took a good many generations to breed bucks that would tolerate sharing their does, but it was the only way for protection."

"You could shut the herds up at night," Meatha said.

"It was tried. They don't like it, these goats want the night and the cold air and the moons to make good coats and strong breeding; they wasted away, shut in. That was why my ancestors came to this place in the beginning, because they thought the caves would be good protection and make their flocks safe."

"It must have been frightening," Zephy said, "with the volcanoes still smoking and the cinders falling."

"Yes, they were afraid. The stories show it, the ones that have come down to us. But they came. They didn't like the Herebian hot on their tails every minute. This was the only place the Herebian wouldn't go at that time, on the site of the old city. There were fire ogres in the caves then, too. They must have been terrified sometimes—but it was better than the warring tribes."

"Why was it better?" Zephy stared at him.

"Because the fire ogres and the wolves were only—well, it was their instinct to kill. But man—the Herebian, the Kubalese—theirs is a conquering out of lust. Man doesn't need to conquer and subjugate other men. When he does, it's a sickness."

They came to the cleft; as they entered, the rocky cliffs closed around them and a cold breath like winter blew out of the dank, sunless fissure. The stream became black and narrow, silent flowing, and a weight seemed to press around them. Yellow moss grew up the sides of the stone walls, and something small scurried out from some rocks and disappeared ahead of them. Zephy glanced at Meatha—but Meatha was looking steadily ahead.

Chapter Eleven

Meatha seemed unaware of the dank, forbidding atmosphere of the fissure as she pushed farther in, leading eagerly. Boulders stood across their narrow path so they must force their way around them; the river slipped by dark as a rock-snake on their left, the cliff walls had little growth except the yellow moss. The fissure, cut by the ancient river and perhaps by lava flow, seemed to Zephy to breathe an evil life of its own.

Meatha whispered something Zephy could not make out, and reached back to take Zephy's hand as one would take the hand of a small child. They came around a boulder with Zephy pulled close to Meatha, and they were standing before a cave that opened black in the fissure wall. Meatha entered it at once and Zephy was pulled along; Thorn followed, silent, watching Meatha with interest.

The blackness became absolute as they thrust themselves in. How did Meatha know where she was going, that there was no drop-off? Zephy pulled back, but Meatha would not allow that, she dragged Zephy on, pushing ahead with calm certainty. Only when Zephy glanced behind could she see anything at all, and then just the rapidly shrinking cave opening; she felt they would leave the world behind completely when they left that feeble light. Meatha pulled too hard in her eagerness, pushing into the darkness as steadily as if she carried a lantern.

Zephy strained to see or to feel with some sense what lay ahead and around them, but she could not; there was only the heavy blackness as if she could remember nothing else, did not know what light was. At one point they heard water running and felt a cool surge of air. There was a wall on their left now, smelling of dirt and satisfyingly rough and real. But what lay on the right? Was there an abyss? Zephy clung to the left-hand wall and felt Thorn's hand on her arm. But whether to steady her from a fall or from her own fear, she did not know.

If you lived in darkness all your life, she thought, and had never seen light, you would not be able to imagine what the world looked like. Do we, Zephy wondered, live in a world where there is something *we* can't see, but is there around us just the same?

The vision in the tunnel had implied that this was so. And the Cloffi Covenants taught that there was another world invisible to them. Before, she had never really believed that. Could part of the Cloffi teaching be truth, while the rest of it was not? But of course, Tra. Hoppa had told them that, that the most successful lies had enough truth in them to lead you into belief. Well, she had *seen* the vision in the tunnel; she had seen that other world for herself.

But then that stubborn doubt nagged at her again: it could all have been imagined. Still she followed Meatha blindly, though her thoughts were confused and uncertain.

At last they began to see something ahead, black shapes in the blackness. The dark was less complete, and Zephy felt as if she could breathe again. After an interminable time more she was seeing the sides of the cave. And finally she could see that they were on a wide flat path walled by earth and stone. It seemed to Zephy now that she could define the murky spaces around her with other senses than her eyes, with the *feel* of the space, with some sense of air on her skin—though she had not been able to in the blackness.

The ceiling was twice as tall as Thorn in some places, and at others rose to a height Zephy could not judge. The tunnel was still growing lighter. It turned and twisted as if it had been cut by natural forces through the softer areas of rock, as if perhaps the river had run here once. She wanted to ask Thorn, but she could not bring herself to speak, even to whisper.

Then they turned a corner and saw brighter light directly ahead; the tunnel widened into a sweeping cave lit from above. Meatha had stopped, but now she broke away from them to stride quickly on. Zephy stood in the entrance, the space opening before and above her; space and light, for the walls of the cave rose to an incredible height and opened to the sky as if a plug had been cut deep down into the mountain, a round hole revealing a drift of clouds. The floor of the cave was sparsely grassed, and the wagon stood at one side, its colors bright against the stone, the two mares grazing near it. A thin line of smoke rose from an open fire like a thread pulled taut to the sky, and on the fire a haunch of meat was browning. The smell of crisp meat filled the cave, making the saliva come in Zephy's mouth.

The light seemed translucent, gave an other-worldly quality to the cave. She stood quietly, feeling the silence and the mystery, the rightness of it—and then she saw Anchorstar standing at the edge of the clearing.

Over his leather tunic and trousers he wore a brown cape against the chill. It swept the ground and was hooded, his white hair showing at the temples. He gave the impression of great height and strength. Meatha stood facing him. Neither spoke, but their expressions were changing softly, as if with shared thoughts, and Zephy was drawn to watch them in spite of the sense that she was intruding, for the silent speaking was wonderful and frightening to her. She stood staring, half-believing in him, and half-afraid.

And then she turned and saw Thorn's expression, and felt his trust and satisfaction in Anchorstar.

At last Meatha moved away and Anchorstar looked across at Zephy and Thorn and smiled, and the tenseness went from Zephy so she relaxed and was engulfed by a sense of warmth.

He was of Sangur, she knew that at once in a sudden flood of knowledge. He had come up from Sangur's cape coast through Pelli and Farr, and then Aybil, singing and juggling in the villages, doing his tricks of magic. And she knew that he had come seeking. She had a blurred sense of faces, children's faces, and of Meatha among them, then a sense of people running—faces full of fear, their open mouths shouting wordlessly: a sense of terror and repulsion . . . then of sadness.

Thorn steadied her, for he had seen it too.

When Anchorstar spoke to them, he spoke in silence from his mind, and they knew at once that he was pleased that each of them responded, had the skill for which he searched. There was a sense of his great wonder as their thoughts filled with his silent words, *You have the gift of seeing, of true seeing.*

"Ynell's gift," Thorn breathed huskily.

Yes, Ynell's gift, Thorn of Dunoon. You think you have only a trace of it, young Cherban, only enough to tease you, but that is not the fact.

Thorn blanched, dropping his head as if he had been chastened.

"And Zephy Eskar does not understand," Anchorstar was speaking aloud now. He clapped a strong hand on Zephy's shoulder and stood looking into her eyes. His eyes were golden, flecked with light, and as she stared into them, Meatha and Thorn faded, the cave faded. There was brightness, a wind. She was swirling, weightless. She was lifted above the land, she was rising on the wind . . .

She *was* the wind; she was looking down on Ere. She was drifting and blown at a great height above the land, could see clouds swimming below her, and beneath them the green sweeping reaches of Ere, bright green hills washed with moving shadows as the clouds passed below in a space, in a distance, that was overwhelming. The land swept below her, the dark bristling stands of woods and forests, the twisting rivers. She could see how land touched sea in a lace of white beaches and foaming surf, see Carriol's outer islands like green gems, see the Bay of Pelli curving in between two peninsulas. And in the Bay of Pelli, beneath the transparent waters, the wonder of the three sunken islands and the sunken city, lying still and secret. She could see the pale expanse of high desert with the Cut running through it like a knife wound, the river deep at its bottom lined with green—a trench of lush growth slashing across the pale dry desert.

How bright the other three rivers were, too, as they meandered down through Ere's green countries from the mountains. And the mountains themselves, black and jagged and thrusting, that circle of mountains, the Ring of Fire, pushed up toward her as if she could touch the highest peaks—snow-clad, some. Then between the peaks a glimpse of a valley so beautiful she was shaken with desire for it, something . . . but it was gone at once, faded, the vision taken abruptly from her.

Something gone, something that had been hidden deep within that valley in the black stone reaches of the Ring of Fire. Something she wished with all her heart she could reach.

Then it was Thorn's eyes she looked into. She felt drained, as if this cave and all in it was an indistinct dream. As if she had been torn away from reality. Thorn waited, and when she really looked at him, she saw that he, too, had seen the vision. And Meatha—she looked up to see Meatha's flushed and trembling face.

Anchorstar stood a little way from them, waiting. They went to him, stood before him. *I am a Child of Ynell,* Zephy thought, shaken. Nothing can ever be the same, nothing . . .

"Yes," Anchorstar said at last, "Nothing will ever be the same. You are Children of Ynell, and you are not to be afraid."

No, Zephy thought with surprise. Fear was not a part of this; this was beyond fear. "And there are others," Anchorstar added quietly. "Perhaps many. In Burgdeeth there are children who wait for you, though they know not what they wait for. All of Ere may one day depend on the Children of Ynell. Others have done their share before you, and now it is your turn. If you so choose. But it will be more painful than you know.

"And it may be," he added slowly, "that time is running out."

I should challenge Anchorstar, Zephy thought suddenly, and now was shocked at herself. But Tra. Hoppa had taught her well: to take nothing she was told as absolute truth until she had sought it out for herself. Yet she could not challenge him, there was not room in her. If this were to be a lie, then she would have to see it in its own time, in its own way. She could see naught but truth in this man, truth in the visions he gave them. "I am no god," he said, laughing at Meatha's unspoken thought. "I am mortal just as you. But a stubborn mortal, child. A mortal with something of your own talents, though latent in many ways. Though I can speak to you, my powers are not constant. They need the help that comes when I speak to another with the talent. For the gifts vary. And you must know that the seeing is stronger close at hand. It is a rare Child, indeed, who can speak at any distance. And a rarer one, still, who can read of the future as you have done, Meatha. The power is a force that, for most of us, takes close proximity, as if it is a spark that falls, dying, at a distance.

"And the power is stronger in these Waytheer years, when the star is close overhead. The star's very presence seems to give a strength that is needed."

"If the power is stronger in the Waytheer years," Thorn said thoughtfully, "and if the Luff'Eresi can be seen more clearly then, are the two connected?"

"They seem to be connected. But there is too much that man does not know. Who knows, even, what a god is? Who knows what we ourselves are or are not? Perhaps the force that put us here has woven an intricacy beyond our understanding, beyond intention of our ever understanding."

"Tra. Hoppa told us once," Zephy said slowly, "that we can only see a very small portion of what there is to see or know. But that—that when the Landmasters deliberately prevented us from seeing, from trying to see, they were committing a sin. And that people who did not try to see were sinning, too."

"Perhaps I should have said," Anchorstar corrected himself, "beyond intention of our *easy* understanding. Perhaps we were meant to question and to seek after answers that would not come easily, that would stretch our minds in the seeking, stretch our very souls." He paused and studied her; but the picture in his mind was of Tra. Hoppa, so that Zephy stared back in surprise.

"Yes, I know Tra. Hoppa," Anchorstar said, answering her silent question. "Tra. Hoppa is an old and trusted friend. I saw her in the crowd on Market Day, and she saw me of course, but we dared not speak. To cast suspicion on Tra. Hoppa in that way would have been more than foolish. To go to her home secretly, watched as I was, would have been too risky. We will meet again, perhaps. I would like that; a meeting in safety, where she is not jeopardized. Do you not know her story?"

They shook their heads.

"Come then, let us sit by the fire. I will make a meal for you and tell you her history." He led them to the fire and brought out cushions from the wagon, then began to carve off slices of the roasting haunch and lay them on new bread. As steam rose from the meat and the juices soaked into the bread, Zephy found she was ravenous.

When they had satisfied their first hunger and were content to eat more slowly, Anchorstar settled back against the cave wall and began to speak quietly of Tra. Hoppa.

"In Carriol when I was a young man, Tra. Hoppa and her husband lived on a promontory overlooking the sea, a wild place with the breakers crashing below. There was always a hearthfire that was welcoming, and they harbored Children of Ynell from all the more primitive countries, Children come to Carriol because there they could be free. The Children would stay there until they could find a place to work, a place to live, a bit of land to farm, or until they went on, perhaps to the unknown lands.

"Then Tra. Hoppa's husband died, and she left this work to another. How she came to Burgdeeth is a long and complicated story in itself. She was in Zandour when she heard from a trader that the old teacher of Burgdeeth had died, and that his apprentice had suddenly left Burgdeeth. It was just what she had wished for, and she came at once up to Burgdeeth. The story was that the apprentice and the teacher had had an argument, something to do with silver and with trading in Aybil. I don't know the rest of it. She came leading a pack animal, tall-seeming in her Carriolinian gown, I was told, and regal. She acted every bit the Carriolinian lady, and let herself be entertained at the Set in a manner that no other woman in Ere, save one of Carriol, might have expected. She helped the Landmaster to fashion some of the teaching myths, as much as she loathed doing that, and made herself useful enough so that, what with his need, his natural abhorrence at engaging a woman was at last overcome. I had the story from a trader, shortly after she became teacher. I have not spoken with Tra. Hoppa since she left Carriol.

"And you three know the rest. That she has taught more than she was told to teach.

"Most of Tra. Hoppa's special children have left Cloffi. A few of them, just as you, were the Children of Ynell. They have done much good in Ere, secretly, though some have left Ere, too, and gone into the unknown lands. Perhaps one day they will return to Ere and to Cloffi. Perhaps one day, together, we can bring truth to the Cloffi cities, make Ere a place where men can rule their own lives as they were meant to do."

"That," he said slowly, "is why the Children of Ynell are feared in Cloffi. Because they could reveal the Landmasters' deception, the false history, reveal the twisted religion for what it is: a tool to enslave. And the Kubalese fear the Children too, as spies. But the Kubalese are clever. They fear them, but they use them." He looked at them for a long time. "In what I am going to ask you to do, I want to make clear that each of you must choose or reject it for yourselves. I am going to ask you to go back to Burgdeeth with deception foremost in your minds, to do the work for which you are better suited than I. You will not be suspected there as I would be.

"I want the other Children of Ynell. I want the younger ones brought away safely, the ones I feel are in greater danger now than ever before in Ere's history. I believe the Kubalese smith is there to take them if he can, and that it will be dangerous indeed to slip them away from him. I want you three—but Zephy and Meatha most, for you are of Burgdeeth—to help me in this, to help all of Ere and your true brothers and sisters in this. But I want you only willingly. If you have doubts, I do not want your promise.

"War may come to Cloffi, and if that happens, I believe

that all the Children of Ynell, even you two, will die or be taken captive for the use of the Kubalese.

"On the day of Market, it was Kearb-Mattus who alerted the Deacons that I might be a menace, who encouraged them to drive me out at once. He trusts me no less than I trust him."

Zephy thought of the gold coin hidden on the black goat, of the game of search-and-seek in the alley, and all at once she saw clearly the answer to the questions that had puzzled her. "He is searching for them!" She cried. "Kearb-Mattus is searching out the Children of Ynell!"

Anchorstar nodded.

"But he—but he . . ." she swallowed, and felt sick. "Three children have died in Burgdeeth. *He has killed them!*" She stared at Anchorstar. Meatha had gone white.

"No," Anchorstar said softly, "Kearb-Mattus has killed no child."

"But he . . . Nia Skane is dead! And the two little boys who drowned. They were all children who . . . bright children, different children! How can you . . ." her disappointment at Anchorstar flared too quickly.

He remained calm, his expression steady and appraising. "Not dead," he repeated at last. "They were taken." He banked the fire and poured wine from a flagon into pewter mugs.

"But I saw her body, Nia's body, and the little boys—"

"Only taken," he repeated. "They were made to seem dead. They were viewed as dead in the ceremonies, white as death with the drug MadogWerg that the Kubalese keep."

Zephy remembered Nia's white face. Surely it had been death she had looked upon. Then she remembered the hunting party in the street the night of Nia's funeral, remembered Kearb-Mattus's dark figure pulling the cape over something tied behind his saddle.

Anchorstar saw her thoughts and nodded. "Taken,"

he repeated softly. "Made captive, prisoner for the uses of the Kubalese."

"*What kind of use?*" She breathed, sweating with sudden fear. "And where? Where are they?"

"I do not know where. It is part of the work to be done, to find them. The mind drug is so potent that the children seem truly as dead, their minds inactive. No other Child of Ynell, seeking them out in their thoughts, has been able to sense the slightest hint of them. But I am certain they are alive. The Kubalese value the Children. They fear them, yes, as spies against Kubal. But they value them, too, as spies on their own side, if they can, with drugs and mind-forming, make the Children twisted in their thoughts so their allegiance is to Kubal alone."

"That is what they want," Thorn said. "That is what you have traveled across Ere to prevent. Spies. Faithful, mind-twisted spies."

"But how can they!" Meatha breathed. "How can they make the Children—even with drugs . . . *I wouldn't, I never would spy for Kubal!*"

"The youngest children will," Anchorstar answered. "Those who can be made to believe untruths about Kubal, just as children are made to believe untruths about the Luff'Eresi by the Temple training in Cloffi. It is easy to train a young child's mind into falsehood if you take time and skill with it and have nothing to conteract the training. The drugs will prevent their knowing the Kubalese intent until it is too late even for the Children of Ynell, until there has been subtle damage to their minds, so that they learn to love the corrupt. A Child of Ynell can be turned to evil just as anyone else can, can be made to lust after falsehood and evil, and desire to control others with his skill; never doubt it. But it would be difficult indeed to train you older ones, if you are strong-minded. Not without a good deal subtler effort than the Kubalese are prepared to put forth.

The young ones are more malleable, and the young ones' own passions can betray them. The young ones, and those older ones who are weak. Kearb-Mattus wants only the Children who can be made to *want* to use their powers for Kubal. He does not want you, you three are a threat to the Kubalese plans, if indeed Kearb-Mattus knows what your talents are." He sighed and laid a hand on Meatha's hair as if he, as Tra. Hoppa, found her delicacy and beauty a source of sadness.

"I believe the Kubalese will not attack Burgdeeth until all the young Children of Ynell have been taken by Kearb-Mattus. Though the last one or two might be taken at the very beginning of the attack. I would think that only a few are left in Burgdeeth even now."

"But how can Meatha and I get them away?" Zephy said. Then she saw Meatha frozen into that inner speaking. Zephy paused and delved deep into the silence, into the voiceless words; and she saw the tunnel, Meatha was showing Anchorstar the tunnel that ran beneath Burgdeeth.

She understood that the Children could be taken there, hidden there until the small hours of darkness when they could be led away to meet Anchorstar beyond the house-gardens. Yes, perhaps it could be done. If only their talent for seeing were stronger. And then she saw the stone, lying in its niche, and she knew they had the power. The power was there, the stone was the key, the weapon that would strengthen their talents. Meatha showed it to Anchorstar, and his exhaltation was great, his look intense as he examined the experience they had had with it; the vision Zephy shared with Thorn now, so he was there with her seeing the gods, feeling the immensity of space and of light.

Then Anchorstar's voice rang deep in their minds, as a prophecy would ring, and Zephy knew he spoke the words he had spoken to Thorn on the mountain when first he came into Cloffi.

I seek a lost runestone, a stone of such power that the true gift would come strong in one who held it. Found by the light of one candle, carried in a searching, and lost in terror. Found in wonder, given twice, and accompanying a quest and a conquering . . . And the time to wield that power may be soon, for there are rumors across the land . . .

Zephy stared at Thorn and felt a chill touch her, of fear and of anticipation. They stood looking at each other, linked, shaken, lifted into a dimension that exhalted and terrified her.

Fire Scourge

There shall be five days of worship at Harvest. On the fifth day, the last Worship of Fire Scourge shall be conducted under the full moons. The fields shall flame unto the sky, and the people shall turn their faces upward. We will see your flaming prayer, and we will judge your worthiness. You shall kneel down before the fire. You shall give the gods proof of your willing destruction of the earthly and unworthy. You shall show your innocence.

Only the innocent will be granted absolution. The guilty will burn for all time at the fires of Urdd lit by the Luff'Eresi to cleanse evil from the hearts of man.

From the *Covenants of Cloffi*, Book of Fire.

Chapter Twelve

"You were not in the west field," Feill Wellick said. He stood over them, cold as winter. They looked back innocently, trying to hide their apprehension. "You were not in the west field all day, not since early morning. *Where* were you?"

"There were too many," Zephy said. "When the other girls came, the line was so long the wagons couldn't keep up with us so we went to the north field, we . . ." His expression cut her short. She stared up at him, her heart like lead.

"No one saw you in the north field."

"We were there," she said boldly. "They would lie to get us in trouble, those girls." She had never talked to a Deacon like this. Her heart pounded; but she tried to look puzzled at his concern.

He couldn't prove anything; not that he needed to, of course. In the end he sent them to pray, so they missed supper. They prayed until after dark on their knees in the square, giddy with the knowledge that he had sent them exactly where they wanted to be. They were so close to the runestone, so close. Their bodies ached from the one position. They longed for darkness to be complete so they could slip down. It would be so easy to retrieve the stone.

Though the thought of bringing the stone up into

Burgdeeth was terrifying. It seemed to Zephy that the runestone would send a brightness out from itself that nothing could hide.

And then when darkness came, Feill Wellick sent two Deacons with lamps to stand over them to hear the Prayers of Contrition. They had no chance to slip into the tunnel. They were sent home to bed very late, with the Deacons watching them go. Zephy climbed into her cold bed feeling utterly defeated.

They don't know anything, she thought uneasily. How could they? It's just that we're too defiant, both of us, and they caught us once for swimming, so now they're always suspicious. But how will we get the stone now? Will they watch us all through harvest?

The next day they worked in separate fields, to allay suspicion, then came together innocently at noon to share their dinners. They sat a little way from the crowd of gossiping women and the clusters of girls. A Deacon rode by and stared at them and went on.

Three children had been taken by the Kubalese. Nia Skane, carried away behind Kearb-Mattus's saddle. Little Graged Orden, who had run away when he knew where the red rag was hidden, drowned with his friend, Gorn Pellva. Or so it had appeared. Had Gorn been a Child of Ynell, too? And what about Elodia Trayd? Zephy could still see Elodia's defiant gray eyes staring up at her. Would Elodia be next?

"And there's Toca Dreeb," Meatha whispered. "He *knew* where the coin was hidden on the black buck." The sun struck across Meatha's cheek as she turned. "And Clytey Varik, maybe. We mustn't let Kearb-Mattus take any of them. Clytey's such a strange girl I can't be sure. But there's something about her . . ."

"But she's always so lively. And with other children."

"All the same, I feel it. Clytey Varik. Elodia Trayd.

Toca Dreeb," she said with certainty. "And one other. Did you ever watch Tra. Thorzen's baby?"

"A *baby?* But how could you tell?"

"Tra. Thorzen was working beside me this morning and the baby—Bibb's its name—was lying in a patch of vetchpea to one side, gurgling. I thought things at it. I could make him smile. And I could make him cry."

Zephy stared at her. "It could have been . . ."

"Coincidence? I don't think so. I thought of food and he gurgled and reached out toward me, then when I thought of someone coming up behind and hitting him, he turned around very afraid and began crying. But when I thought he was warm and comfy and fed, he settled back and smiled and went to sleep."

Zephy frowned. "How will we steal a baby?"

"And what will we do with him? I've never taken care of a baby."

"The first thing is to get the stone. We'll have to try tonight, after harvest. When you take the donkeys back, turn Dess loose and slap her."

"We've done that before."

"She *can* jump the fence, though. We've seen her."

So they let Dess loose, heading her toward the plum grove, and in the search for her, Zephy slipped down into the tunnel while Meatha searched for the donkey above, in the opposite direction from Dess.

With the boulder rolled over the opening, the weight of blackness took hold of Zephy, making her shiver. She struck flint to candle, and in that trembling moment before the flame steadied, she knew, coldly, that if they were caught with the stone they would be killed for it; that somehow the Deacons would know what it was.

Yet the quest gave her a feeling that nothing in her life had ever done. She touched the cool walls, passed the first timber support, brushing dirt and stone with her fingers.

When she reached the niche at last, she had convinced herself the stone would be gone and could hardly bear to look. Then when she held the stone wrapped in her handkerchief, she had to unwrap it to be sure. Her desire to touch it overwhelmed her, but she wrapped it again and made haste to get back; she could put them both in danger with her dawdling.

They caught Dess knee-deep in Tra. Llibe's vetchpeas, gorging herself, and dragged her away toward her pen as if they were very angry, elation and terror making them nervy. Then they crept into Zephy's mawzee patch, and she unwrapped the stone, couching it in her handkerchief.

"Touch it, Zephy. Touch it once with me."

"I'm afraid. Wait until we can use it on one of the children."

"Maybe we could see if the Kubalese plan to attack. Maybe from Kearb-Mattus's mind. Anchorstar said—"

"But Anchorstar said you have to be close—"

"Not with the stone. With the stone we can do it. Oh, please let's try. Think of Kearb-Mattus as hard as you can, think of his face."

Zephy touched the jade reluctantly and felt Meatha's hand next to hers. She tried to see Kearb-Mattus's face. She could not, but she could feel the sudden sense of him so strong that she started. Whether that was the seeing, or only her memory of him she didn't know. She tried to go in, like drifting smoke, as Anchorstar had shown them. She tried to mingle her own self with Kearb-Mattus and in a moment of dizziness she knew that she had—and then she saw the soldiers.

They were mounted on great horses, their sectbows and swords slung over their saddles. She saw them riding hard over broken ground; she saw them making camp; she saw them assemble before a leader. Then there was only grayness, she could see nothing—but now a knowledge was growing in her mind, fledging out as if it had been there all the time unseen, now unfolding itself as a moth unfolds from the cocoon. And she knew, in that moment, the Kubalese plan. She knew the dark partnership into which Kubal and Cloffi had entered. She saw the exchange of strengths of the two countries, and she knew their intent.

To rule all of Ere! A ruling oligarchy powerful beyond any man's dream. An oligarchy made of Kubalese and Cloffi leaders. She stood gripping the stone, her knuckles white. In return for Kubal's strength in fighting men, so much fiercer, so much crueler than the Cloffa, Kubal would receive—had been receiving—the Children of Ynell, to use as spies.

And she saw that Kearb-Mattus was more powerful than she had supposed. The Children of Ynell must be very important, indeed, for Kearb-Mattus, as one of the Kubalese leaders, to come seeking them himself.

The Children had been feared by the Landmasters lest the day come when they broke away from the false Cloffi religion and made others see the truth. And now they were feared, too, lest they discover this new plot against Cloffi's freedom.

But why couldn't Cloffi and Kubal just have joined, without the threat of war? The Cloffi citizens were not strong enough to prevent it. And then she saw that if there were war and Cloffi seemed to be conquered, the Landmaster could feign honesty, could treat the alliance as making the best of a bad situation. Where if he simply joined Kubal, even the docile Cloffa might become too angered or disgruntled to be tractable.

And then she saw the last ironic part of the puzzle, and knew that Meatha saw it, too. The missing piece that even the Landmaster didn't know, that only the Kubalese leaders knew. She saw plainly that when—not if, but when—the Kubalese conquered Cloffi, the Landmaster and his family and the Deacons would be enslaved or put to death.

She stared at Meatha, sick. How could the Landmaster be such a fool? Meatha's eyes blazed; and then she began to smile, a twisted, bitter little smile, and she said coolly, "The Landmaster has baited his own trap."

The low sun glinted through the mawzee stalks in shafts of light that moved constantly on the wind; the scent of mawzee was strong, like baking bread.

"Could we—could we speak to Anchorstar?" Meatha whispered at last. "Could we speak to him with the stone?"

They tried, but they could not; it was all of darkness.

"We must try to see the Children," Zephy said nervously. "We must find the Children . . ."

They started with surprise at the ease with which the vision came. It was Nia Skane, and Zephy caught her breath—but this was Nia before she was taken. Zephy saw a montage of children playing and running in the street, and she knew she was seeing through Kearb-Mattus's eyes, for she could still feel the sense of him strongly. She saw Nia walking alone down the lane from Temple, and she knew Kearb-Mattus's intentions. There was a wild flashing of scenes as Nia ran, was grabbed, as something was forced over her face. Zephy saw the child fall, saw her lying pale and still and twisted beneath the painon tree. She dropped the stone and turned away, sick.

"You can't let go like that!" Meatha turned on her in a fury. "You *can't;* not and be able to help!"

"I—I'm sorry. I'll try." But the vision had shaken her terribly.

"Don't you see?" Meatha said more gently. "We *saw* him do it. Now you *know* Anchorstar was telling the truth."

Zephy stared at Meatha, ashamed she had lost control, ashamed she had doubted Anchorstar. Ashamed that Meatha knew.

* * *

Chapter Twelve

THEY FOUND Clytey Varik sitting on her sculler steps shelling out some vetchpea pods. Twelve-year-old Clytey had a sliding blue-eyed glance that made her seem as devious as the older girls. She was wily and gay and popular and was always surrounded by her peers and by a good many boys. But still there was an odd quality about her that made her different somehow. Of the Children Meatha had named out to Zephy, Clytey was the most puzzling. "The others," Meatha had said, "little Toca, Elodia Trayd, the baby—we could almost be sure of them without the stone, though I know we must try it. It's Clytey I don't understand. She flirts like the older girls, she laughs and—and yet I don't know. It's just something different. We'll see," she had added with more confidence than Zephy had felt. I wish, Zephy thought, I wish . . . but what was the good of wishing?

Clytey tilted her head and looked at Meatha now with an expression almost of defiance. Zephy paused, but Meatha went to her with the stone cupped and hidden, then bared it suddenly and held it against Clytey's fingers.

Clytey looked puzzled. Then slowly her eyes widened. She laid her hand over Meatha's, covering the stone. She grasped the stone and pulled it away, and her expression had come alive in a way Zephy had never seen—then suddenly a darkness crossed Clytey's face, too. Her look turned from awe to terror; so alarming a terror that Meatha reached for the stone. But it was too late. Clytey was staring at something behind them. "The fire, they're coming through the fire," she screamed. "They're behind the fire, the swords . . ." Her cry catapulted between the stone buildings.

She flung away from Meatha into the street, dropping the stone in her agitation. But it seemed to make no difference, whatever the stone had summoned held her in a white terror. "They've killed them," she cried, staring at empty space. "Oh, the blood . . ." Zephy reached her first and clamped her hand over Clytey's mouth. Meatha grabbed up the stone, wrapping it hastily. Zephy had Clytey in her arms now, but it was too late; others were coming, running, drawn by the commotion, then stopping to stare at this child who was obviously having a vision. The word rumbled among the onlookers.

Zephy muffled Clytey with her arms, but Clytey flung away from her in a pale, panting terror that seemed to see nothing else, crying, "The fire—great Eresu, the fire, they defile the fire . . ." Clytey covered her face with shaking hands as others pulled at her, at Zephy and Meatha. Zephy fought, turned to bite, and sunk her teeth into someone's arm. People were flocking into the street shouting. She was held, pushed and trapped in the crowd, could not see Meatha; saw Clytey's face once more, then she was dragged, flailing, into an empty alley and she saw Kearb-Mattus's face close to hers. She felt herself jerked and twisted, forced down the alley away from the mob. Clytey screamed; the crowd's cry rose; she could hear the Deacons' voices. She kicked to get free, and thought she heard Meatha's scream, too. She hit out, and Mama was there holding her hands, dragging her up steps . . .

They forced her through the sculler door. She could hear screaming, still, and she cried in response, "Let me go! Let me . . ." Something in her told her to be still, not to fight, but her fury was too great; her fury, and her terror for Meatha.

Kearb-Mattus wrenched her arm behind her and forced her through the longroom and up the stairs—one flight and the next, brutally. She could not resist completely and feel her arm broken, she was not strong enough, the pain defeated her. She felt herself pushed up the ladder, shoved, heard the trapdoor close behind her and heard the old bolt, forever unused, wrench free and slide home with a scraping noise.

Then there was silence in the loft.

She crept to the window.

Below, the crowd was thick. All Burgdeeth was there in the street. Zephy could not see Meatha or Clytey, but two donkeys were being led up toward the place where the Deacons stood: Dess and Clytey's little gray donkey. The crowd parted slightly for them, then parted very wide, in deference, as the Landmaster rode up. Elij was with him.

Now an opening was made in the center of the crowd, before the Landmaster and the red-robed Deacons. The donkeys were brought up, to stand with their ears back, not liking the excitement. Then the girls were there, being stripped of their clothes by the head Deacons.

Clytey and Meatha stood naked and ashamed before all Burgdeeth.

Slowly, then, they were dressed in rags, the filthiest rags the Ragsinger could produce. Clytey's mother came running, crying, and Zephy could see that Meatha's parents were being held back by the crowd. Clytey fought as they dressed her, but Meatha held herself like steel, cold, frozen. Zephy's heart lurched for her, she wanted to cry out, she wept inside in a sickness she had never known, as if all her insides bled in one terrible quailing illness for Meatha.

The girls, rag-dressed and smeared with muck and dung and butcher's blood, were lifted up in a macabre ritual by four men each, and laid across their donkey's backs, face down, like sacks of meal. They were tied, then the crowd began to smear on more muck from the gutter, and to dump buckets of slops on them. Zephy turned away and was sick into her chamber pot.

When she came back to the window, the donkeys were being led away toward the Temple for the last sacrificial rites.

Zephy knelt on the stone sill, shivering, for what

seemed hours, until the procession came back down the street. It was led by the Landmaster riding his gray stallion, his red robe garish above the children's rags. The donkey's heads were down as if in shame, though more likely it was the commotion. The crowd that followed chanted the dirge with a strength and vehemence that made Zephy shake with fury.

Long after the procession had gone, long after the town had stilled, Zephy crept shivering into her bed and lay curled tight around herself, unable to drive the pictures from her mind. When Mama pushed open the trapdoor and came to her in the darkness, she turned her face to the wall and held herself rigid.

"Did you want to die there, too!" Mama whispered. "You could not have helped her. You could not have helped either of them. *Did you want to die with them, for nothing?*"

Zephy could smell the food Mama had brought. It nauseated her. She did not speak, or look at Mama, and Mama turned away at last. She must have paused, though; perhaps she turned back toward the cot. "Whatever you think of Kearb-Mattus," she said evenly, "it was Kearb-Mattus who pulled you out of that. It was Kearb-Mattus who saved your life. For me, child. He did it for me. Not for the love of you."

When Mama had gone, Zephy sat up in the darkness. She was sore with anguish and wanting Mama badly. But she would not call out to her.

She could not seem to sort anything out, could not come to grips with anything. Vaguely, she sensed that she was the only one left, that she must do what was necessary without Meatha, without the stone. And this was impossible. She stared at the black oblong window and wondered where the stone was. But it didn't matter, it was over; the things that Anchorstar had told them, had shown them, they did not matter now.

The shock of her own thoughts stirred her at last. She knew the pain of Meatha's death like a knife—and she knew there was no choice, that she must do as Meatha would have done. She rose, her hands shaking as she fastened her cloak against the night. Had Meatha dropped the stone in the street? She could not have kept it hidden, stripped of her clothes as she was. Had the Deacons taken it from her?

But Meatha would have flung it away somehow, she would not have let them know. Had she been able to cast it into the gutter? Zephy went to the window once more and leaned against the cold sill, waiting.

Much later Shanner came, looked at her strangely, flung himself into bed, and slept. He seemed like a stranger to her. When at last Burgdeeth's lights were snuffed and the town was silent, she crept out and down the stairs and into the street, lifting the door to keep it from creaking. She kept to the shadows. Waytheer was caught square between the two moons. She thought it should give her courage, but it didn't. She felt numb and mindless.

In front of Clytey's house she knelt and began to search in the gutter. Her hands were immersed in cold dishwater, spit, little boys' pee, animal dung, garbage. Her legs and tunic became splattered. *Could* the stone be here? Or would it be lying, still, among the cobbles even after that crowd?

When she finished the gutters on both sides she crossed and recrossed the rough cobbled street on her hands and knees. She was terribly exposed, alone on the moonlit street. She felt around the steps of each house and even searched hopefully in the bowls of grain that had been set out at each door for the Horses of Eresu, for luck on this night before Fire Scourge. Could Meatha have slipped the stone into one of the bowls before she was bound? All the doors had been decorated with tammi and otter-herb and the leaves of the painon, which gave off a wonderful scent, and with swords hanging point downward to show respect.

She searched futilely until first light, then crept back to her own sculler to scrub off the muck from the gutter. Then she stood watching the first rays of sun through the open window, listening disconsolately to the sounds of Burgdeeth stirring as people came out to begin the third morning of Harvest.

She knew the girls' clothes had been burned at the last rites. Had the Landmaster found the runestone among them or perhaps at the bottom of the sacred fire, black among the ashes? If he had found it, had he any idea what it was?

And were there more Children to be gotten out of Burgdeeth than Meatha had guessed? Was Elodia Trayd too old for Kearb-Mattus to bother drugging, did he mean to kill Elodia as he must have meant to kill Meatha, at the time of attack? And me, too? Zephy wondered. Does he know about me? Or does he think it was only because I was Meatha's friend that I tried to help her?

She went to harvest as she was expected to, sick and shaken. At midmorning she sought out Elodia in the fields, then Toca, and stood staring at each in turn, then went away again silently. Elodia had glanced up from her work, staring back for moment with that steady gray-eyed gaze that made her seem so much older than a child of nine. But Toca, a rosy little boy, had only looked at Zephy and grinned and gone on snatching up bits of whitebarley behind the wake of his buxom mother.

Zephy did nothing more about the Children, on this harvest day or the next two. She could think of nothing else to do. Her mind seemed to be in limbo, resigned to the idea that she would fail, that she would be responsible for the deaths of the very children she was committed to save. By Fire Scourge night she felt so drained and uncertain of herself that she was constantly on the verge of tears. Mama, thinking she was grieving for Meatha, left her alone. Zephy could not have held up if Mama had put her arms around her, had asked her what was the matter. She thought of Anchorstar with the terrible knowledge that she would fail him, thought of Thorn with sick shame.

After supper on the eve of Fire Scourge, she dressed herself in her good tunic and her cloak and brushed her hair carefully, then went to join the procession to Temple. But her eyes were cast down in more than submission; and her heart scudded uncertainly as she followed along in the twilight, hastily making a plan.

Chapter Thirteen

One candle burned in the dark temple, in the center of the dais. When the first prayer began, the Landmaster's voice rang out alone. Then candles were lit one by one, flame after flame leaping, and when a bank of candles burned across the dais, the Deacons' voices rose. "Bless these our people, and bless this flame we raise to you. Bless this fire and bid it cleanse our lands. Lay your sanction upon your humble servants this holy night." And the people answered in a quick staccato, "The fire, the sacred fire." The Deacon's voices raised an octave. "Bring upon our land the peace of resignation." And the people answered, "Bless us, we are humble." The flame burned higher. "Look upon our submission," moaned the Deacons. "Look down upon our reverence and bless this sacred flame. Oh Revered Ones, bless the ground this flame will sanctify."

"The Fire, the sacred Fire."

Zepny mouthed the prayers, but her mind was filled with a terrifying coldness. Would she be brave enough? She knew, as surely as the stone brought true vision, that tonight would come the attack. With all her strength she fought the very submission the Deacons were praying for.

What would happen if she failed? Or if the attack came too soon? There would be little time, there in the field as the fires were set. She had a wild, terrible urge to snatch the three Children out of Temple at once and make off with them. She sat with pounding heart, willing herself to be still.

She saw Elodia turn once and stare at her. Did the child sense something? Did she know? *Was* Elodia Trayd a Child of Ynell? Or was she only different? Brighter, rebellious, but without the sight?

"Bless our Master for he is holy. Bless our crops and our works. And keep our children from worldly affliction. Keep them from the Curse of Ynell. Pity us in our trials and sanctify us in our duties."

"Bless us, we are humble."

The sacred grain was poured into the chalice. The flame burst forth and was blessed. The Deacons' voices rose in the litany, and in prayers to Waytheer, in special obligations and beguilings on this year of Waytheer.

"Bless us, we are humble. We kneel before Waytheer in humility."

Then at last the Deacons' hands raised in the final benediction. The grain was blackened now, but the flame still burned. The Landmaster took up torches and began to light them in the flame. The Deacons raised their hands, and the crowd rose, to file forward one by one and receive the burning torches. Zephy seized this moment to slip forward in line to just behind Toca Dreeb and his mother. The top of Toca's head shone yellow in the light of the flame. The back of his childish neck looked tender, very sweet. She shivered for him; he was so small and vulnerable.

Elodia was at the beginning of the line. And the thin, bent figure of Tra. Thorzen was there in back, carrying little Bibb over her shoulder as if the baby had gone to sleep during the ceremony. Zephy wondered again if she should be so sure about a child yet unable to speak. It was lucky, she thought, that half the men of Burgdeeth would ride guard this night, and among them Tr. Thorzen and Tr.

Dreeb—she had winnowed that information out of Shanner who, though curious, had talked freely enough. Shanner! she thought, and a pang touched her. What would happen to him this night in the attack? He rode front guard in the Burgdeeth Horse. Shanner could help me, she thought for the second time. If I'd asked him, somehow he could. But she would not have dared to ask him. And he would never have believed her, anyway; not about what Kearb-Mattus planned for the Children of Ynell; not about how he had stolen them. He would only laugh, in spite of his hate for Kearb-Mattus, and say she was imagining things. And he would never believe about Anchorstar or the stone; surely not that she was a Child of Ynell; nor about the wonder of the vision she had seen.

Where was Kearb-Mattus now? The Kubalese never came to Temple. What was he doing, had he slipped out of Burgdeeth to join the Kubalese army? Or was he lying in wait, to create havoc when the time came? She moved forward, received her taper, felt shaken with guilt for her thoughts, and followed the line down the steps.

Ahead, the moons touched the statue just behind the Luff'Eresi's wings. The blowing, moonlit clouds were pale as silk. All their lives she and Meatha had walked this procession together, carrying their lit torches side by side. All their lives they had watched the sky, but on this night most of all, for sight of the Luff'Eresi or the Horses of Eresu, moving on the moon-washed clouds. And they had thrilled beyond speaking when dark winged shapes did move there, silent on the winds, looking down on Fire Scourge.

The marching line of guttering torches wound beneath the statue's raised hooves, then moved away toward the cut whitebarley field that had been chosen for the ceremony this year; the other fields would be burned in secondary ceremonies after the flames from this field died.

The chant of the Deacons was soft now, sibilant, their low voices making a prayer that was snatched away by the breeze and muted by the shuffle of feet. The line was beginning to curve, to make the circle of the field, winding like a fiery snake. Zephy's heart scurried—not yet—not yet . . .

Her torch smelled of rancid oil. She followed Toca's low-held torch, nearly paralyzed with fear. The stubble of the cut field crackled under her feet. She shivered, then suddenly bile came into her mouth and she ran, stumbling, and heaved her supper into the irrigation ditch.

The line had moved ahead. She hurried, swallowing the ugly taste as people near her turned to stare. She found Toca and slipped in behind him, sweating and shaken. Toca marched on, perhaps unknowing, perhaps not. She tried to shield her thoughts from him, to calm them, to think only of the ceremony, the fire, and not what she was about to do. But in her memory she saw Clytey's pale face and heard her cry, "The fire, they are behind the fire." She almost grabbed Toca and ran; *not now,* she thought. *Not yet.*

How could she get all three Children away when they were so spread out? And then she knew that she must try to speak to Elodia silently. Even without the stone, she must try. Could she make the younger girl understand? Washed with doubt, she stared at the licking flame of her torch and tried to center her thoughts, to bring her very being into Elodia, to feel she was Elodia . . .

She could not make words, words did not come. Only a feeling. Of desperation and fear and of challenge. She tried to give Elodia what she had felt with Anchorstar, to press a sense of urgency upon her. Elodia marched resolutely, staring straight ahead. Zephy had no idea whether she was reaching the child. She thought of Elodia slipping out of line and following her unseen, thought of her wanting to. But Elodia only walked on with her usual straight, light pace, her taper held high, away from the heads of her elders. *Follow me,* Zephy thought. *Follow me when the field is lit.* She tried to think of herself as someone else would see her, tried to make a yearning for herself in Elodia, a desire to follow. The procession had wound almost completely around the field now, the ring of fire wavering and bright. Zephy could see the dark shapes of the Burgdeeth Horse riding behind the marchers. Were the Kubalese there in the night too? But the moons were higher now, and brighter; wouldn't such riders be seen? They could be in the groves, though, or behind the rises north of the housegardens. But the Captains of the Burgdeeth Horse must have thought of that. She shivered. In spite of the Landmaster's traiterous plan, she felt sure the men of the Horse did not know. At least she felt Shanner didn't. Could the Captains be part of it? Surely they must think that the Horse would all go free, then; that the battle would be but a mock one. And that was not the case.

She felt a cold terror for Shanner.

And Anchorstar was there among the hills waiting for her and the Children. Were the Kubalese there around him, had they discovered him? But she couldn't think of that now. Her distress and uncertainty made her falter. *I can't do it,* she thought suddenly. *Think of Elodia,* she cried silently. *Bring Elodia to me . . .*

The snake of fire had joined itself, the field was surrounded by flame. There was a hush as the Deacons stepped forward. They raised their arms to begin the blessing of the field. The Landmaster's torch blazed high above his head against the sky. The cry of the Deacons rang out in a prayer harsh on the night breeze, high and piercing.

Then at last the gentler litany began, like a honeysong, like a true blessing, and the voices of Burgdeeth rose with it in unison and in joy, in thanks for the successful harvest and for another year of safety and surcease from the wrath of the Luff'Eresi.

When the prayer was finished and the Deacons had stepped back, the Landmaster knelt, and all Burgdeeth knelt as one around the edge of the field. They brought their torches forward and struck the fire in unison so the field burst into flame with a sharp crack. Zephy stood frozen, then dropped her taper in a panic and turned to little Toca. "Come with me, Toca, I have a surprise. It's beautiful . . ." She searched Toca's blue eyes, trying to think what would rouse him. He looked up at her blankly. This moment when his mother was praying and not attending to him would last but an instant. "Come on," Zephy breathed, smiling. "We will go to Elodia and find the triebuck in the moonlight . . ." and she thought hard of the triebuck standing with his head lifted and his three horns gleaming the way she had always pictured it. The little boy's eyes grew huge. He put his hand in hers and stepped out of line, away from the blazing field.

They ran across the stubble in the darkness behind the line. When they reached Elodia, Toca flung himself at her shouting, "The triebuck, we're going to see the triebuck," so that Zephy dropped his hand and clapped her own hand over his mouth. "It's a secret," she whispered, terrified. "We must keep it a secret." A few heads turned and stared, but most were too caught up in the ceremony.

Elodia gave Zephy a strange, cool look and rose at once. She put her hand in Zephy's without question and her arm around Toca and began to pull the little boy away. When they were somewhat back from the fire and the kneeling line, she said softly, "You spoke to me. You spoke like Ynell." Zephy said nothing. She could feel Elodia's trust and her fear mixed. She wished they could run now, at once, get away. But there was still the baby. "Bibb," Zephy whispered. "It's Bibb Thorzen, too." She searched the younger girl's face. "Can you see him?"

"There," Elodia said, pointing. "Lying on the ground by his mother . . ."

Bless Eresu, the woman was not holding him. "Wait for me!" Zephy put Toca's small hand firmly into Elodia's and was gone.

She came up behind the slight, kneeling figure of Tra. Thorzen, clapped a hand over the baby's mouth, snatched him away, and ran—headlong into utter confusion, dark horsemen pounding toward her, the worship line broken and people running, women screaming, the clash of sword on sword, the fire flaring up behind. Zephy ran toward Elodia, grappling with the strong, struggling baby. He smelled of wet pants. She saw Elodia's terrified face, grabbed Toca's other hand, and they plunged away, half dragging the running little boy. Three huge Kubalese horses loomed before them, they swerved, there was a cry of pain and terror behind them.

The baby was fighting to get away. Perhaps his fear was magnified by Zephy's own. Toca was pulled off his feet, she tried to scoop him up and nearly fell. they plunged into the housegardens where the attack had not yet come. The cries behind them were terrible.

They stumbled among tangles of vetchpea in their frantic flight, blundered into mawzee, terrified at the noise they made, but pushing frantically toward the north and the upper housegardens—they must get past them, to Anchorstar. Then a platoon of Kubalese horses filled the night before them, they turned and fled in panic. Had they been seen? Zephy pulled the Children into the Husbandman's cow pens, but there were men there, soldiers. She dragged Toca and Elodia out, the baby heavy as lead in her aching arms. Where could they go? They *must* get past the upper housegardens, they *must* get to the north and Anchorstar; but the fighting was there now, trampling the gardens, and there was fighting in the village streets to their left. Frantically she pulled Elodia back in the direction they had come . . .

Chapter Thirteen

They ran, panting, toward the plum grove.

In the darkness of the grove she could not tell what might be waiting; but the grove was silent, no horses plunged, no voices shouted. She found the boulder at last, wrenched it free, and shoved the children though as a dark shape moved between the trees. "Hide," she hissed. "There's nothing to fear in the tunnel. Don't come out, not for anything. I'll come back for you." She shoved the boulder back and ran. Could she lead whatever it was away from there? She dodged and nearly fell, could hear hooves behind her now. The air in her lungs was like fire. She swerved down the main street and into a group of fleeing women, then spun into the Candler's open doorway, and stood gasping for breath. A horse pounded hard behind her, lurched past. She stood shaking uncontrollably. There was shouting and commotion ahead of her, screams. Then she watched as women were herded back down the street by a mounted Kubalese soldier.

Before she could flee again, a group of soldiers wheeled their horses into the street and began to jerk the swords from the doors and whack at the shutters with them, the horses trampling the little bowls of grain that had been set out for the Horses of Eresu. She watched as the shutters were wrenched off the windows and flung down, and pieces of furniture, clothing and pans and tools, were pulled out and trampled. She saw the weaver's loom smashed into sticks. She could smell honeyrot where a keg had been broken open, and she heard laughter as the soldiers sucked up the liquor. She heard a soft noise behind her, turned to run, and a hand was clamped over her chest and an arm encircled her. She was held tight. Then her captor lunged and fell, pulling her down beside him.

She was lying in wetness, in blood.

It was a Kubalese soldier. He stared up at her unseeing. Her only instinct was to crawl away from him. She pulled his tunic back and went sick at the sight of the wound then she freed herself and rose, to slip through the open doorway. The room smelled of wax. She tripped over a chair then at last found the back entry, and pushed it open to slip out into the narrow alley then along it in the shadows. She could hear women screaming again, and a sharp crack. She moved quietly toward the plum grove.

She had gone several blocks, was nearly at the edge of the housegardens when she came around the last row of houses and up against a Kubalese soldier standing silent in the shadows. She had no chance to escape. She struggled and he hit her hard so she saw flashing lights and blackness. He pulled her across the square between milling horses and men, past screaming women and a group of Burgdeeth men tied together—she sought for Shanner but could not see him. She fought and kicked and the soldier hit her again. She could taste blood. She was shoved into a group of women, cried out blindly for Mama, then was prodded with a sword as they were herded, stumbling, toward the Set.

At the Temple they were forced at sword point to spit on it, then were prodded through the gate of the Set, toward the prison.

THROUGH THE PRISON BARS, Zephy could see the moonlit dome of the Temple. She was in the cell where Thorn had been kept. Women were huddled against each other, staring blankly. Some were bleeding, and a few had skirts blackened from fire as if they had tried to run through the flaming field. The smell of burned cloth mixed with the smell of filth. A woman began to weep, and someone began to whisper the Prayers of Contrition. They could still hear screams from the square.

Then Zephy saw, over the top of the Temple, the angry red sweep of fire on the mountain and knew without question that the Kubalese were burning Dunoon.

Chapter Fourteen

DUNOON WAS BURNING. The fire leaped high against the night as the Kubalese soldiers spurred their horses in a circle around the flaming huts.

While the main bulk of the Kubalese army had swept through Burgdeeth herding the populace like chickens, a small, select cadre had cut out fast up the mountain to enter sleeping Dunoon and, from ambush, lay fire to the thatched rooftops and pen the huts in a cordon to prevent escape. They narrowed and closed this circle until the Kubalese soldiers rode bridle to crupper, cheering the leaping flames.

But they saw no man run from the burning huts, heard no scream. When at last the flames died, the Kubalese soldiers dismounted, their weapons ready, to stamp into the huts to kill those left living or drag them out for their sport, to tear apart the furnishings and to loot, if there was anything worth the taking.

But there was no man, no child or woman there; the huts were empty, their contents smoldering untended.

Had Dunoon's goatherds, at the first sound of hoofbeats in the dark, run away in fear? Or were the men of Dunoon hidden among the black peaks, laughing down even now at the Kubalese? Seething with fury, the Kubalese band spread out and up to search in the dark among the crags and shadows.

But on that rough terrain in the darkness, the Kubalese

horses could only stumble and grow confused; they were struck from unlikely places, they leaped away in terror at strange sounds and thrusts, unseating their riders who, heavy in their war leathers, lashed out clumsily at nothing. The Kubalese soldiers fell and could find nothing but boulders with their flailing swords.

And the men of Dunoon advanced, quick and sure in the darkness, knowing their own land, attacking without sound, one here in the shelter of an outcropping, one to slip a Kubalese from his mount as silently as a breath. Thorn slaughtered three, and another; a quick knife to the loins, to the heart, a fallen body. The huts no longer flamed, were smoldering now, and the moons were cloud-covered.

When Thorn paused in the fighting to pull his sword free of a Kubalese body, he saw, down the mountain, that the flames had died in Burgdeeth's field. If Burgdeeth had been taken this night, were the Children of Ynell safely away? He saw Zephy's face in a quick, painful flash, then he plunged deeper into battle.

He dodged a Kubalese soldier and drove his sword into the lunging man just as the Kubalese horn of victory bellowed. Were the Kubalese mad, calling victory? Shouts rang across the night and made him swing around to stare. Then a Kubalese voice barked coldly, "Your leader is taken, men of Dunoon. We have Oak Dar. Lay down your arms or he dies."

But it was a trick! How could the Kubalese have Oak Dar? How could they believe such a ruse would fool Dunoon?

He slipped forward past men arrested in battle, past Dunoon swords touching the Kubalese but waiting in their readiness to plunge. He moved toward the source of the shout and paused as a torch was lit in the clearing, then another. He could see the captive now, the man that two Kubalese soldiers held slumped motionless between them.

He clenched his fists and stared at the sword lifted above his father's throat.

He strode into the clearing.

Facing the Kubalese captain, he thought too late that if Oak Dar were dead, this gesture was stupid beyond measure, to have made himself vulnerable so. He stepped forward and put his hand on his father's cheek. The Kubalese did not try to stop him. He felt along his father's neck for a pulse. Yes, Oak Dar lived. He moved to take his father's weight upon his shoulder, but the Kubalese leaders blocked this, staring down at him with merciless eyes.

"What do you want, Kubalese, in return for my father's life?"

A slow smile spread across the evil face. "Son of Oak Dar, is it? So be it then. Now *you* rule Dunoon, lad. What say you to that?" The voice was deceptively soft. "Do you bring your people willingly to slave? Or does your father die this night?"

"No one *brings* my people, Kubal. They choose in these matters for themselves. And what do you mean, to slave?" Though he knew well enough what was meant.

"You will live here freely, son of Oak Dar. You and your people. Only Oak Dar will be held under guard. You will herd your meat goats for us and will slaughter them at our bidding to feed our camp at Burgdeeth. If you do not obey us, Oak Dar dies."

Thorn stared at him and turned away. The plan his father had laid so well, had carried out with such quick skill, had come to nothing. They were defeated. And his father seemed injured in a way that terrified Thorn, so limp he was, near lifeless.

He bowed his head, looked up once more at the Kubalese, then gestured toward his burned hut. "I will accept your terms, Kubal. But only with my terms laid on. My father will have the care he needs, all that we can give him.

We will come and go to his hut freely, as we choose. Otherwise—you are bidden to kill him at once." His voice caught, infuriating him. "Our men still wait in the shadows. They will be more than glad to take up the battle once more. And glad to see you die."

No emotion showed on the Kubalese face. The man stared at him for so long that Thorn thought he would surely kill Oak Dar. But then he nodded woodenly. Thorn stepped forward, motioned to another herder, and together they lifted Oak Dar and began to carry him toward his burned hut.

"No! Leave me alone. Let me go!" Zephy tried to twist away from the soldier who held her. His grip was beyond her strength. Enraged, helpless, she flung herself on him and buried her teeth in his arm.

He screamed; she tasted blood, he struck her across the face so she reeled backward sick with pain, nearly fainting.

When she righted herself the other girls were staring at her coldly. Not one of them had resisted being herded out of the cell. The older women, still behind bars, stared too, without expression. They had been huddled that way all night, silent and expressionless, as if the shock of the attack and of the capture of Burgdeeth had left them dumb. Or was it only that, used by men all their lives, they found this defeat not so different?

Mama looked at Zephy as if willing her not to fight. She had been brought into the cell very late, and now was summoned out again, to cook for the Kubalese troops. The girls were to wait table, the soldiers said, snickering. When the guard reached for Zephy again she lunged at him, and when he turned to strike her she kneed him in the crotch. He let her go, bending over double. She dodged by him but was grabbed by another, and his blow on her ear made her head ring. She crouched at his feet, blackness engulfing her.

Chapter Fourteen

When she could again make sense of her surroundings, she thought she heard Tra. Hoppa speaking sharply beside her. "Let her be. If you take *her* for your sport, you'll answer to Kearb-Mattus, soldier. She's one of his, can't you see that!"

Zephy shook her head, trying to understand. The soldier stood over her, staring at Tra. Hoppa. "One of *his,* old woman? What are you trying to say?"

"Don't act stupid, soldier. This one is a Child of Ynell. Take her to Kearb-Mattus if you doubt me. Take her to him, or you'll know what Kearb-Mattus's anger can do to a common soldier—if you haven't learned that before now."

Zephy could only stare at her.

"You'll come too, old woman. And if you lie . . ." the soldier jerked Tra. Hoppa into the line of girls and prodded Zephy with his boot.

She rose, still staring at Tra. Hoppa. But Tra. Hoppa would not look at her, the slight old woman stared straight ahead, ignoring Zephy. How could Tra. Hoppa do this? Surely she knew that Kearb-Mattus promised no good for a Child of Ynell. Though maybe she didn't know that he would surely kill Zephy; Zephy had told the old woman nothing, had had no chance. There was nothing for her to do now but follow the Kubalese's orders. What would happen at the Inn? If she were not killed, she knew she and the other girls would be used badly. She looked and looked at Tra. Hoppa, but the teacher would not look back. They were herded into a tight line and prodded along beside the wall of the Set, toward the gate.

This was the second time they had left the cell. Five days ago, the morning after the attack, they had been led out to bury Burgdeeth's dead. The older women had gone, too, everyone in the cell. Only not all of them had come back: the prettiest girls had been taken up to the Inn. There had been screams in the night and drunken laughter.

But that was after they had dug the pitiful graves in the blackened whitebarley field. They had been joined by Burgdeeth's surviving men, who came marching chained together like animals. All of them had been given spades. They had dug graves for all Burgdeeth's dead, the soldiers, the women, and children. Shallow graves among the burned stubble where the bodies must lie forever prone in the bare earth.

Shanner's grave, cold and lonely.

She had seen him lying dead, a crusted wound across his chest so she had turned away sick. Mama had not seen. And Zephy had not told her. Ill with it, she could not bear to think long of Shanner's death; yet when her thoughts turned from it, they could only dwell again on the burning of Dunoon, and despair would grip her harder, a cold immobilizing fear.

It was growing dark as the soldiers herded them along the wall. The Kubalese horses, tied in a row, munched idly at their fodder, great dark shapes shifting and blowing as the group of prisoners passed. Ahead of Zephy, two girls turned as they went through the gate and stared boldly at the Kubalese guards.

The cobbled path was strewn with manure and straw, not spotless as the Landmaster had always demanded. Ahead in the square, the statue loomed bold against the darkening sky. Were the three Children still in the tunnel beneath it? But there was no food or water. Had they come out, hungry and thirsty, and been captured? Why hadn't she thought, before Fire Scourge, to take provisions there, in case they would be needed? Two drunken Kubalese soldiers lounged against the statue just beside the secret door, their honeyrot jug propped on top the hedge.

Why did Tra. Hoppa call me a Child of Ynell? She doesn't know that I am. And why would she say it anyway?

Does she think, if they felt I had the gift, I would be used less harshly than the other girls? Tra. Hoppa knew nothing about what Zephy and Meatha had planned or about their visit to Anchorstar. Zephy had wanted to tell her, in the cell, but even a whisper had seemed like a shout in that crowded place.

The nudge on her arm was so soft; she turned, and Tra. Hoppa gave her a look of silence, pressing close. "Climb the statue, hide there between the wings. Go when I distract them. Wait until the small hours, then get away. Get away from Burgdeeth."

Zephy gasped, started to speak . . .

"Shhh—watch me. Go when the soldiers run."

Tra. Hoppa moved away from her, slipping between the girls. Then suddenly she broke free of the line and ran, her skirts and tunic flapping. The rear guard came running past, pushing Zephy out of the way. A big girl, taking Tra. Hoppa's example, broke out in the other direction and others followed. There was shouting, someone screamed. Zephy thought she was frozen to the spot, looked around blindly. Then she ran, terrified.

She reached the statue and pushed between the bronze bodies. Were the two Kubalese still on the other side? She couldn't see, hadn't time to look; she clutched for the Luff'-Eresi's raised foreleg and scrambled to pull herself up. Her hands slipped on the smooth bronze; she gripped the edge of the Luff'Eresi's wing and struggled, pulled, until at last she scrambled up between the god's rising wings, sick with fear. His back was still warm from the heat of the day; she was hidden as if in a nest of bronze where his wings and human torso rose up. She could not see below her, could see only the wings rising like curved walls on either side of her.

Finally when no one clutched her ankle, when no face appeared, she relaxed and pulled herself forward on her belly until she could peer down between the Luff'Eresi's wing and his waist.

The two Kubalese soldiers were gone from beside the hedge. There was still angry shouting from several directions; but she was well concealed, and the warmth of the statue felt good. Where the Luff'Eresi's back changed from horse to man, the muscles were smooth and taut. His wings rose from this joining place, their feathers, as long as her forearm, overlapping in intricate patterns. And the wings themselves soared as if they felt the wind, the windblown clouds above seemed to stand still and the wings to move beneath them. Waytheer shone once between blowing clouds thin as gauze, then was gone. She wished she had her cloak. She had sat on it in the cell, and left it there sodden with muck from the stone floor.

The soldiers' voices faded, at last were gone. The line of girls who had not escaped, and Mama, had already reached the Inn. Had Tra. Hoppa been captured? If she was free, would she go to the tunnel? Zephy looked at the Horse of Eresu next to her, his dark shape lifting in the moonlight, then left her perch to climb onto his back, nearer to the tunnel entrance. His horse's head rose above her, his mane flung out. She could see only one light near the square, in the Deacons' house across the way. What had happened to the Deacons? And to the Landmaster? The Landmaster's Set had been plundered. From her prison Zephy had watched as silver and carved furniture and Zandourian rugs had been thrown carelessly onto the cobbles, then loaded in bundles onto the backs of Burgdeeth's own horses, to be carried to Kubal. Jewels had been tossed from soldier to soldier, glinting in the sun then stuffed into saddlebags. And the serving girls had been used cruelly by the Kubalese. Quiet girls who had spent most of their lives in the Set, living quite apart from Burgdeeth. Once, they had seemed only shadows to Zephy if she thought of them at all. Now she remembered them with pity.

When she had seen Elij grooming the Kubalese horses, she had felt only surprise that he was not locked in a cell or dead. And she had wished him dead instead of Shanner.

There was a dull pulsing of laughter from the Inn, and then shouts. She could slip down the side of the statue now, and go into the tunnel. But she knew she could not. She must wait until all the soldiers slept, then make her way to the Inn. For she could not leave Mama.

Chapter Fifteen

SHE SLID DOWN the side of the statue in shadow, and stared around her at the unsheltering, moonlit square. There was a long, unprotected distance before she could slip into darkness beside Burgdeeth's buildings. It would be so easy to slide open the door to the tunnel now and hide herself there. She felt as if eyes watched from everywhere. She pulled off her shoes and raced headlong to the first deep shadows, by the Weaver's. She crouched by the broken loom, her heart pounding.

She began to move carefully along the wall among the tangled, broken debris from Burgdeeth's homes. At the edge of the moonlight, a carved doll lay forlorn atop a broken washtub. Food was scattered, good mawzee spilled and honeyrot sticky where casks had been smashed open. In front of the Forgemaster's, smith's tools lay covered with blood so she stood, shocked, for a long moment. She felt sick for Shanner, sick with his death, and sick that the tools he had loved were here like this. There was a child's tunic hung from the corner of a building and some hides had been thrown into the street. The Kubalese soldiers must have been very drunk, indeed, to destroy so wantonly. Even they would need tools, need food and equipment.

A tangle of brooms and cookpots and broken benches lay across the Inn's porch, in full moonlight. From the shadows she stood looking, then quailed as she heard movement inside. In one of the upper rooms? A girl laughed, and a door banged. Maybe all the girls didn't find the Kubalese so distasteful. She started forward then drew back in terror as the door opened noisily and a Kubalese soldier stepped out.

He stood on the porch looking around him. He seemed to look right at her. She thought he must hear her heart pounding; she felt like a trapped animal. He belched and scratched himself, then started down the steps. She shrunk from him, pressing herself into the rubble as he came toward her. But he kept on, lurching past her so close he could have touched her, and went on down the street toward the square. She watched him cross the square, a black figure striking across the pale cobbles toward the Set.

She listened for other noises from inside. When all had been silent for some time, she swallowed dryly, slipped up the stairs, and began to lift the heavy door. She got it open without sound and stood in the dark hallway. Where would Mama be? Not in her own room, surely. But she turned, and began to push open Mama's door, willing her eyes to see.

The moonlight through the window cast itself across a sleeping form in Mama's bed. Zephy crept in. The figure was big, and as she stood listening, it groaned. She edged backward, to get out. A whisper stopped her.

"Zephy?" Mama's hand was on her arm, pulling her away from the bed, from the moonlight. Then Mama's arms were around her.

At last, shaken with crying, they huddled in the far corner of the room away from the sleeping Kearb-Mattus who, wounded, had been brought to the best room in the Inn. It was to tend Kearb-Mattus that Mama had been sent for. He had awakened only once since Mama had arrived, but his bandages were clean now, and his wounds had been doctored with dolba leaf. "There are other wounded in the longroom. I am to nurse them and Kearb-Mattus. Tra. Hoppa cooked their supper." They had caught Tra. Hoppa, then.

"Where is she?"

"In the loft. Sleeping in the loft."

"Mama . . ."

"You must go away, Zephy. I don't know whether what Tra. Hoppa said was true, I don't want to know. But they will surely kill you, the Kubalese will kill you if they find you. They won't wait for Kearb-Mattus."

"We can go now, we—"

"I cannot go with you."

Zephy froze, staring. "What do you mean?"

"I am needed here."

"Needed! Needed by the Kubalese?" Her voice raised so that Mama grabbed and hushed her. "Needed by those who have destroyed us?" she hissed.

"I am needed by Kearb-Mattus. No matter what the Kubalese have done, I cannot leave him."

"But you—"

"You can slip food from the sculler if you're careful. Take Nida, she can carry blankets and a waterskin."

Zephy clung to her. "What if he dies? What will they do to you then?"

"I will not let him die."

"I could stay with you . . ." Did Mama feel for Kearb-Mattus the same pain that Zephy herself felt for Thorn? Would a grown woman suffer the same awful agony?

"You cannot stay with me. You must go now. Tomorrow they will kill you. It won't be forever, Zephy. Go to Carriol, you can go along the edge of the mountain. You'll be safe in Carriol. Cloffi—Cloffi cannot stay enslaved forever."

Did Mama know about the Kubalese plan for conquering all of Ere? Had she known, before the attack? Zephy could not bring herself to ask. Mama's back was to the window, Zephy could not see her expression. She clung to Mama, but at last Mama pushed her away. "Hurry, Zephy. You cannot stay here."

"Then I must take Tra. Hoppa."

Mama stared at her in the near darkness; Zephy could feel her concern. Then she turned silently, and led Zephy toward the door.

As they started up the dark stairs, it seemed to Zephy that Mama had pulled away from her in a subtle way; as if they were no longer mother and daughter, but were equal in something. As if each must do what she must, without taking heed of the other. It was hard, it made her ache inside. But it was fine, too. Mama was letting her go, shoving her out. If she was not ready to leave, that could not be helped. The time dictated the need.

Together they climbed the steps and the ladder. They found Tra. Hoppa sitting in the window just as Zephy had sat so many nights, staring down at the littered, moonlit streets, at the sacked town.

They stripped the beds of blankets and Zephy's goatskin robe, then went silently out the front and down the alley to the sculler, where they gathered food to fill two baskets. At last Zephy and Tra. Hoppa were out on the street. It was but an instant since she had stood encircled by Mama's arms, and now Mama was closing the sculler door between them for what might be forever.

Zephy went ahead. They did not speak. Each was loaded with bundles. Tra. Hoppa took her sleeve once, when she saw which way Zephy was headed. Zephy stopped to whisper, "There are Children in the tunnel." They went on again in silence. The moons were sinking.

When they reached the square, they froze, then backed

deeper into the shadow of a building, for there were soldiers there, dark shapes gathered before the statue silently working at something. They had tied great ropes to the extended arms of the Luff'Eresi, and around his wings, and around the heads of the Horses of Eresu. Now suddenly they began to heave forward on their straining mounts. They were trying to pull down the statue. They meant to destroy the people's god-image—and in so doing, they would discover the tunnel. The men shouted, the horses hunched, the statue creaked. Zephy clutched Tra. Hoppa's hand and they ran back through the narrow streets, then through the gardens, dropping their bundles there, ran on until they reached the plum grove.

Zephy wrenched the stone back, and they plunged down into the darkness, gulping for breath. "Elodia?" Zephy cried over the creaking of the statue and the wild shouting of the Kubalese. "*Elodia!*"

There was no answer from the tunnel. They ran blindly. Zephy thought unreasonably that if she could find the niche, the stone would be waiting, that it would help them. Despite common sense, she felt along the wall and stopped at last, plunging her hand in.

Of course it was not there. She was wasting time.

Then she heard Elodia speaking softly in the darkness. The baby whimpered. She heard Tra. Hoppa speak to him as if she had taken him from Elodia. She felt Toca's small hand in hers, and they were running as the statue groaned above them.

The baby began to cry, then stopped as if Tra. Hoppa had clapped her hand over his mouth. They stumbled and bumped each other in the darkness, then at last they saw moonlight through the hole. Zephy pushed ahead and crawled up into the grove. Nothing stirred there; though in the shadows under the trees . . . She snatched the heavy baby from Tra. Hoppa; he was warm and soft against her, and he smelled bad. The others climbed out and they ran across the gardens, grabbing up their bundles, the dry mawzee rattling around them.

When at last they reached the pens, the donkeys were stirring restlessly. Zephy held the others back and stood listening. Could she see a shape in the blackness? Then Tra. Hoppa's hand pressed her down. They crouched, hardly breathing. The smell of rotting charp fruit was strong around them.

There was a soft snuffling but that could be the donkeys. Then a low grumble, so muted that Zephy could not be sure whether it was human sound or animal. Then they heard a sharp snort, a pounding of hooves, a harsh Kubalese swear word; and a steady cantering away, toward the square. There had been a mounted Kubalese soldier there, the animal must have shied. Zephy removed her hand slowly from across the baby's mouth. They could hear the horse brushing through the gardens, then clattering along the cobbles farther away. It must have been a guard, waiting out his stint there in the darkness. Would another come now, even though a predawn light had begun to glow in the east?

Then they heard the other sound. The groaning, a wrench of metal, and the crash. The statue had been brought down.

Zephy rose and found the shed, groped for Nida's saddle and halter in the darkness, and began to saddle the fidgeting donkey. Dess, who wasn't being touched at all, kicked at her evilly.

The saddle felt strange, mucky, as if it were coated with dirt. But it was surely Nida's saddle, Dess' pack bars were different. Besides, she could feel the tear in the skirt, where straw oozed out. Then she realized the Deacon's must have taken Nida's saddle instead of Dess's to carry Meatha. She leaned over and smelled the leather. It smelled of the gutter, all right. She shuddered. But she continued to fasten the straps, there was no time to change. Besides, Nida was used to her own saddle, it fit her right. Dess backed up to kick again, and Zephy drove her off with a slap.

When the saddle was secure and the packages tied on, she lifted the fat baby on top—he smelled no worse than the saddle—and they started off through the upper house-gardens; they must cross the northerly whitebarley field. Toca crowded close, stepping on Zephy's heels. When the baby began to fuss, she covered his mouth with her free hand, lurching against the donkey.

"He feels our fear," Elodia whispered. "Think of something safe and warm." Zephy tried, but she was far too afraid to make her thought convincing. When they stepped out onto the stubble of the whitebarley field, the crackle alarmed her so she drew back quickly, pulling the donkey away. "We'll have to go around," she whispered, and started east along the edge of the field. Already the sky was too light. She pushed Nida to a faster walk, then a trot. She could hear Tra. Hoppa's quick breathing. It must be hard on the old woman, no sleep, the fear and tension, and now this lunging flight.

When Toca began to lag behind, Zephy set the little boy up behind Bibb. "Hold onto the baby, Toca. Not too hard," she added, at Bibb's indignant grunt. Then she froze . . .

Behind them a horse had snorted, and now there were galloping hoofbeats. "Run! Oh, run!" she whispered, pushing the donkey into a canter and trying to hold Toca and Bibb both as she ran along side; they ran until they were breathless, but when Zephy looked back she could see nothing; then the ear-splitting wail of a donkey rose behind her, and Dess lurched into view, running at full clip.

Zephy pulled Nida up, exhausted, exasperated, and

glowered at Dess. The fool donkey had surely alerted the Kubalese.

Dess fetched up close to Nida, shoving Zephy aside. Quickly, Zephy stole a rope from the blanket pack, secured her, and gave the responsibility of her to Elodia. They went on to the top of the first rise as fast as they could and down it as the sky began to lighten in earnest.

They had put three rises behind them when the Kubalese patrol came riding out along the east edge of town and up in the direction of Dunoon. Three soldiers loomed on the skyline as the little band knelt in a shallow. Zephy could not make the donkeys lie down, never having needed to before, and only hoped their gray color would hide them. Tra. Hoppa held Toca's hand, and winked conspiratorially at him. Elodia had taken the baby in her arms and was concentrating on keeping him still, pushing a feeling of quiet into him until he lay relaxed, staring happily up into the little girl's face.

After an eternity, Zephy crept up the side of the rise and looked over, then sighed thankfully. The patrol was a dark line going up the mountain.

But what did they want in Dunoon?

When she looked back toward the east, the sun was coming up. They could not climb the rises now, it had grown too light: they must go around, in the low places.

It was a slow tedious business, making their way so, and the day was indeed bright when at last they slipped behind the first boulders at the foot of the mountain. Zephy half expected to see the Kubalese patrol waiting for them, but there was nothing, only the tall black boulders and some stunted grass, and the mountain, sheer as a wall. But there were breaks in that wall where the thrusting columns of stone overlapped. Now they could travel unseen, among those jutting columns. And now Zephy must decide: would they go east to safety or west toward Dunoon, where her heart tugged? To the east lay Carriol, and shelter. To the west was a burned, defeated village patrolled by the Kubalese.

She led the band straight into the mountain between tall black stones, then began to wind among the jagged pillars until she found, at last, a protected place where the donkeys could rest and graze. Dess lurched at once into the tallest stand of grass, her ears flat back to her head. Above them, the sablevine was already turning copper with the coming of winter. Zephy undid the food bundle and set it on a rock and passed Elodia the milk jug. The younger girl's sandy hair and gray, steady eyes made her look older than nine. Or maybe it was her expression. There was a touch of sadness about Elodia that was not childlike. "How did you manage without water?" Zephy asked. "I half expected . . . I thought you might be gone, that you might have come out."

"We did come out. In the night, late when it was quiet. Or, I did. I took water and food from Tra. Hoppa's house," she said, grinning at Tra. Hoppa. She pulled up her tunic and showed them the lumpy linen package hanging from her waist. It contained scallions and dry bread and a bit of berry cake. She shared this out equally, and they sat eating and staring about them at the lifting, monolithic stones that stood black and silent around them.

They could see a bit of the valley, and Burgdeeth directly below. They could not see Kubal to the east or the low hills that separated it from Cloffi. And the desert lands on their right were cut off by an outcropping of stone.

Zephy watched Elodia as the child began to draw away from them in her mind, her face turning inward. She was seeing something, or she was hearing something. They all became very quiet; Zephy tried to make herself receptive, but she could not. Elodia's hand stroked the dirty leather of Nida's saddle as if she were stroking something else entirely, in another place. And when at last she came back to them, she did so suddenly, seemed to see Zephy so suddenly that she gave a start. Then she said flatly, "Dunoon is burned. The patrol rides through it, all black. There is no one. They are going to go back down the river. They—they make a fear in me."

"*No one?*" Zephy said. "No one?"

"I don't think so. Not in the village, the huts are empty!" But now Elodia's voice was uncertain.

Zephy rose and went to stand among the boulders. When she came back to them at last, she could say only, "I must go to Dunoon. And you must wait for me."

THEY CLIMBED THE ROCKS until they found a secure place so high it seemed nearly at the top of the Ring of Fire, though of course it was not. They pushed between boulders until they found a minute valley with a shallow cave at one side. They rolled several stones across the valley entrance, then turned the donkeys loose. The baby drank the last of the milk from the jug and went to sleep at once.

This was foolishness, to leave these four alone. But she knew she must go to Dunoon; she could think of nothing else. And she must not send them on ahead. Tra. Hoppa did not try to change her mind; it seemed to Zephy that Tra. Hoppa knew there were currents and forces moving around her that she herself could not touch. And Elodia—the feeling from Elodia was one of silent support. As if the younger girl read, could touch, the depth of whatever pulled at Zephy so strongly.

She had made no explanation to them about Anchorstar, about the stone. Something held her back. If something happened in Dunoon, if she did not return, they would be safe in Carriol. They had the donkeys and food. When she returned, she would tell them. She thought once that perhaps she should make her pledge Elodia's pledge, too, so the younger girl could carry on. But then she turned resolutely away, looking toward Dunoon.

She took a little food, accepted Elodia's cloak, and started off alone. She took no waterskin. She could move lighter and quicker without, and there were places among the black rock where little springs seeped down. She could hear the sharp call of a flock of otero diving after insects above her, and once the sweet clear cry of a mabin bird, filling her with a terrible longing. There was no other sound save an occasional pebble she dislodged. The sun was moving down toward the horizon ahead of her so its brightness blinded her except when part of the mountain cut it off.

Then she came around a tall stone shelf to see another group of Kubalese soldiers coming straight up toward Dunoon, riding fast; she was close enough to Dunoon now to catch an occasional glimpse of the clearing and the blackened huts. She stood in the shadow of a stone, watching the ascending riders; only when they were just at the lower pastures of Dunoon, below the village, did they spread out so some were riding directly toward her. She spun around, frantic for a place to hide.

She found only a small chink between outcroppings and she wedged herself there, where a horse could not come, and stood still, hardly breathing, wondering if her light tunic would be like a signal flag; she pulled the cloak around herself, wanting to run; but she knew she must be still.

She heard them come: a clatter of hooves struck stone close to her; she could smell the sweat of the horses and of the men. She heard them climb above her, then stop suddenly. There was a sharp command to dismount. She stood as helpless and palpitating as a bird caught in a net.

Then at last she heard the command to climb, and some swearing. They had not seen her after all. They were up there scrambling over the rocks and had left their horses tethered.

She could take them!

Yes, and be tracked from here to Carriol. And what could Kubalese horses do, climbing these mountains? Like a cow on a window ledge, she thought. She collected her wits and slipped quickly down toward the plateau where Dunoon lay blackened, listening for signs of their return. She must keep to the shadows until they were gone, lest they see her from above. She must keep close to the mountain.

When she came around the last stone spire that hid the plateau, she saw the other five. She could hear their voices but could not make out what they said, or what they searched for among the huts. Could they be looking for her and Tra. Hoppa, or perhaps for missing Children? She strained to understand their words, but only an occasional one was clear.

They mounted at last and went on up the river and into the black canyon. Zephy looked back and up, but could not see the first band. She ran headlong for the huts, then stood hidden in the doorway of the first, peering back up the mountain.

The stench of the burned thatch made her eyes water. The sight of the burned furniture, the broken crocks and blackened bits of clothing, sickened her. Did human bodies lie here? She could not bend down to look and backed out feeling sick.

Yet she knew she must look.

The thatch was all burned away above her head, only blackened wisps against the sky. She went from cottage to cottage not knowing what she expected to find, and unable to stop herself. Again and again she paused to stare up the mountain, thinking each time to see dark shapes descending.

She came at last to Thorn's own cottage. She entered, staring around her helplessly at the mass of blackened rubble, the burned table, a chair. At last she went away again out along the edge of the village toward the river.

On the other side of the fast water, some little gray nut trees spread their branches to the ground, offering cover. She pulled off her shoes, ran to the river, and crossed it. The water was deliciously cool on her feet. She came out reluctantly and slipped behind some rocks, then started up along it in the cover of the trees.

Did the shadows of the cleft seem too dense? Did something move there? But in spite of her fear, she felt drawn to the cleft, and when at last she entered the dark canyon, it seemed quite empty; it was silent until, as she slipped through its shadows and turned into the cave, a whirring noise made her go cold.

But it was only a startled bird. She entered the cave, her heart pounding, and stood in the darkness to listen.

Chapter Sixteen

THE LIGHT AT HER BACK cast her shadow into the cave to meet the heavy darkness. She tried to walk softly, so she could hear. Were the Kubalese waiting in there?

But where were their horses, then? She knew she was being silly and forced herself ahead, clinging to the left-hand wall as the darkness closed around her.

It was very different without Meatha's steady guidance. The blackness could be a narrow trail, could be a drop of empty space, she had no trust in the fact that she had walked here before. She felt out with each foot before she was willing to take a step. And her fear of something unseen shook her so she could hardly force herself ahead. But the inner cave drew her; she pressed on, the blackness muffling her senses.

Perhaps even the wall she clutched would deceive her, would take a wrong turning so she would be led in a different direction. She tried to remember a break in this wall, but her memory of that other passage was mostly of Meatha's sureness.

She strained to see in a darkness where no vision was possible, strained to hear where the fall of her own footsteps filled her ears.

And in her sudden blindness, she thought she understood better what Meatha must have felt all her life. Meatha, who knew that something more existed around her than what she could see. I could only guess at what she felt, Zephy thought sadly. I didn't understand what she sought after, what she yearned so hard for sometimes that she was pale and lonely with it. I could never help her.

The darkness was growing less dense, she could see the walls a little; then the cave was there ahead. She ran headlong into the cave, loving the light, staring up gratefully at that far, small patch of sky overhead.

Then she turned and saw the wagon. Did that mean Anchorstar was here? But there were no horses, no sign of fire . . .

She stood still for a long time, a cold little fear stirring within her. At last she started toward the wagon. She stopped again before the red door and stared up at it, reluctant to climb the steps and push it open; yet knowing that she must. And when she did, there was a heaviness in her and her heart was pounding for no reason.

The wagon was lined with cupboards painted red and decorated with patterns of gold. The wood of the ceiling gleamed, and the bunk . . . how strange, everything so neat, nothing out of place, and yet the bunk's covers were heaped and tangled as if . . . She stood staring—as if someone were sleeping. "Anchorstar," she whispered. Yet she knew it was not Anchorstar, for now she could see a thatch of red hair beneath the goatskin robes.

She crept forward, afraid to speak, afraid to touch him. He lay so still as she pulled the robes back. His face was pale as death; but when she touched it, it was hot with fever. His lips were cracked, and there was a long slash across his cheek scabbed over with clotted blood. The red stubble across his cheeks made her think he had lain there for several days. "Thorn! *Oh Thorn!*" He did not stir. She knelt and picked up the waterskin from the floor. It was quite dry.

She felt panic, did not know what to do. While she tried to think, she searched the wagon for more water. She found none, nor any food, only a lantern. At least there was flint. She lit the wick, then took up the waterskin and hurried back through the tunnel as fast as she could manage without putting out the burning oil in its own sloshing. She could see now that the tunnel was quite safe, broad and flat.

When she drew near to the mouth of the cave she set the lantern down and shielded it with rocks so it made only a faint glimmer. Peering out, going quickly, she filled the waterskin at the dark, evil-looking little stream. It was the same water as lower down of course, it was just the light here in the cleft that made it so dark; yet she disliked taking that water back to Thorn.

When she stood once more beside the bunk, Thorn had turned onto his side so the gash was covered. She felt relieved that he had moved. It was some time before she was able to wake him, and then he was as groggy as if he had been drugged. She held the waterskin to his lips, and he drank thirstily.

"Is there pain?"

"In my leg." His voice was gray and strange. "Pull the covers back and tend to it."

She set the lamp in a niche above the bed and drew back the goatskin to reveal the dark bloodied bandage around his left calf. She searched for clean cloth, found a little, then went rummaging into Anchorstar's cupboards for some salve, for crushed moss or dolba leaf to pound.

But she found only a little dried-up ointment of cherla in the bottom of a crock. She mixed the red paste with water, then began to remove the bandage. The wound smelled bad. When she had the bandage open at last, she went sick with the sight, for the leg was festering. It was a long deep wound running from below his knee down through the calf. There had been a lot of blood, the bandage was thick with it and impossible to remove entirely, and there was dried blood soaked into the straw mattress. She cut the bandage away as best she could, then began to wash the wound with water. Thorn winced with the pain.

"How did it get so festered?"

"I don't know. The rags maybe—some filth. I took them off a dead Kubalese, it's his tunic. I took it when we buried him."

"*We?* If there were others, why didn't they help you?"

"I sent them on, Loke and the others. I told them I was all right. It was only a wound, I didn't think. . ." he stared at her. "Where is Anchorstar? You're supposed to be with Anchorstar."

"He—the attack came too soon, right as the fires were lit. I'm afraid something has happened to him."

"Maybe—maybe he just couldn't reach you. But the Children . . . Where are the Children?"

"They're with Tra. Hoppa. On the mountain. They're all safe. All who are left. Meatha—Meatha and Clytey are dead." She swallowed and looked at her hands. "Meatha tried the runestone on a girl, on Clytey Varik. She . . . Clytey had a vision of the attack and started screaming and . . ." she looked at him helplessly. "Oh, Thorn. They took them to the death stone."

"I see," he said, and they remembered Anchorstar's words: *It would be difficult to train the older ones—Kearb-Mattus does not want you, you three are a threat to the Kubalese.* They stared at each other, the pain of Meatha's death linking them.

"And Shanner?"

"Shanner is dead." She swallowed. "I dug his grave, in the burned field." Tears came then, and she knelt by the bunk, crying against him.

It was not until the wound was cleansed, Zephy fretting over what to do for the festering, that they realized they had been speaking to each other in silence, feeling revulsion at the Cloffi ways and at the Kubalese tyranny, and sensing a commitment, too, that increasingly grew and held them.

"And the stone," she responded at last, though she had tried to avoid thinking about it. "The stone is gone." And she knew he felt, with her, the searching in the gutters, her despair.

"The prophecy," Thorn said, "the prophecy about the stone—*found by the light of one candle, carried in a searching, and lost in terror . . .*"

"It was lost in terror. That has all happened. And then," she said, remembering Anchorstar's words, "*Found in wonder, given twice, and accompanying a quest and a conquering . . .*"

"Found in wonder," he said with an effort. His pallor had not diminished. "And who will find it? Given twice?" His eyes searched hers.

"*And accompanying a quest and a conquering . . .*"

Would they see the whole prophecy come to pass?

"I brought food," she said at last. "Let me help you sit up." She laid out the mawzee cakes for him. "But you can't walk. I'll have to soak your leg, it won't be better until I do."

"Soak it with what?"

"Birdmoss, maybe."

"There's birdmoss in the river near the village."

"There are Kubalese on the mountain, searching for something—for your people, do you think? For you?"

"I don't know." He turned to look through the wagon's little window. "We'll wait until darkness. I can't run, we'd be sitting targets. See what you can find in those cupboards. Weapons, rope . . ."

She gathered together everything that would be of use

to them, and when darkness came, they made a pack with the blankets and slipped out. She had found a small hoard of mountain meat, and some tammi leaves to make tea.

"What if Anchorstar comes back? What if he needs this bit of food?"

"I hope he has gone on along the mountain or is waiting for us. I don't think he would come back here very soon, with the Kubalese searching."

If he is alive, they both thought. *If they haven't killed him.*

Getting down the steps of the wagon was not easy, and when they had gone only a little way across the grass, she began to wonder if they could manage. Thorn's weight against her was considerable, and his jerking pace jolted them both. His shallow breathing, from the fever, made her heart lurch with pity, and she could feel his effort and exhaustion increasing even before they entered the dark cave.

It seemed an eternity, that trip to the mouth of the cave. There they rested for a long time, Thorn exhausted and Zephy aching from her effort. But night was coming down; the darkness would protect them. They started at last along the river, and where it foamed in a pool above Dunoon she found birdmoss and knelt to wrap his leg.

"It stings."

"It's supposed to. Should we go through the village?"

"Up behind it at the edge of the rocks where there's some cover, where it's hard going for horses."

It was hard going for them, too, and longer this way, the dark climb slow and difficult. She wished she had stolen the Kubalese horses. "Be careful, can't you!" Thorn growled. "You jammed my leg against a boulder."

"I'm trying, Thorn. You're heavy as a dead donkey."

She could feel him try to take more of his own weight then, and she was sorry she had said anything. At last, high above the plateau, they rested among the sheltering rocks.

"Why would a wound make me so weak and give me such a fever? Even if it festers, it—"

"It's filled with poison. That's why it festers. The moss will draw it out." She sounded more certain than she felt. His weakness made her afraid. She had kept seeing Thorn in her mind standing tall on the mountain, his face ruddy with health, his green eyes challenging her. Now his eyes were so pale, and he seemed to have little challenge left in him. Their blind hopping progress must make the pain a hundred times worse. If only they could have a light. But they could not have brought the lantern, it would have been like a fire on the mountain for the Kubalese to see.

At last the moons began to rise, lifting up over the sea beyond Carriol and lighting the stones ahead of them, casting a silver wash across the grassy clearings and up the peaks and cliffs on their left. Now with the moonlight they could go faster. They rested less often, surer in their progress and not blundering into boulders. They felt much easier when they were well away from Dunoon, pausing once beside a trickle of water to fill Thorn's waterskin and sit on a boulder, staring down at the moon-touched land below them. A few lights still burned in Burgdeeth. Was one of them the Inn? Zephy had a terrible longing for Mama, was gripped by emptiness when she thought of her, alone at the mercy of the Kubalese; without help, if she should need it. Zephy turned away from Thorn, biting back tears.

"She wanted to stay," Thorn said softly. "She's a grown woman, Zephy. It was what she chose to do."

She stared at him. He had seen it in her mind as if it were his own thought. She shook her head and tried to smile.

He put his arm around her, and they sat silently, the comfort of his concern washing over her. His strength, in spite of his illness, wrapped around her so she was soothed by it.

The moonlight made the cleared fields below look pale as ice, the land all awash with patterned silver like the dreams she had once cherished, as if Chealish castles lay there, and wishing springs and the towers of sacred cities.

"As it should be," Thorn said.

"As Carriol is," she whispered, her heart lifting.

He looked at her with surprise. "But Carriol's not like that, not magic, Zephy. It's only a country, it has bad as well as good. Don't think to find it perfect."

"I only thought—the way I always imagined it. . ." It had been magic, the way she'd thought of it. How foolish, she'd never realized. "Still. . ."

"Yes. Still it is free. It is a place to grow in, to become what you were meant to be, maybe."

"Yes. What we were meant to be." Then, "Where would Kearb-Mattus have taken the other Children? To Kubal, do you think? But that means," she said slowly, "that we must go there too."

"Yes. We must go into Kubal."

It was nearly midnight when they came at last to the little clearing with the rocks across its entrance. Zephy strained to push them back. "No, wait, I can climb them," Thorn said, pulling her away. He slid up, surprisingly agile on his hands and one knee, and she handed him the pack.

In the shallow cave three figures sat up in the darkness; the baby stirred and whimpered. Elodia took Zephy's hand and Toca clutched at her tunic. But Tra. Hoppa looked only at Thorn. She put her hands on his shoulders and turned him so the moonlight touched his face. Then she led him to her goatskin robes and helped him to lie down. She prepared a drought for him, soaked the wrappings on the moss, then brought him bread and charp fruit. Zephy was hungry too, and bone tired, but the old woman's concern was all for Thorn.

A thin rain had started, making Zephy shiver, and she was close to tears with fatigue. Elodia pulled her in under her own covers as if she were the older of the two; but even warmed by Elodia's closeness, it was a long time before Zephy was able to sleep.

And when at last she slept she dreamed and woke in a cold sweat, but unable to remember; then she slept again, and when she woke the sun was shining into the green clearing and glinting off the black stone cliffs. And high up the cliff Elodia was clinging to the stone, picking morliespongs. Zephy lay half dreaming still and saw that Thorn still slept. She brought herself more fully awake and sat up to look at him. His color was better, and he seemed to breathe more easily. She smiled and lay back and was about to sleep again when she smelled their breakfast cooking.

She rose and found Tra. Hoppa laying breakfast on a stone in the center of the clearing. The fried morliespongs smelled wonderful, and there was mawzee mush and a little of the mountain meat. The eager donkeys had to be tied to a boulder to keep them out of the food. Dess, who had pushed in greedily, sulked now with her tail turned to them in fury.

The baby had been bathed and properly fed, his napkin washed and laid across a rock to dry while he sported a piece of Tra. Hoppa's petticoat; he seemed much happier; certainly he smelled better. Toca held him solemnly, his blond head bent over the child, then looked up at last with a lonely, hopeless expression on his face. "He wants his mother," the little boy said sadly. "It's like . . . it's an ache in him you can feel."

Zephy put her arm around Toca. "And she must want him too. She must ache for him terribly." She paused, studying the child. "But he is like you, Toca. He's like all of us. We're different. We would have been killed had we stayed, or made slave."

"Children of Ynell," Toca said solemnly, his six-year-old face serious and pale. She could see the fear in him; she thought the sin of his difference must have frightened him all his short life.

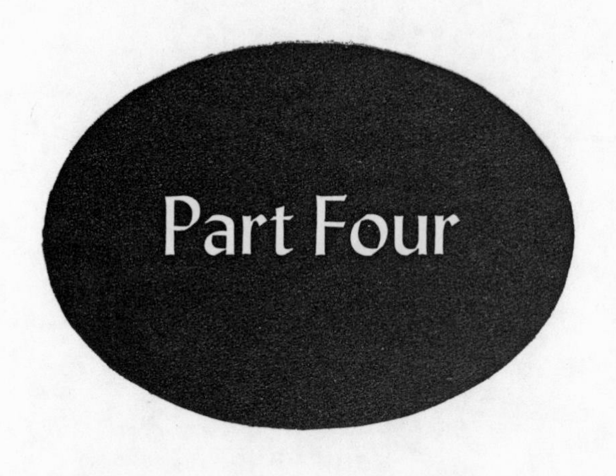

The Luff'Eresi

For the spirit moves onward, born yet again in a form we do not understand, born yet again on a plane farther removed from Ere than the plane in which the Luff'Eresi now dwell. So are the planes of the universe. One and another and another beyond all counting by man. And each of you must move from the one to the other in lives that shine like hours in our mortal days. Must move or, trapped in a lust for cruelty that destroys the spirit, must die bound in one body forever.

From *Prophet of Death,* Book of Carriol.

Chapter Seventeen

For four days they lingered in the valley, cooking sparingly and fanning the smoke into the wind so it would not be seen. Thorn grew stronger, and the wound cleansed itself at last. The fever left him, and as he began to feel his strength returning he told them of the conquering of Dunoon, and how he came to be lying wounded in Anchorstar's wagon.

"We had planned, long before, a ruse to deceive the Kubalese, and it would have worked," he said, "if my father had not been wounded. We had taken food and stores to a secret valley we knew, high in the Ring of Fire, in a place no horse could climb, only the goats. We took the herds there, we had moved all of Dunoon when the attack came.

"The refuge is a meadow whose only access lies narrow along the edge of a lake of molten fire. No Kubalese coming through that narrow pass could survive our arrows and the boiling lake as well. It is a dangerous place, animals —and children—can fall and be burned alive, and there are fire ogres still in the caves, though those caves still hold relics in some places of an old outpost of Owdneet, too. The heat of the lake warms the pastures so they are lush and green, and the rock cliffs rise sheer on every side for protection. The Kubalese could not stand against us there. This might once have been a secret place where the Horses of

Eresu grazed, perhaps where the Children of Ynell came to shelter in times of war.

"The herds and the women and children remained there, but the rest of us returned to Dunoon. We slept in the caves, but we lighted all the cookfires of the village each night to make it seem we were still in Dunoon. And we posted sentries.

"When the band of Kubalese came—my father had counted on a small band, on most of the army staying in Burgdeeth, and he was right—when they came they set fire to the cottages. The village was in flames almost at once. They thought they would drive us forth and shoot those who did not burn to death, but there was not a man, not a woman or child in the village, and no herd to slaughter. When they discovered the ruse, they began to mill about and to go in forays among the rocks and up into the cleft, searching. When they had dispersed, we attacked. And we killed many.

"But then in the midst of battle my father was wounded, swept up by the Kubalese and dragged to the center of the burned village. By his height and his leading of command, I suppose, they knew him for Oak Dar. He was crippled in the back and unable to move. If they had not carried him, the injury might have been less severe; I have seen animals wounded like that."

It was a moment before Thorn could go on.

"If it had been any other man in Dunoon, the battle would have continued. The Kubalese demanded that the herds and all of Dunoon return. They ordered that we tend the flocks as we always had. And because my father lay paralyzed and helpless, all of Dunoon did return, the herds, every woman and child. We became slave to the Kubalese, for those few days that Oak Dar lived.

"When—when my father died it was by his own hand. For though his legs were paralyzed, his arms were not. And his mind was clear. He waited until most of the Kubalese soldiers had returned to Burgdeeth, leaving seven of their cruelest guards in Dunoon. We found my father, on the morning of the third day, with the . . . with the skinning knife through his throat. He would not live captive and be the cause of the captivity of his people.

"We covered him and let him lie there as if he were sleeping, until the two guards came to the cottage for their breakfast. Loke and I took them from behind and killed them. The other five gave us more fight, but we had all the men of Dunoon, and though they had left us no weapons we had slabs of painon wood and stones.

"We buried my father on the mountain. We buried the Kubalese at the foot of Dunoon. I was bleeding so badly that I took the shirt off one to staunch the blood. That, I suppose, is how the festering began, with Kubalese dirt in my blood.

"We lay them in a common grave and marked it with a message the Kubalese will not soon forget. Then all of Dunoon—all of the men who were left, and the women and children, and all the flocks—began the trek over the mountains once more to the lake of fire. My mother, too, mourning, and Loke beside her. I stayed, though she rankled at me about my leg. I told her I would rest a bit, and I went to the cave, to the wagon, to dress the wound again before I started out to find Anchorstar, and you. I never came out again until Zephy found me. The fever came on me as quick as a breath, and I woke to find myself sprawled on the wagon floor, freezing, not knowing how long I'd been there. I got into Anchorstar's bed, and the next time I woke was when Zephy called my name."

Toca stared up at Thorn with a look of adulation; and that day, he began to bring Thorn's plate when the meal was prepared in the evenings, and he kept Thorn's waterskin filled in an urgent child's ritual. He helped Tra.

Hoppa each time she removed Thorn's bandage to soak and treat the wound. How much of Thorn's own thoughts the child reached in to take, Zephy had no idea. But all of them—except Tra. Hoppa, of course—were becoming more sensitive to each other's thoughts.

"You are very much a success," Zephy said to Thorn when they were alone. "Toca worships you, and I think Elodia finds you very interesting, young as she is."

"Well what else could they think of this handsome face, so beautifully scarred in battle? The children are not without taste."

"You're a horrible Cherban."

"Zephy, the four of us are coming very close in our minds. Tra. Hoppa sees it, she watches us with that funny little grin. It's as if some force is increasing, the longer we are together."

"Yes," she said thoughtfully. A force that made the thoughts of each increasingly open to the others. And a force, too, that had strengthened Zephy's dreams until they were vivid and unsettling. She dreamed of Meatha's face in the darkness and woke overcome with grief. And she began to dream of other things, some frightening, and some as wonderful, as full of light, as the vision in the tunnel.

In the dark dreams she thought she woke inside an enclosure, dank and sunless, a place that felt so evil she shuddered and drew back. Each time she dreamed it, she would see nearly lifeless creatures lying like cadavers on narrow shelves and feeling without hope, without *sense* of any kind, and yet as if something within them lived, a brief flicker . . .

And then again she would be on a path of smooth white stone like something poured and hardened that wound its way up the mountain between the rough black lava; she would be climbing eagerly. Or she would be in a cave of sparkling light, with water cascading around her catching the glint of the sun, and there would be ice falls where the foam of the water broke, and she . . . Oh, they were dreams that made her wake with a lilting hope and wonder. And once she dreamed she stood by a crystal pool and saw Meatha coming toward her.

Then there were the other dreams of Meatha, dreams she did not like to remember.

Sometimes the others touched one of her dreams so they would wake knowing the same agony or joy that she had felt. But it was Thorn who, when she had a particularly bad dream of the dark place, gave her comfort when she woke, coming outside the cave to sit with her in the early dawn and hold her close against the fear that swept her. She knew he had seen, had felt the same fear and revulsion she did.

"We have seen the captive Children," he said quietly. "There is an evil there . . ." he looked at her steadily. "An evil we must battle with every strength we can find."

Then Elodia, sleeping with her head cradled on Nida's saddle, woke in the night to tell Zephy more about the dark cave—an enclosure made half of earth and half of stone walls, she thought—and the feeling of almost-death was rank and terrifying. Never a demonstrative child, Elodia pushed her face into Zephy's shoulder and shook with dry weeping, this stoic little girl who always seemed so in control of herself. And she kept repeating, "I felt sick—so sick." She stopped crying, her face white, and looked up at Zephy. "It was like something had hold of me from inside myself, making me the same as dead."

"The drugs," Thorn said later, "the drugs the Kubalese use."

"In Carriol," Tra. Hoppa said, "such drugs are well-enough known, dechbra and wellshing and epparoot. And MadogWerg. They make the mind sleep, make it unwilling to wake itself. They were given to stop pain; but when the pain was past, they were taken away again with great suffering. If they are used too long, they can kill. There were no roots or herbs to counteract their effects. But a Child of Ynell could make one whole again, make a mind want life again, by the strength of his thought. Some were trained for that work; it is harsh and very demanding, to reach in like that. It saps the strength of those who are able—and too few are able."

"But drugs," Zephy breathed. "How can they make spies of the Children, train them to spy, if they must keep them drugged?"

"Maybe that's part of the plan," Thorn replied, "to sicken them first, then bring them back when their will has been destroyed and they won't resist any longer."

Zephy stared at him and felt sick.

"It could mean permanent damage in their minds," Tra. Hoppa said. "It could mean that some of them can never be whole again. The force that springs from that place, the way you two describe it, seems to me more than the cruelty and lust of the Kubalese—something even darker. Could those Children, perhaps one among them, have grown so twisted with the drugs that he has already turned his mind to the bidding of the Kubalese, turned to darkness itself?"

"It feels like that," Thorn said. "More devious even than the Kubalese." He rose and turned away from them to stare out through the fog toward the shrouded mountain. Then he left them, needing suddenly to be alone, climbing the rocky barrier.

Soon he was above the fog, looking down to where it lapped like a white sea to cover the land below. He thought of what lay ahead of them, and he knew he wanted to go into it alone. Yet he knew, too, that the girls had strengths he did not have. What lay ahead was a terrifying foe that took the body and mind from within. If there was only one thing that could battle that darkness, it might take the strength of all of them together. By their own stubborness they must reach into those minds. Would they have the strength, even together?

Thorn could not judge Zephy's powers, not now, they had come too close. Their minds met now so easily that he could not be sure what was her own power and what his—or what had grown out of their increasing solace in each other.

Who was to say that all of them would not end up bound in a living death like those they dreamed of, laid out on cold stone slabs, their minds taken from them?

The fog was beginning to blow around him, to move higher on the mountain, though lower down it was still so thick it covered Ere. Soon wispy fog had surrounded him, and he found it somehow soothing.

Something dark moved in the fog above him, high on the rocks. He stood looking, alarmed. There—the fog curled back; he could see the outstretched neck, the dark muzzle, the great wings, the Horse of Eresu snorted in alarm and thrust upward, his wings taking the sky . . .

He was gone, into the fog-drowned sky.

Thorn stood staring, his heart pounding.

Then he climbed upward, scraping his leg so the pain came sharp. When he could go no farther for sheer cliff, he stood on a narrow, jutting rock no wider than his arms' reach. He knelt and saw the sharp round hoofprint. One print where the Horse of Eresu had struck the hard earth between stone as he leaped away.

When he returned to the valley enclosure, the donkeys were pressed against each other nervously, staring up at the mountain from which he had come.

And Zephy stood waiting for him. She put out her hand and took his hand quietly. "What did you see?" she breathed. "Something—something wonderful and—something *winged,* Thorn. Near you. I felt it, I felt you turn. But it was gone too soon, it was gone . . . " Her eyes were tragic with the loss.

The passion of the vision, of her intensity, gave him a passion for her, too, so he wanted to take her in his arms. He stood staring down at her, his blood rising. And then Toca came running, shouting, his tousled pale hair every which way and his face wet from the scrubbing Tra. Hoppa had been giving him. Thorn saw Elodia, too, by the cave entrance, watching intently. Toca slammed into Thorn, his eyes huge. "Show me what you saw! Show him again, show him to me!" he demanded. And, when Thorn had, "More of him! I want more. Make him come down here!"

"I can't *make* him, Toca, it's only what I saw." What did the child think, what interpretation had he found in that six-year-old mind for the ability they had? "It's only what I saw, not what I can make it be."

The little boy looked unbelieving. "I can," he said, almost sullenly.

"You can what? What can you do?"

"I can . . . " The little boy stared at him hard. "I could make him come here, if *I'd* seen him!"

"What do you mean? That you can make animals do things? Like what?"

"I can—I can make Dess kick Nida," the little boy said slowly.

"Why not make Nida kick Dess?"

"It's easier the other way. Nida doesn't like to kick."

"Show me."

Toca turned toward the two donkeys and became very still. Nothing happened for a long time. He remained motionless; then all at once Dess turned, lay back her ears, and let fly so hard that poor Nida dodged only just in time.

They all stared at Toca. No one said anything. Toca

looked back at them with quiet superiority. At last Thorn said, "Can you do that whenever you want? Any time?"

"Only—only since we ran away, more. It used to only work sometimes."

"What else can you do?"

"Just with animals, mostly. I can make birds come to me."

"It's as if," Thorn said to Zephy later, "as if your very escape from Burgdeeth has in some way made each of you stronger. Or maybe it's our all being together, maybe each of us draws strength from the others."

When they left the little valley, it was to travel slowly, Tra. Hoppa insisting Thorn ride when he wanted to be walking. Though as much as he growled at being treated like an invalid, his respites on Dess's back were welcome enough, for his leg still throbbed when he used it much. Zephy had cleaned Nida's saddle so it smelled better and mended the rent in the skirt so the straw had stopped coming out, using Thorn's knife for a punch, and twine unravelled from their rope. But after a day of the sharp-cornered saddle, Thorn put it back on Nida to carry pack as it was intended, and rode the cantankerous Dess bareback. He would ride behind, watching Toca and Bibb wedged atop Nida's pack, and watching Zephy's dark brown hair, sleek as a river otter, where she walked beside him. The flush on her cheeks and the brightness in her dark eyes seemed to have increased since their journey began. He put it down to her sudden freedom, away from the stifling influences of Burgdeeth.

Each day he was able to walk longer distances, but still their progress was slower than he liked. For one thing, they must stop early in the day, whenever they could find a resting place, for they were travelling along a steep, dizzying drop, and often there was no wide, safe bit to be seen for many hours. The mountain was blanketed with fog much of the time, so their way was more uncertain still. The drop looked less alarming hidden so, but in reality was the more dangerous. When the fog lifted briefly one day, they could see Kubal spread out just ahead, for they were now crossing above the low hills that separated Kubal from Cloffi.

Their food was growing short, though Elodia was clever at finding morliespongs, and twice Toca had called down the fat otero so that Thorn could snare them. There had been wild scallions and tammi where the mountain was gentler; but on the precipitous parts, little grew. One night they slept head to toe in a thin line on the narrow path with the donkeys tied up short and the rock dropping away sheer and terrifying just feet from their blankets. They tied the baby to a stone outcropping to keep him safe.

Zephy slept, that night—if I slept at all, she thought afterward—very conscious of their frailty there on the edge of the cliff. And conscious, too, of Thorn's closeness. She felt the warmth and protection of his thoughts surrounding her, touched an assurance in him that seemed to be sharper because of their danger.

The next day the path began to drop, to make its way lower along the mountain; they were descending toward the banks of the River Urobb.

The fog was only a mist when they reached the river's edge, and dusk was coming on. They came around a sharp curve so that the river was before them quite suddenly; and Zephy caught her breath and stopped to stare. It was exactly like her dream.

The river fell foaming between black rocks to swirl in pools, then fall again. The boulders that formed the pools were nearly white, smooth-washed. And along the river's edge ran a path of pale stone, smooth, disappearing above in the mists.

It was her dream; it spoke to her so she trembled. No

one said anything. Thorn looked at her and felt a tightening of his throat as if something he feared, or longed for, lay up that mountain.

At sight of the river, Toca flung off his clothes and raced in, paddling about as happy as a river-owl. They were all in need of a bath, and Thorn had pulled off his bandage and his boots and was about to take off the rest when Tra. Hoppa and the girls hastily departed upriver.

When they had bathed they made a small fire to cook supper, its smoke quickly lost in the fog, and the flame hidden by stones so it could not be seen from any distance. They were now almost halfway to the River Voda-Cul and the border of Carriol. And they were, all of them felt it, close to a place of meaning, perhaps coming closer to where the Children were held. For they were above Kubal now; and they were, in some way, atune with the darkness that beckoned. Elodia felt it; she was so quiet, as if she reached out again and again in her mind toward that darkness, touching, probing. But all of them felt a lightness, too, a rightness about this place that had nothing to do with the dark—that was the opposite of the dark—as if two forces met here.

When Zephy went to sleep, with her head cradled next to Elodia, she dreamed of Meatha in the fog; and the dream was so real she could well have been awake, standing by the fog-shrouded river, then moving up the pale stone path.

Chapter Eighteen

It was a dream that was not a dream. Afterward Zephy could not say whether it had been a vision, or whether she had been fully awake. And if what she saw was true, then somewhere in Ere, Meatha was surely alive.

In her dream she had risen and slipped out from under the blanket shelter and was standing on the bank of the river in the fog. She felt a sense of movement without effort that was dreamlike, and the fog swirled like water around her as she began to walk forward up the smooth path.

When the fog thinned, she could see that the sun was shining; and soon it became so bright she could hardly look. Then through the glare the dark shapes of mountains began to appear close around her. And she was approaching a rough spire, a monolith. It rose pale against the dark mountain; and as she drew near, she knew it was the death stone.

Meatha was there, tied to its base. She was dressed in smeared rags. Clytey was being led forward by red-robed Deacons. As Clytey was being bound, Zephy tried to go to Meatha, to speak to her; but she could not. She was held unmoving by something—as if she were not real there, as if she were on another plane.

The Deacons were saying a prayer over the captives, performing some last ritual unknown in Burgdeeth. They appeared to be genuflecting to each other rather than to the sacred valley of Eresu that she knew lay in the mountains above. They turned at last and, leading the two donkeys, started down the path toward Burgdeeth. They passed so close to Zephy she should have been brushed aside, but they did not see her. She saw Nida's saddle on Dess, the straw sticking out, and both donkeys smeared with dung and blood. Then the vision was gone, the air shimmering and the mountain and death stone indistinct—all was clear again and it was late evening, the light soft and welcoming. Meatha and Clytey were still tied, looked exhausted as they slumped against the cutting bonds.

And there were gods there, standing huge before the two bound girls.

The Luff'Eresi surrounded them. Shifting and indistinct they were, but their human arms were outstretched, and their men's faces stern—tall and awesome beyond anything Zephy could imagine. Was this the sacrifice, then? Zephy turned her face away in dread; but she could not help but turn back. She stood staring, in a terror of apprehension, trying to push forward, to somehow stop what would happen, but unable to move.

A god came close to the children but did not touch them, she sensed that he could not: he seemed not real in the same way that Meatha and Clytey did, seemed not so solid. But then came a figure from beside the Luff'Eresi, a human figure stepping out dressed in pale robes. She came to the Children; Meatha's face was white as the woman touched her. Yet as Zephy watched, Meatha's face lost its fear. The woman released Meatha's bonds, then those of Clytey, and stepped back.

Zephy watched Meatha and Clytey approach the Luff'-Eresi as if they were enchanted, saw them reach up to the closest god in awe—and saw they could not touch him. It was as if they were touching air.

Then a Horse of Eresu came forward and bowed his head and knelt. Zephy could feel his warmth as Meatha and Clytey climbed onto his back. He rose in a gesture that was startling and beautiful: from his kneeling position he flowed to stand, then his wings took him into the sky in one liquid motion. She could feel, as if she rode there, the rough silk of his mane in her hands, the wind sweeping her. She moved with Meatha and Clytey as they were carried above the mountain, above incredible peaks; the Horse of Eresu's strong wings knifed and turned the wind; the mountains, jagged, swept below. Then the valley came into view, a valley so terribly green . . .

She saw Eresu and it was as if her vision were many-faceted. She saw the green secret land honeycombed with terraces and bowers, saw the valley and inside the caves and bowers all at one time, moved within the lighted caves with their tumbling falls of water; and it was as she had dreamed. She saw the Luff'Eresi moving freely on the wind above the cliffs and terraces and on the low green hills. She saw Meatha happy among them and others like her. This was Eresu, so Meatha must be dead; yet Zephy didn't understand how that could be, for the Luff'Eresi had not killed her.

Then something began to happen to Meatha, Zephy could feel the change in her. She gathered with the other Children of Ynell, Clytey, the girl who had released her, all of them. There were no more than a dozen—boys, girls, men and women—and they began to march out of the valley. Zephy could see them going along the white path and down along the river, down and down along the hills, walking silently. Then there was sudden darkness, and she heard Meatha cry out to her in her mind; then a silence that was terrifying in its emptiness. She could see Meatha no more; only the sense of her remained, and Zephy thought she was whispering, *Now you will come. Now you must come to help us.*

Meatha's words faded so Zephy was not sure they had ever been. Her sense of Meatha became quickly contracted as in the darkness of an unhappy memory. As one might remember someone long dead.

Did Meatha live? Zephy had no sense of how to distinguish what death was. The atmosphere around her began to grow more solid. Then it was suddenly as if what had gone before could now be seen as a dream, and she had awakened at last to stand, fully in charge of her senses, in the valley of Eresu.

Five winged gods came away from the rest in the valley, and she trembled as they approached her. They were more magnificent than anything one could have imagined. The dignity and the joy in their faces was as if joy was the very essence of life. Their faces might have resembled human faces except for their perfect strength and for that joy. She was drawn to them so she could not look away, even had she wanted.

Their movement was like water over stones, their golden bodies shifting with light and their wings—their wings were tapestries of light glinting, shattering; it was as if she saw them through a curtain of shifting air, not steady as Meatha had appeared. Yet so real, more than real. And there were Horses of Eresu there among them. And though the Horses of Eresu mingled with the gods, they were solid to look at; Zephy could see them clearly, where the gods shifted as light shifts on blowing leaves. The wings of the Horses of Eresu were not blinding, but were wonders of velvet-toned grace. They still looked like horses despite their differences, while the gods were like no animal or man, not like any creature of Ere.

Then one Luff'Eresi shifted and was standing close above her, huge, his horselike body far taller than her head, his human face solemn, his eyes, from their great height, holding her completely. Above the silken coat of the horselike body—a dark, burnished shade—his torso was muscled and full of powerful grace, and his terrible strength made Zephy tremble. His expression and dark eyes sent a wave of awe and wonder through her that made her kneel; but his voice roared at once in her mind, *Rise, child, do not kneel before me!*

When he spoke, it was as Ynell, silently in her mind; and it was as if all her life she had waited for this. She rose and stood before him, and thought only, *You are the god of Ere!*

Mortal! His silent words thundered in her mind. *I am mortal! Not a god, Child of Ynell. I am as mortal as you!* She stood staring at him, not believing him. Yet he was forcing her to believe, to stretch her mind to believe him. Her thoughts would not come in any kind of order, only in the overwhelming sensations that swept her. *If you are not a god,* she thought at last, *then there can be no god. There can be no being meant for us to worship if you are not he.*

I am a mortal creature. The Luff'Eresi spoke this time so sternly that she drew back, chastened. *I am mortal just as you. I am only different. To call me a god is to humble yourself, human! And yet*—and his voice-thought grew softer now, gentler. *And yet there is the spirit, the spirit that all mortals yearn for. But it is not here on Ere, Child of Ynell. No god is here. The gods we seek—and all of us seek them, Zephy Eskar—the gods we seek are spirits so far removed from Ere and from this time and place, that few can guess at the reality of their beings. To be mortal is to understand mortality. But beyond that, the next step of your spirit's life can only be grasped when you are ready.*

Zephy felt as insignificant as a grain of mawzee—yet she felt, at the same time, a sense of continuity, of a stretching out before her, felt a lift and exultation as the Luff'Eresi showed her the meaning of his words, gave her the sense of layers of life, of intricacies she could not unravel but which laid a richness on her mind, a richness and maturity on her very soul.

At one moment she felt she could almost touch the varied planes of existence, the plane, different from her own, where the Luff'Eresi dwelt, the plane that came closer to Ere in the Waytheer years. She could almost understand the physical differences that made their two worlds not quite touch, not quite mesh. She could almost embrace, for a moment, concepts quite beyond her experience, could almost make sense of them.

But why—if this were true—why didn't Cloffi and all of Ere teach this true wonder, make prayer for the reality instead of—instead of . . .

Instead of worshipping false gods! The Luff'Eresi bellowed into her thoughts. And the feel of his laughter overwhelmed her. *Instead of worshipping us. You are right, Zephy Eskar. Your people have been led as donkeys are led. You have been given chaff when there was whole good grain to serve you. You have been lied to, to feed the evil lust for power that the Cloffi masters have nurtured like a sickness in their breasts.*

"But why?" she said aloud. "Why, if you knew? . . ."

He did not respond with a voice in her mind now, but with a surge of direct knowledge that nearly overpowered her, with a feeling that lifted her, made her see the life of Ere, all of Ere as the Luff'Eresi saw it: a slow, ordered—though there were times that seemed without order—rising and growing of the generations that came one after another. A slow laying on of knowledge and then in places the breaking down of that knowledge, and the destruction of it by falsehood, by deceit, so that people for many generations afterward foundered, led by falsehood and avarice and laziness, led by warped emotions where they should have seen clearly. Until, here and there, a few broke away, and knowledge was built again slowly, and stronger.

She could see those who understood come, over the centuries, to stand at the gates of Eresu. Like a tableau, Ere's history flowed past and around her, a tapestry woven of the warp of truth, but laid over with the weft of human frailty and fear, with the human need for security even at the expense of truth; then with the brightness of the human spirit rising like flashing colors here and there against the easy dullness of human sloth and greed.

They must come at their own times, at their own terms, Child of Ynell. If we were to go into Ere and change the way men live, change willfully what they believe, we would destroy something in those men. Once we told men we were mortal, for generations uncounted we spoke to them of this and tried to give them truth. But they would not drink of it. The suffering men do to themselves in believing their myths can only winnow out the strong and the loving and make them stronger still. They who search for truth will come seeking. And they are welcome here.

"But the death stone—why. . . ?"

The death stone, Zephy Easkar—yes, we have influenced man sometimes. We have taken our liberties—to save those rare few who are the true wealth and hope of Ere. Before the death stone, they were killed in temple ritual with the populace looking on. Now they are brought here and they stay in Eresu or go elsewhere as they choose. Your Cloffi landmasters are not sure enough in their minds of any truth to resist us in this. And they may truly believe that the Children die here. At least they are conveniently rid of them . . .

And she was suddenly awake, standing by the fog-bound river shivering, longing for the Luff'Eresi, for the words she had lost . . .

She had wanted to ask more, so much more, to ask help. But she had been given all she had a right to ask. The saving of the Children through the use of the death stone had been all the help the Luff'Eresi found it fit to give. Any more would have weakened the very strength of the human condition that the Luff'Eresi, by their reticence to interfere, had nurtured over the generations.

Her feet were wet. She could hear the river churling.

There were tears on her cheeks. She heard a stirring and saw the campfire come to life as if the ashes had been uncovered and tinder added. Thorn came through the fog and stood looking down at her, and she knew he had seen what she saw, for it was with him still.

"Yes," Thorn said huskily. "I saw it. I was there with you."

And then she was in his arms as if he could give her rest from that terrible longing for the almost known, rest from that terrible awe.

When they gathered before the fire with the others, Thorn was able to tell, more lucidly than Zephy, the sense of what the Luff'Eresi had said, the sense of wonder they both had known as they faced him.

He was able to describe better the sensation of cold dark that had pressed around them, too, with the last vision of Meatha. He watched Tra. Hoppa's increasing excitement and eagerness, watched Toca's pallor and Elodia's serious, pale silence as the children tried to deal with the word pictures and the strong, direct thought sensations.

It was Toca, grasping at the vision and words as another child would grasp at a magical tale, who spoke a few words of the Luff'Eresi haltingly, taking them from Zephy's mind, ". . . *can only winnow out the strong and the loving and—and make them stronger still. They who search for truth will come seeking. And they are welcome here.*" It seemed strange to hear the words from the little boy's mouth. How had they come this close to each other in such a short time? Was it partly the fear they shared, fear of the Kubalese, of being captured? Fear of the darkness that lay ahead of them?

When they discussed Meatha, surely fear was there. And later as Zephy and Elodia tried more skillfully than Thorn to reach out for Meatha, a sickness came around the children, too. But there also came a sense of direction quite apart from that, a sense of something pulling from the low hills to the south, a taut insistance, heavy with urgency, as if the darkness wanted them, would swallow them.

Thorn grew increasingly uneasy. Tra. Hoppa and Bibb and Toca should go safely into Carriol now, and find shelter. But he felt Tra. Hoppa's stubborness. And Toca could be stubborn too. Even the baby seemed awash with the emotions of the others, for when their thoughts and talk were frightening, he cried. Much of his crossness could be the lack of milk, though. Dried mawzee mixed with water was meager food. "He needs milk," Thorn said, "We can't take him into Kubal." He stared down the hills where the fog was lifting at last. "We can't take a baby there."

"We must stay together," Tra. Hoppa said, "There are farms in Kubal. We can steal milk."

"Get caught stealing milk, our throats cut, and never find the Children," Thorn scoffed.

But Tra. Hoppa's blue eyes flashed. "We must be together. We need each other now."

"If something happens to me and Thorn," Zephy said evenly, "why should it happen to all of you?" But Tra. Hoppa's stare defeated her. The old lady, at least four times their years, had perhaps four times their stubborness, too.

Elodia simply remained quiet, with no intention of being diverted.

There had been no trees on the mountain, only stone and grass. Now as they followed the downward trail beside the River Urobb, they left the stone boulders and outcroppings and came into a forest of zantha trees whose silk hung long and pale like a woman's hair. They could not see the valley for trees and hills, but the river rushed beside them. The zantha branches cut off the sky, and the trail looked as if it was seldom used, tangled with dead branches and thick vines that would have tripped human and donkey if Thorn had not cut them away. They made slow progress, Thorn slashing at the heavy growth. Then late on the eve of the second day, the zantha trees disappeared and the hills became bare and rocky once more, dropping quickly to the valley of Kubal. Here the river left them in a sudden waterfall that tumbled to the valley floor.

They stayed hidden as best they could among the stony hills and dry grass. When they came to a place where two flat boulders met overhead, they made camp in their shallow wedge, setting the donkeys on the most sheltered grazing and rolling out their blankets under the stones.

They made no fire, but ate cold mawzee soaked in water. Then Thorn took Toca and set out, as darkness dropped down, to scout the country below for a farm.

As they started off down the rocky slope, they could hear the falls, then the river running below them. Their progress was hesitant. Thorn, slowing to keep pace with the little boy, fingered the length of rope wound around his waist, felt for his knife and hoped he wouldn't need it. It seemed, as they moved downward and darkness increased, that a strange unease reached up to touch them, though he thought it might only be his apprehension at going into the hostile land. Toca was very quiet. They came at last to a widening of the river and saw it curve off sharply to their left. It would meet the Voda-Cul farther on. The rich Kubalese pasture and farm land lay in this curve of the river.

It was perhaps an hour later, as they made their way along the edge of the hills, that Toca whispered, "There's a farm there, cows are in the field. And horses in a shed, I think." He took Thorn's hand and guided him away from the shelter of the hills onto the open fields, then along them until they came to a fence, nearly ramming into it in the darkness. They stood there in the blackness, silent, while

Toca tried to pull the cows to him. The little boy's hand tensed in Thorn's and grew sweaty. Then after a long uneasy time, "I can't. There's something the matter. It's not like—like when we're together. It's not so strong now, I don't know if I can."

Thorn felt it too, as if something were awry; felt a weakening of the security he had grown used to as they travelled, the wholeness and gentle strength that had surrounded them when they were together. Now it was fragmented, shattered.

"Maybe you're trying too hard." But he knew that was not it.

"We have to go into the field. I can do it closer."

But even in the field and quite close to the cows, it was perhaps half an hour before one reluctant animal, snorting softly with uneasy curiosity, came to Toca from the dark lump that marked the little herd, and let him put the rope on her. She stood tensely for some time until the two of them had soothed her, though when Thorn began to milk her at last, Toca, at her head, seemed to have endeared himself to her sufficiently so she let her milk down all right. They got near a full waterskin—a hard job, milking into the small mouth of the waterskin, and her fidgeting. As Thorn finished, a light burst out in the dark field, and they saw that a door had been opened, that there was a house there. A figure stood in the light for a few minutes, then the door was closed. Thorn and Toca slipped away, through the fence and up into the hills as quickly as they could.

"It was different," Toca repeated. "It isn't the same as with all of us together."

"*How* different, exactly?"

"The strong is gone, the strong thing."

"What strong thing?"

"The thing that makes—that helped me call the birds down, the thing that makes you stronger."

Thorn looked down at the child and knew he was right. It was as if Toca's increased strength, Zephy's increased ability for visions had grown as the four of them grew closer together. Had grown as strong, he realized, as if they did indeed carry the runestone as they had intended to do. As strong as if they had had the runestone all the time—Zephy's vision, Elodia's dreams . . .

He stood staring into the night. What had Meatha done with the stone? Stripped of her clothing, then tied across Dess's back, what could she have done with it? She had been so silent, Zephy said. Meatha had not fought back, she had not screamed as Clytey had . . .

Could she have held the stone in her mouth?

Could she have held it there all the way to the mountain, held it until she was left alone at the death stone? But Zephy's vision had not shown that. He tried to see Meatha again as Zephy had seen her last in Burgdeeth, to see Meatha's hands and feet being tied, to see her lifted across Dess's back, see her face pushed into the dung and grime that was smeared across the donkey and saddle, see her face turning away, pressed against the leather . . .

And then he knew.

He pulled Toca up, and they began to run hard up the hills.

AFTER THORN AND TOCA had gone, Zephy lay for a long time beneath the rock shelter, wakeful and uneasy. The others were sleeping. The baby woke once and fussed, and she took him up and calmed him, then lay him back beside Elodia. Her growing restlessness made it almost impossible to lie still. She tried to feel if Thorn was in danger, but she could be sure of nothing. At last she rose and went outside, to stand gazing down at the dark valley and at the two rising moons.

Then when Thorn came at last, charging over the crest of the hill suddenly, with Toca some distance behind him, she could only stare. He pushed past her into the shadow of the shelter, she heard Elodia groan, then out he came dragging Nida's saddle. She watched him, perplexed, as he pitched the saddle down where the faint light from the moons could touch it. His knife flashed, and she stared in amazement as he ripped open the stitching she had done. An excitement was growing in her; she knelt beside him eagerly as he reached into the straw. Toca stood over them, a silent little figure.

When Thorn drew his hand out, she reached to touch the stone that gleamed in his palm, and at once they were locked in the vision that rose and swept them, the moonlight gone, locked in utter blackness. Torchlight was drawing near them; there were figures dark and still on the stone slabs. Now they saw faces, though, saw Clytey first, then Meatha, saw the faces of Children they did not know. And dark thoughts were there among them. And there were grown men and women, the Children of Eresu who had marched out from the valley with Meatha. And then they saw the tall figure lying still and silent and alone, his white hair catching the torchlight. Zephy's very soul cried out to him, tried to wake him . . .

The three of them knelt there as one, their hands touching the runestone, willing Anchorstar to wake, willing with all the strength they possessed to wake him. But he did not stir; and as morning began to come, they let go, exhuasted and discouraged. They laid the stone down and stared at it, gleaming dully beside Nida's saddle. Elodia, who had awakened, came to hide herself in Zephy's arms. From the shelter the baby whimpered in a kind of sleeping panic.

At last Zephy picked up the stone in her hankerchief, tied it, and handed it to Thorn. He fastened it to his belt, and they returned to the shelter to prepare for the journey ahead.

Chapter Nineteen

THEY HAD GONE a long way by noon and stood at last where they could see an unnatural formation marring the hills below them. Where the hills dropped to the flat valley, the cleft between two separate hills seemed to have filled in: the broad mound was wider than any of the surrounding, rounded hills; it was grassed over, but it was flat on top and out of keeping with the rest. Was this their destination?

As they travelled, their sense of forboding had grown stronger, drawing them on. Never had their attention wavered, not once had any of them gazed off across Kubal and wondered if they were going in the right direction. They had simply followed that feeling of darkness that had increased, that depressed them now so each was quiet and withdrawn, staring down on that wide mound.

Thorn knew Zephy was frightened, her brown eyes were dark and calm, but she had begun to bite her lip at one side so it was drawn in, in a twisting pucker. Elodia seemed to have become hardened; the line of her face looked more determined. Toca was the same as always, a sturdy little boy following Thorn unquestioning, steady as earth.

They waited until it began to grow dark before they continued, coming at last to a shallow ravine where the donkeys could be hidden. It was nearly bare, though one end was blocked by a small stand of brush that would break the view of it from below. Tra. Hoppa could stay here with the baby—and with Toca, too, perhaps. Thorn dug out a trough below a trickle of water that came down the hill so it would collect for drinking. He settled the donkeys among the brush, and the children helped Tra. Hoppa hide the packs in brush, too.

They made a cold meal hastily, during which Toca made it clear that he was not to be left behind. Slowly, Thorn took up one waterskin, the knife, the rope. He looked at Zephy, and she nodded. There was no point in delay, it would only make them edgy. They could rest the night and start fresh, but none of them would sleep. They had the runestone, they had all the help they could have. He kissed Tra. Hoppa on the cheek and turned away.

When they started down the hill, the feel of darkness met them like a wall so all of them wanted to draw back. Thorn took Zephy's hand, and when he turned to look at her, she was too calm and very pale. He wanted to say, *Stay here, stay safe.* But he knew that he could not. She had committed herself just as he had. She was biting her lip again. He stopped and put his arms around her and held her close. Her warmth dizzied him, he wanted desperately to stay with her there and keep her safe, to find his own safety with her. They stared at each other, stricken.

When they reached the mound between the hills, they could see no opening. Thorn began to wonder then if this was a natural formation after all. But the sense of darkness was too strong, and all of them had begun to catch glimpses of stone slabs and still figures, like mist across their vision. Over and over it came, the two places seen at once, the real and the vision seen together as the sky darkened and night came down.

There was no visible way into the hill. They skirted

it expecting a door and found none. They examined the grass-covered earth where it rose abruptly from the valley floor like a wall, but there was only earth and grass. They climbed the hill then, uneasily.

On top it was like a flat field, with tufts and hillocks and rabbit holes. Nothing more, no opening. And the black rabbits themselves, long-tailed, wily creatures, darted away across the hills as they approached, then paused to watch them.

Then at last, in a hill removed from the mound, they found a narrow cleft like a scar, a wedge into which Thorn went alone to find a larger opening inside, then a tunnel and at the end of that a door, dirt encrusted and heavy. He pulled it open slowly, scraping dirt.

Beyond was darkness. He struck flint to a candle, then went cautiously along the bare tunnel, moving at last into the dark mound. The others followed him.

Once through the tunnel, they found themselves in a larger passageway that all of them recognized from the visions. Shallow indentations along the walls held stone slabs and silent figures. The shock of finding in reality what they had seen in the visions made them silent; reality and vision seemed confused suddenly, their minds could not cope.

Then Elodia stepped forward and laid her hand on the bare arm of a child her own age; and they all started at the sense of warm skin, of living flesh.

"The stone!" Elodia breathed, her intensity like a knife. At once Thorn was beside her laying the jade in her hand; they touched hands and touched the runestone to the figure, willing the child to wake.

She was a pale, fragile girl of about Elodia's age. Her skin seemed almost transparent, as if her life was frailly held, indeed. She stirred at last, and her face seemed to go whiter with the effort she made. Her chest rose in barely visible breathing; then a movement down the passage made them start. A greasy light came from around a corner of the passage and grew brighter. They could see the flame of a torch approaching.

They snuffed the candle and drew back into the smaller tunnel, clustering against its wall to stare toward the approaching light. They could hear a faint scuffing and an occasional grumble as if the torchbearer was not happy at being pulled from a cozy place, to walk the damp tunnel. If he was after them, if he had heard them, he was not being very quiet about it.

As he reached the first niche he stopped and leaned over. They could see him clearly now, a big Kubalese bending almost double to lift a child to sitting position and hold a cup to its lips. At niche after niche he stopped; but when he reached the little girl she drew back from his grasp. She must have refused the draft, for after a moment he growled in agitation, shook her, then held the cup again, her head higher this time. At last he grunted with satisfaction, released the figure carelessly, and came on down the passage.

When he had done all the sleeping figures and gone on, they followed him, moving in the opposite direction from the sleeping girl. Surely he was giving fresh drug. Now all would be harder to awaken. How often did he make these rounds? Was he the lone keeper or were there others? Passages opened both left and right, and Thorn knew they could easily become lost. It was time to act. He unsheathed the knife, loosed the rope from his belt, handing it to Zephy, then slipped ahead.

It was all done so fast, his thought to hers, no time to panic. Thorn loved her in that quick moment when she leaped ahead with him, steady and fast, never faltering; he crouched behind the Kubalese, jumped, plunged his knife in as Zephy flew to wind the rope around the soldier's feet and pull it taut. The man cried out, Thorn found his face as he fell and muffled him, and he was down heavy as lead across Thorn's legs. Zephy was binding him, but Thorn steeled himself and cut the man's throat. They were safer that way.

"He might have told us something," Elodia said, coming up. There was a quantity of blood. They all felt sick.

"He might have lied, too," Thorn answered. He righted the torch and handed it to Toca. Then they moved the nearest figure, a half-grown boy, into another niche beside a young woman, and the three of them were able, just, to lift the Kubalese up onto the slab. The blood was slippery, and they were splashed with it, wiping it off on his clothes before they left him.

Now ahead of them lay half a dozen figures that had not had their dose from the cup. The cup itself Thorn protected carefully for there was an ample draft left that might somehow be useful.

Again they tried to awaken a drugged sleeper, and again there was a stir from the young woman, but she did not open her eyes. As they became more sensitive to the sleepers, they began to experience their need, their crying out for that draft that Thorn carried, an aching hunger that tore at them all in its intensity. They experienced the longing nearly as if it were their own, which perhaps weakened their own determination as they tried to rouse the Children of Ynell. But the need was stronger in some than in others, and in those from whom it came the weakest, their efforts to arouse were most rewarding.

After some time they had amassed a small band that followed them like sleepwalkers down the corridor, children and adults ambling, blank-eyed. Among them was Clytey Varik.

Thorn and Zephy, Elodia and Toca proceeded silently, their mental effort turned to reassuring those who followed, to keep them following, to make them yearn for life . . .

They found that the narrower tunnels leading off the main corridor were short for the most part, some going into empty rooms or caves and others simply stopping; some with a few niches, but most unoccupied. Most of the drugged Children had been kept in the corridor where they were easiest to get to. At the far end of the corridor was the place of most danger.

For by reaching silently forward together, by feeling outward together, sensitive to each other and to what lay ahead they had been able to see into the mound's depths. And at the end of the corridor was a room where the MadogWerg leaf was brewed in a cold-still, and where two Kubalese guards played at a game of dice sticks. Thorn could feel Zephy's fear of the place, of the guards, and feel her hatred too and her rising determination to aggression that was very like his own. He could feel Elodia's singleness of purpose so finely steeled that her abhorrence and tenderness were shielded. And Toca—Toca simply went on, made his stoic effort one-minded, following Thorn. Thinking nothing of good or bad or distasteful, but simply encrusted with a small fierce discipline, soldier-like and so touching that Thorn, in spite of himself, put an arm around the little boy's shoulder, then knew at once that Toca was better left untouched just now, that the shield was not that impenetrable.

The sleepers who had not been roused must be attended to later, yet the mental strength of the four to wake them was waning. Thorn thought that without the runestone they might never have been able to do it—might not yet, he thought. Won't be able to if I don't stop dreaming and pay attention to where we are. For the brewing room was around the next curve.

The possible plans were several, but they chose to divide the two guards. When they saw the wooden door ajar and the candle burning within, they all slipped back down the tunnel save Thorn, who moved quietly in the shadows to the other side of the opening and stood still.

When the mumble of voices continued and the click of dice and sticks did not cease—and when their minds were touching—Thorn thought that he was ready; and down the tunnel in the darkness Elodia let out a scream that made the blood go cold. A scream of pure terror that he had felt her building, getting ready to deliver, for some minutes. It was so good a scream he wanted to laugh with the pleasure of it, but there wasn't time; the two guards boiled out. He caught the second in the knee, in the groin, felt him twist, pulled his arm behind him, and heard the other shout where he had bolted down the corridor into the children. Thorn stabbed again, felt the guard go limp, and pelted after the first, found him fighting rope and girls and Toca in a melee so confused it was all Thorn could do to sort out the right thing to hit, afraid to use the knife. The drugged Children stood looking on, like shadows.

When they had the man down, Thorn decided to let him live, tie him and question him. The man was gone in drunkeness; Thorn could smell the liquor. Disgusted, but glad for the advantage it had given them, he tied him well, and they dragged him onto one of the slabs.

Now the brewing room was empty. They made quick work of the MadogWerg, mixing the ground leaf with dirt, then burying the whole mess. There was quite a lot of it, the dry, bronze leaf crushed to a fine powder, and some not yet crushed, gathered into small sheaves, the round separate leaves quite beautiful, just as Tra. Hoppa had described—the most potent of all the drugs.

They poured the brewed liquid into the Kubalese's liquor cask. A little welcoming draft for the next Kubalese who came along. But Thorn saved back that in the cup, he did not know why.

The drugged Children who had followed them stood

clutched together like moon-moths in the doorway, clinging to each other. Thorn brought them in, pushing, gently cajoling until they were seated, close together still, on the lower bunk. Nine of them, frightened and pale and confused—even the four adults—by the lantern light and by being awake and walking, by the world which they all seemed to have forgotten. When they smelled the reek of drug from the cold-still, they stared toward it longingly until Thorn tipped it over with one blow and smashed the tin cups and the tubing under his heel. Then they looked terrified indeed, whether at his violence or at the destruction of the still, no one could be sure.

The cave was fairly large, with the table in the middle next to a supporting post, the bunks by the door, clothes on pegs, and a tangle of things at the back—crocks and barrels and a small cooking stove like an iron pot, with a bit of chimney that attached to three tubes in the dirt ceiling. Thorn examined these. "They're no bigger than rabbit holes," he said admiringly. "And there were plenty of rabbit holes up there. A little bit of smoke, carried off by the wind . . ."

There were half a dozen black rabbit skins hanging, dry, on one wall, and rabbit carcasses, dried and smoked, hung from the main beam of the room. Zephy opened a barrel to find it filled with golden-colored grain. "Would we dare to eat the food? We'll have to feed the Children. They wouldn't have drugged all this; they must have needed it themselves. What did they feed the Children? Besides the . . . besides the MadogWerg. It must have been liquid, they were hardly awake," she said, touching a big iron pot. "They had to feed them, Thorn, they would have died otherwise."

"Could you make some soup?"

She and Elodia set about it at once, tipping water from a barrel and adding the grain and dried rabbit and some tammi and kebbel-root. The fuel for the stove was dried cow dung, hot burning, that filled a linen bag. She wished she had milk for the children.

The Children's eyes had followed her as she investigated the room, and at the words MadogWerg they had seemed to tense, their faces to harden and to become slyly eager—the most alive they had looked since they had been awakened. She could feel their thoughts, their increasing desire for the drug as they came more fully awake and felt the sharp pangs of withdrawal. She felt, with them, the ugly quick pains in her body, in her legs and hands. She should have felt sorry for them, but she could only feel repulsion. She wished they could be shut away, she realized with shock. Oh, how could she think such a thing. She stared at Clytey Varik's blank face, and felt a horror at her own emotions. Yet the Children were so like something dead that the feel of them, sick and negative, was almost more than she could bear. It was as if their very spirits tainted everything around them with a heavy intensity of lifelessness, with such a pall that joy and love were made somehow indecent in the presence of their intense death-wishing.

She looked up and found Thorn watching her and knew they had shared this. And she knew that their very sharing was repugnant to these drugged, sick Children. She felt a passion to get away from them, and then a gripping pity that made her turn and stare at them, so she almost cried out in agony at what they were.

As one, Toca and Elodia rose, and the four of them took hands and stood as before touching the runestone and trying to waken the Children more completely, awaken them to life, to wholeness. They breathed such passion into their effort, into the Children, breathed the very souls of their spirits into them. But they pulled away at last exhausted, near dropping with fatigue and discouragement; for the Children had remained as they were, their eyes and spirits willfully unseeing; blank and defiant.

Now Thorn looked at Zephy for the first time without that spark of challenge and assurance. He seemed to have lost hope suddenly. She stared at him with chagrin. "They don't want this," he growled angrily. "They don't want to be better. We can't make them want it, we're not strong enough."

"We are! You're stupid to say we can't! You'll undo everything!"

"Undo what? They're dead—they'd be better dead. Look at them! They want to be dead!" He swung to face the silent row where they crouched on the bunk, staring dully. "*Look at you!* You're nothing. You've lost your very souls, you've let them be taken from you. You can't even fight for your life! All you want is a morass to wallow in. To die in!" He turned away furious, his eyes dark with anger and his fists clenched as if he would like to hit them.

And Zephy, watching the Children with apprehension, saw the blonde young woman's eyes go clear suddenly, saw her looking back at Thorn with life in her face. Zephy caught her breath, cried silently to Thorn, saw him turn and take the woman's hands.

The woman looked at Zephy, now and smiled. Tremulous, uncertain, but aware. Very much aware. Thorn pressed the stone in her hand and they held it, the three of them. Zephy could feel the change then, could feel that now, at last, the bodily pains and depression did not matter, that something else stronger had taken hold. That life had returned, the stubborn eagerness for life.

At last the woman said her name, Showpa, and that she was of Quaymus. And they set about, together, bringing the others back. For with Thorn's anger, all of the Children had begun to reach out, to feel out toward his strength. And toward the runestone. Had begun to fight at last.

Chapter Twenty

ZEPHY WOKE cold and stiff from sleeping on the stone floor. She could not tell whether it was night or day. The constant darkness of the cave depressed and upset her. She had awakened several times, longing to see daylight. She rose and went into a side corridor, where there were several holes in the cave ceiling to let in air, and stared up at the barely light sky. The cold, predawn air felt so good. She had a terrible desire to leave the cave and run across the hills, free.

Instead she hunkered down against the stone wall, waiting for some sign of life from the others, thinking that otter-herb tea would taste wonderful, wishing she could wash herself properly.

None of them had wanted to sleep on the stone slabs. Certainly the Children who had been drugged had not. They had all chosen the floor instead, with Tra. Hoppa and two of the women occupying the bunks in the brewing room. Thorn had brought Tra. Hoppa and the baby down, and Showpa had taken to Bibb at once, relieving Tra. Hoppa of him.

But now, instead of Bibb, Tra. Hoppa had Nia Skane and the two little boys from Burgdeeth to look after. All three children had been found in a deep, nearly closed tunnel with a supply of watered MadogWerg so diluted that they were semi-conscious. They lay bound, with their drug-water in bottles beside them, being used in some terrible experiment that sickened Zephy. Thorn thought it had been done to see at what level of consciousness these three young ones would keep themselves voluntarily, when the drug in the sweetened liquid was all the food or drink they had. Tra. Hoppa had taken them at once into her own care, until she fell asleep from exhaustion. No one realized, perhaps, what a toll the journey had taken of her. She had looked tired and drawn when Thorn brought her in.

Now, with twelve Children awakened from the drug, they should surely be able to wake the others. But Zephy felt an unease all the same, for the sense of evil that clung about the caves had not diminished as the Children were awakened one by one. On the contrary, the feel of dark had increased. They all felt it, the sense of dark they had touched from afar, now grown strong all around them. Why? Why? She scowled, perplexed and frightened, and found she was clenching her hands so tight they had gone quite numb.

She rose at last when she heard others stirring, and went to the brewing room to make zayn tea. And all through the day and the next day as the remaining Children were found and awakened from the drug, she puzzled over the feel of the foreboding that lay rank as a bad smell upon the caves. But it was not until she found Meatha at last that she felt the darkness surround and touch her like a live thing.

She had discovered Meatha quite unexpectedly, after she had nearly given up hope, in a crevice so deep she might well have missed her. As Zephy stood staring, then knelt so the candlelight fell full on Meatha's face, she could see no indication of life, nor could she feel the sense of life that had come from the others. Furiously, she tried to force her own sense of living into Meatha, her terror making her frantic. She poured every ounce of her strength into the pale girl, but the darkness gripped Zephy and held her, and seemed to swing a curtain between herself and Meatha; and she could do nothing.

When Toca found her, she was close to tears and exhaustion, and she thought she had lost Meatha.

Toca came to her silently and stood quiet for a time. She was so preoccupied she paid no attention to him. Then slowly she began to sense a kind of animal need and possessiveness coming from the little boy, something quite beyond her own power, and directed at Meatha. Something so basic and simple—like a baby demanding its mother's attention with righteous fury. She drew her own thoughts back and waited, letting Toca take hold as he would.

She sensed, as his very spirit gripped into Meatha, that part of what he was doing he had learned from the baby, from Bibb, that demanding, uncompromising indignation; and that part of it was from his own experience. He was still so close to babyhood that he could more easily bring it forth: a charged, young-animal insistence to life that *could* not be ignored.

Nor was it ignored. For at last, where Zephy's strongest efforts had failed, Toca's were responded to. Zephy felt the darkness drawing back, knew that it was being held off; and finally Meatha opened her eyes, staring blankly.

Zephy, shaken, could have wept over Toca. She took his hand in her own and knew that he was complete and special, and admired him—and let him know that she did.

When Meatha was able to rise, able to walk supported by them both, she clung to them as if the very touch of something living was necessary to nurture the flow of her own life forces. As if she had been very close, indeed, to dying. When she had been fed, in that dormitory that the brewing room had become, leaning against Tra. Hoppa, taking a hesitant spoonful at a time, she was stronger. She and Zephy looked at each other silently, and a lifetime seemed to have passed. Truly a resurrection of life had taken place and neither could speak of it; and the strangenesses that lay between them brought them closer. For fear bound them; the gift of Ynell bound them; the darkness bound them.

Before the last Children were awakened from the drug, Thorn began to post guards—Children made well and willing to remain at the farther reaches of the tunnels, away from distractions of the mind, to sense anyone coming above on the hills. But no one came, they were not disturbed; and finally Thorn wondered if the three soldiers—the two dead and the one still captive—had not been set to live here alone for a very long time indeed.

The bound Kubalese refused to talk. He would not give them any idea of when more guards were due or from what direction. When Thorn questioned him about the feeling of evil, of dark, he would only stare as if he didn't understand. He accepted food grudgingly but told them nothing, so that Thorn half wished they had killed the man after all and saved the trouble. To pity the Kubalese, the drug giver, would have been hypocritical to Thorn, as it was not to Elodia, who felt some strange human kindness for the captive.

It was Elodia, though, who to save the others danger, had successfully shielded her thoughts, taken a knife, and crept out into the night with Toca, through the hillside door. They went alone to locate a band of horses that Toca sensed, grazing untended, to the south. The little boy would have gone by himself, recklessly. They returned with the news of a small band of Kubalese horses and a wagon at what appeared to be an iron ore depot. And, a fact that shook them all, two smaller Carriolinian mares, butternut, all butternut. This news made them renew their search for Anchorstar, though he could not be sensed. Why had they felt him before they ever reached the caves, but not now? Their efforts brought an increased feel of evil only, an aura of malignancy. Their great fear was that, drugged and perhaps unfed, Anchorstar had died. Or that he had been deliberately killed, as too threatening in some way.

"I could not sense him here when we came to the caves," Meatha said. "We could feel nothing but the evil. But we could feel no Children either, though we knew they were here. *You* saw them in your visions but we never did, we only had the knowledge of them. Maybe you did because you had the stone. When we came, there was just the feel of evil. And then almost at once a dozen Kubalese soldiers were around us, forcing us down to drink of the drug, making us swallow, holding our mouths open and pouring it so we choked—and they laughed, they were doing that to us and laughing. We could not resist them. Then afterwards I wanted the drug. I wanted it again and again," she said, ashamed. "And when I was in that sleep, I didn't care about Anchorstar, about anything. I—I wanted him to be like us . . ." She hid her face in her hands, torn with sobs.

"But I don't understand," Zephy said. "What made you come here from Eresu? Why didn't the Children come before, if they knew about the captive Children?"

"They didn't know. They could only feel the darkness, the danger. They don't know everything, even in Eresu. They felt the evil, but they didn't know what it was, where it was.

"But when you drew near Eresu on the mountain, I could sense you. I knew I had left the runestone for you to find, and now I began to feel that you had it. As you came nearer I began to see you sometimes. It was only after we began to sense you and the strength of the stone, that we began to feel that the darkness came from these hills in the south, and that there were Children here. It was as if before, with the Children drugged, there was nothing strong enough to reach out to us. The drugged Children were as dead; there was nothing in them to reach out and echo in our own thoughts. Perhaps when the runestone was closer, and magnified it, the sense of them in the darkness was clear.

"And then it seemed to me all at once that it was Anchorstar, too, who led us. Suddenly I could feel him here in the south. Maybe he had just been brought here as captive, I don't know. But all at once, there was the presence of Anchorstar in my thoughts and of Children in danger, Children sleeping, drugged. It was all around us suddenly, and we started out at once. I know Anchorstar was here. But when we came into the cave there was only the darkness again." She pressed her fist to her mouth. "We must find him. Have you searched everywhere? But you can't have."

"We have," Zephy said. "But we'll search again."

They set about it systematically, each person taking a tunnel, scraping at the walls, examining the stone for loose mortar on the chance that there lay, behind a wall, a tunnel they had not discovered. Still there was the feel of dark around them, indecipherable, threatening.

"He must be very special," Yanno Krabe said, looking down at Meatha as they sat at supper, "a very special man." Tall, dark-haired Yanno had taken to Meatha at once, had followed her since she awakened, seemed to idolize her so that the others smiled a little, watching them, feeling his eager worship.

"Anchorstar is very special," Meatha said. "He is . . . If it were not for Anchorstar, you would have died here; all of us would."

"How do you know that?"

"Because it was Anchorstar who told us what the Kubalese had in mind, what they were doing. It was Anchorstar who determined to search for you and to get the others away from Burgdeeth. And then it was Anchorstar's message that told us of the danger and drew us here. He, and the sense of darkness that we felt."

Zephy watched them and thought Yanno a handsome boy. But he was too worshipping, his mind too full of Meatha. She tried to keep her thoughts private, a thing she was learning was very necessary with so many living close together. Necessary and difficult. They all tried to shut away and not intrude on each other, but sometimes it could not be helped. Now she saw a slight twitch come to Yanno's eyebrow and thought, guiltily, that he knew of her disgust. She glanced up and knew her thoughts had been open to Thorn. He grinned. And later when they were alone he said, "Wouldn't you like a pandering man to follow you around making cow eyes?"

"Oh, yes," she bantered, "would you care to do that? I would like . . ." But he didn't need to be told what she liked. She stared at him and suddenly the emotion that had grown between them rose like a quick tide so she glanced down hastily. "Cow eyes," she said with distaste, to hide her own confusion. "Thorn, do you think he felt my thought?"

"I don't know. Maybe not. It doesn't matter." He put his hand on her shoulder, leaned to kiss her, and their minds met in a tide so sweet, so engulfing that she could not pull away, felt lost in him as if they were one. He kissed her and held her, and when they parted they were together still in their minds. And they thought, How can we be like this, be so happy when Anchorstar may be lost.

They had tried not to think he could be dead. If Anchorstar were dead, if there were no point in searching further, they should all be away at once. For surely other Kubalese would come. And yet they could not bring themselves to abandon the search.

"The not knowing about Anchorstar keeps us here so

we may never get out," she said miserably. "It's as if the very thought of him puts us in danger . . ." Then she broke off and stared at Thorn, appalled at herself. "Oh, I didn't mean it that way, not really, not like it sounded.

"Or did I mean it? Oh, Thorn, did I? I'm so tired, my mind is so tired trying to revive the Children: trying . . . I think what I mean is, if we don't get out now, will we ever be able to? Will we just grow weaker and tireder until—until the dark—until the dark . . ." she shuddered, collapsing in tears suddenly. And she only knew that he held her, was stronger at that moment, as she clutched at him as a drowning person would clutch. She cried in great heaving gulps, couldn't stop, and when the tears went dry at last, she gasped and gasped for breath, heaving, panic taking her . . .

He slapped her, set her reeling. He caught her against falling, pulled her to him, and held her so her sobs subsided at last. How could he remain so strong?

"Another time," he said softly. "Another time, it'll be me falling apart and you to hold me. The way you brought me out of Anchorstar's wagon, with my festering leg. One will always have the strength for both when it is needed —one, we are one . . ." And he kissed her then so there was no darkness, there was nothing save themselves in a perfect sphere of time.

Then at last he lifted her face from his sodden tunic and kissed her again. "Now," he said as she stared up at him, "now we have work to do. We must find him, Zephy. We must find Anchorstar before we leave this place."

But it was not until there was danger on the hills, that Anchorstar was found.

For suddenly in the night the Children who stood sentry both below and above sensed Kubalese soldiers on the move. The destination of the riders was uncertain. If they were to come to the caves, the caves must be cleared. The Kubalese rode hard, were tired, wanting rest. But they could rest on the hills . . . it was not certain . . .

The riders came up the flat valley at dawn, toward the hills, a dozen armed men. As they approached the caves, they slowed. Yes, the cave was their destination, it could be felt now, their thirst for liquor, their longing for hot food. A longing, too, for sport that made the Children look at each other and shiver.

In the cave the brewing room was left as it had been found, dice sticks scattered, bunks rumpled, smelly clothes on pegs, dirty plates. Some of the Children went back to the slabs where they had lain drugged so long, and laid down on them once again, going quite still when they heard the soldiers. The rest moved together into three short corridors near the cave's entrance, and there they waited silently. They had left the captive guard, drugged with MadogWerg, lying on his own bunk looking drunk. They left food on the cookstove, aromatic and hot and laced with MadogWerg. And the liquor cask waited invitingly.

If Thorn had a twinge of revulsion at giving Madog-Werg to anyone, even Kubalese, he put it down. He took Zephy's hand in the darkness and knew she, too, wondered if they sinned, doing such a thing. Then he felt her resolve as she thought of the Children like living dead who had lined the walls of the tunnel.

They could sense the Kubalese outside, dismounting, hobbling their horses, ducking as they came through the low tunnel, hot and tired. They could smell their sweat as they lumbered past shouting for the Kubalese guards.

"Ag-Labba! Ag-Labba, rouse your filthy soul, you worthless Karrach! Fill the mugs, fire the stew pot, you've a crew here starving and lusty!"

"Sewers of Urdd, it's a dark and stinking place!"

"Bleed it, man, bleed it! Roll out a new keg, we've had

no drink in a dog's fracking time, you suckers!"

"Bring ogre's breath, you sons of Urdd! Roll out the ogre's breath!" There was coarse laughter and much stamping, and a loud guffaw that ended in a belch.

Zephy felt Thorn laugh at their crudeness, then felt the cold fear they both shared with the others as seven Children slipped out the entrance behind them, to lead the Kubalese horses away quietly. Zephy sensed the care the Children took as they loosened the horse's saddles, cooled them, watered them, and took them to graze and rest on the hills—it might be a long night for these mounts.

Then Zephy felt Elodia touch her in the darkness, felt the alarm of the others suddenly. Something was in the tunnel with them. It was the darkness they had sensed so often; but it was close now, not held back. Very close and real, and one of the Children was slipping away. The dark was *there*, concentrated in that one, they could feel it now as if, in unusual effort, the dark Child could not keep his evil diffused. Who was he? Which one of them? Zephy could feel Toca's fear. She slipped out behind Thorn after the dark one. She could feel Meatha and Elodia beside her. Toca took her hand. She could feel Clytey and the others following.

They could hear the soldiers in the brewing room, grumbling because two guards were missing. "Where the fracking Urdd? . . ."

"Dallying with the sleeping girls, I'll guess! Ag-Labba! Rouse your filthy self. Poke him, Herg-Mord. Roll him out of that bunk!"

"Get up you fracking sot. Serve us up some supper. Pull yourself out of there!"

Behind the shouting, Zephy and Thorn could feel the urgency of the Child who hurried through the dark passage, could feel the warning forming on his lips. Thorn was ahead, running, Zephy on his heels. They could hear the mugs clink, then Yanno shout—and Thorn had him, his fist in the young man's mouth, his arm around his throat; it *was* Yanno! He spun back, his eyes terrified, the feel of darkness like a stench on him, to stare at Thorn in terror, then to grab at Thorn's knife and twist it out of the scabbard.

Thorn hit him so he went limp.

They crouched there, listening, expecting the Kubalese to burst out of the brewing room. But the men were still cursing the missing guards, toasting each other loudly, laughing and swearing by turns. They had heard nothing.

They dragged Yanno into a side tunnel to question him, and Zephy could feel Thorn's fury as he propped him against the wall. "Where is he?" He hissed, his fingers twisting into the man's shoulder so Yanno cringed in pain. "Where is Anchorstar? What have you done with him?"

But Yanno, limp now with fear and pain, seemed to have gone as empty as a shell. No evil reeked from him now. Only fear. He would not answer Thorn. He seemed to have drawn into a place where Thorn could not reach him. He had given up, yet at the same time he clung to something that would not let him speak. Zephy felt that he would die soon, that they could not prevent it, that he would carry Anchorstar's secret with him.

Then at last Meatha went into his mind in a way the others had not. She seemed suddenly able to strip away layers of emptiness and lay bare, at long last, the final dark kernel of Yanno—to lay bare the knowledge they had sought.

And they, going at once back to the entrance of the tunnel and through the cleft to the outside, found the second cleft, tucked behind the first like a wrinkle in the earth. And Thorn pushed in to find the second door.

This one seemed locked or bolted from within. Finally

it gave slightly as if the bolt were weakening. Or as if the door were not bolted, but held. They pushed harder, ramming the door in unison until at last it gave and swung in. Two boys stood before them, the reek of evil strong about them. Yanno's counterparts. Yanno's dark partners, Children lost in their minds and turned inward around a kernel of evil that now ruled them.

And behind them on the slab lay Anchorstar.

Hardly a heartbeat had he. Zephy and Meatha knelt beside him, and Elodia brought water. Thorn, with Yanno dangling from his grasp, faced the two dark Children coldly. "Yanno. Ejon. Dowilg," Thorn said in a flat voice, divining their names. The stench of their evil filled the cave. The three stared back at Thorn with empty, hate-ridden eyes. The other Children faced them in a circle, a small cold army. Zephy shuddered, and turned back to Anchorstar.

Meatha's arms were around him, Meatha's tears on his face. Then Tra. Hoppa was there, she had brought herbs and brew. But they could not wake him.

"He only sleeps," Tra. Hoppa said. "He only sleeps, he's not dead. You *must* wake him. You must make a strength between you that you have never made before, all of you. You must *not* let Anchorstar die!" Her voice rang cold and compelling in the cave: a command they could not have resisted. The Children, having trussed and secured the dark ones, gathered now, and commanded life, demanded life of Anchorstar as they had not done even for one another. They strained, they sweated with their effort as a man sweats moving boulders.

But they could not wake him. There was no stir, no sign of color or of change in his almost-imperceptible breathing—until at last, the prisoners were taken away and the darkness left the cave. The evil left with them, left the Children free to demand life of Anchorstar without the fetters that Yanno and the two others had put on them.

At long last, after many hours more, Anchorstar moved his hand. Then later his pale, weathered cheek seemed to have a little color. They knelt then, all of them, never moving, willing him to live. When it was clear that he would live, some of the children went to clear the brewing room of the drugged Kubalese soldiers, and Tra. Hoppa made a broth of rabbit, with the herbs. In the small hours of the morning Anchorstar was able, with his head supported, to accept a few drops of this. His eyes were open but dead-seeming. It tore at Zephy to see the blankness with which he regarded them.

They kept the stone beside him as they watched in shifts through the day and the next day and night. The deep, patient prodding was taken up by one group then the next, never ceasing.

And when he woke truly at last, and looked around him, the others who had gone to rest woke at once, were called out of sleep, and came to him. Meatha was there kneeling beside him, crying. Toca, all the Children hurried out of sleep to gather before him. With their silent urging, with the stone and with love pulling at him, Anchorstar looked around him at last with true recognition. With surprise. And then with great good humor.

It was several days more before he was strong enough to travel. Fresh rabbits boiled into soup strengthened him, and all the Children took turns caring for him. When Zephy sat with him one night, he told her how he had been captured, and she thought him very patient, for surely he had told many of the others. He had waited in the dark beyond the housegardens as they had planned, on the night of Fire Scourge. And he had been surprised as he crouched there in a low depression to hear a dozen Kubalese troops suddenly thundering down on him. They had not seen him, but were following the plan of attack. And he, having no way to escape running horses, for his own horses were farther up the mountain had crouched lower, hoping he would not be discovered.

But one Kubalese horse had shied, startling others, and one of the soldiers dismounted to investigate. Anchorstar did not dare move, but remained frozen, hoping still he might be missed, his knife ready in case he was not.

He had been found, had killed one Kubalese soldier and wounded two before he was overpowered by the rest. He had been gagged and locked then in a tool shed and left there for three days, until some Kubalese corporal remembered he was there, and told his superiors.

Then Anchorstar had been force-fed MadogWerg and had waked days later in the dark cave longing nearly to madness for MadogWerg. He had not cried out for it and had refused it when the guard came. "But it was all I could do," he said. "And in the end they forced it down me." He looked at Zephy with such defeat—and then with that wry humor at himself. She had bent and kissed him, more touched than she could admit.

While Anchorstar mended, the Children waited patiently; and the Kubalese horses waited, hidden in the hills. Their masters, with the great quantities of MadogWerg they had imbibed, had needed burying on the hilltop. Then at the very last moment Toca and Thorn took the runestone and went down out of the hills into the valley, where Toca called the two Carriolinian mares and the larger horses into a band that submitted quietly to the ropes and harness they found in the wagon there; the band of horses followed them docilely up the hills in the evening light.

Food and blankets had been packed onto the two donkeys, and now the Children mounted two and three to a horse on the big Kubalese animals. Anchorstar, with Thorn behind to steady him, was helped up onto one of the two mares. He handed the reins of the other mare to Zephy and Meatha, and they scrambled aboard so eagerly Thorn could not help but laugh.

The little group, double-mounted, triple-mounted, children's legs sticking nearly straight out on the broad backs, moved up over the Kubalese hills in the darkness, the horses forced quickly on and the two donkeys pulled ahead in spite of their reluctance. Tra. Hoppa, astride a broad black Kubalese mount behind a tall young man, seemed to cling like a fly. Toca, squeezed between them, could hardly be seen.

They did not stop for rest or water, but kept riding hard, forcing the horses until the animals began to blow and fight them. With the heavy burdens, the horses were easily spent, and just before dawn, they were forced to rest. There had been a little light while the moons still hung in the sky, but now it was dark indeed. They had crossed the Kubalese valley and the river Urobb and were now at the foot of the mountains. They dismounted and removed some of their harness to rub the horses down and cool them; then watered them from the trickle of brook they had been following. When dawn began to come, they could begin to see the valley stretched out behind. Thorn was withdrawn and silent, thinking of the three dark Children he had executed. He had asked of them, "Why did you have Anchorstar captive? Why was he so important that you let him live? Did you guard him at the direction of the Kubalese?"

"Not the Kubalese," Dowilg had croaked, as if he didn't care what he told, as if it didn't matter any more. "*Our way,*" he said, staring at the others. "It was our way . . ."

"He was a *leader,*" Yanno said as if leader were a filthy word. "There was light around him."

Thorn had stared at them, feeling their revulsion for

Anchorstar and for himself and the Children. "Then why did you let him live?"

"We thought to make use of him," Ejon said. "We thought we could turn his mind and make use of him against you." He had laughed with a bitter, cold sound that had turned Thorn's hatred to disgust.

"But why didn't you warn the guards of our coming? You were on their side, surely."

"Not on their side," Yanno said. "They would use *us.*"

"We were to ourselves," said Dowilg. "Before the stone came, we were someplace dark, to ourselves." He seemed unable, or unwilling, to explain that other mental state but Thorn sensed it; the feel of it came strong around him, and he understood that when the stone came, these three had awakened to a new level, where their evil became concentrated once more on the Children and Anchorstar. "But he kept us bound with his mind even in sleep," Dowilg said with cold hate. "We were not strong enough."

Thorn had killed them quickly and buried them in the mound.

Now he sat by the little spring, holding the reins of five resting horses, feeling sick at the memory of what he had done; but knowing he had had no choice. To kill in battle was one thing, to kill in cold blood quite another; but to turn that evil loose on Ere would have been unthinkable. When one mare raised her head, then another, he paid little attention. The animals stiffened and began to fidget and stare down into the lightening valley. Then suddenly he was on his feet, fastening harness, shouting to the others . . .

A band of Kubalese soldiers roared up the valley toward them, yelling for blood.

Children leaped up; harness was secured hastily; the horses milling and shying. Thorn shoved Children onto rearing backs; three riderless horses pulled away and went plunging up the mountain. They heard the Kubalese shout as a darkness came over them all; the soldiers were blotted out by the darkness in the sky, all was seething confusion . . .

The darkness in the sky dropped around them; then flying dark shapes landed, pawing, snorting at the other horses. Thorn lifted Children up onto winged backs now, pushed Zephy up, saw the Horses of Eresu leap into the sky seconds before the Kubalese pounded up the last slope, shouting. The abandoned horses were milling, some heading for the mountains. A winged shape landed before him; he lunged to mount, felt a hand grab him from behind and pull him back. He whirled to face the Kubalese soldier. He lashed out, his fist hardly grazing the man, drew back grabbing for his knife, was hit so hard in the head he reeled; he found some mark with his blade, jerked away and leaped wildly for the winged back . . .

The others were specks above him, Zephy's terror for him sharp in his mind as the winged horse lifted to meet her.

They were over Ere. They were on the wind, free; the wonder of the flight obliterated the terror they had felt. The land dropped below them, lit with the coming dawn. They saw the sweep of valley from Kubal to Urobb. The sun, lying just below the sea, sent a sharp orange light onto the outer islands of Carriol far in the distance. Back toward the mountain, Thorn could see the Kubalese riding hard, only specks now, after the escaping horses. He caught a glimpse of the two donkeys, turning off into a protected ravine. Maybe they would be missed. He touched the runestone, safe in his jerkin, and smiled across at Zephy, sensing the wonder of flight that held her, the fierce joy. He could see Tra. Hoppa farther away clinging to a dark roan, holding Toca tight. The child gripped a handful of mane and stared down in wide-eyed wonder. All of them were safe;

the sweep of dozens of pairs of huge wings before him, behind him, lifting and soaring on the wind so effortlessly, held him spellbound; the sweep of land beneath him, another world so far removed from this tide of wind, made him drunk with glory.

The river Voda-Cul cut below them now, through the pale loess planes of Carriol. A deep woods lay between the white expanse and the sea, and in the loess hills themselves he could see carven clusters of dwellings, with the smaller river Somat-Cul wandering down between them toward the lush green pastures that made up most of Carriol. He could see the sparkle of cities there as the sun lifted red; and the names Blackcob and Kirkfalk and Plea came to him, though he didn't know which was which. He knew which was the city of Fentress, there on the largest of the three islands; and that must be the ancient ruin lying on the coast south of Fentress. He peered down between the sweeping wings, mane whipping in his face and the smell of the horse he rode warm and sweet. He laid a hand on the silken neck and felt the strength beneath, and the muscles pulling in flight. He turned to look at Zephy again, though he didn't need to see her face to know her joy; She was thinking of the stone, too. *Given twice? But it has not been. And carried in a search and a questing? Have we done both, Thorn?*

You gave it to me once, he answered. *When we found it in the saddle. We have had a search all right. Was that a questing too?*

Or is there more? She thought.

There is always more. There is a whole lifetime of questing. He did not know whether the others heard their thoughts. It didn't matter. Carriol was there below them, a sanctuary, a place of freedom, and new beginning; and they rode on the winds above it as they had dreamed, as all of them had longed to do. He laid a hand on his horse's neck and felt again the warmth of the strong body beneath him, saw the horse's ears go forward as he chose a distant landing. They descended, and he felt Zephy's longing to stay wind-borne forever; their two horses swept close together, playing in the wind, nipping lightly, and then settled into a long glide that, Thorn thought, would take them down over Carriol's islands. Crouching beneath the dark wings, he could see all of Ere for a moment, the deep Bay of Pelli, the deserts beyond. It was not so large and forbidding, seen from the sky; nor would it seem so large again, ever.

The winged horses descended, dropping down over the coast of Carriol. The sea swept away to the left. Thorn felt his horse tense, saw the land come up quick, felt the great wings catch at the wind in a new way—felt the jolt as the Horse of Eresu landed on a high mass of stone and crumbling walls that rose from the cliffs above the sea. The stallion's wings, at sudden rest, folded over Thorn's legs and beside his body. The others were landing, plummeting down.

They were high above the sea and cliffs on a patch of green supported by ancient walls and towers. They were high in the ruined city, the ancient city Carriol. Below them the ruins crumbled away. Above them a broken tower rose into the clear sky. To the south they could see the pastures of Carriol, a city, farms, then a bay and far in the distance the huge neck of land running out into the sea; this would be Sangur. To the right of Sangur lay the wide Bay of Pelli. But this was all very distant, softened by mists. Close at hand, on Thorn's left, the sea beat a strange soothing cadence as breakers crashed upon the cliffs. Zephy came close and stood with him. They looked out at the three islands, Fentress and Doonas and Skoke, and at the dwellings clinging there, and the little winding streets; and to their right, below the broken walls, the sweep of Carriol. The winged horse still stood close to Thorn, nuzzling him now, then raised its head to look out over Carriol, too, with a soft nicker; nuzzled again, then lifted its wings. Thorn rubbed its neck, loathe for the stallion to leave but knowing he must. Zephy clung to her own horse and there were tears in her eyes. Then all in an instant the horses reared and were airborne, wings sweeping, were leaping into the wind, rising, were gone on the wind, a seething flock there above them, vanishing in cloud. The Children of Ynell crowded closer together, and gazed down over the waiting land.

the end